Classified

Books by Fern Michaels:

Fate & Fortune
Sweet Vengeance
Holly and Ivy
Fancy Dancer
No Safe Secret
Wishes for Christmas
About Face
Perfect Match
A Family Affair
Forget Me Not
The Blossom Sisters
Balancing Act
Tuesday's Child
Betrayal
Southern Comfort
To Taste the Wine
Sins of the Flesh
Sins of Omission
Return to Sender
Mr. and Miss Anonymous
Up Close and Personal
Fool Me Once
Picture Perfect
The Future Scrolls
Kentucky Sunrise
Kentucky Heat
Kentucky Rich
Plain Jane
Charming Lily
What You Wish For
The Guest List
Listen to Your Heart
Celebration
Yesterday
Finders Keepers
Annie's Rainbow
Sara's Song
Vegas Sunrise
Vegas Heat
Vegas Rich
Whitefire
Wish List
Dear Emily
Christmas at Timberwoods

The Sisterhood Novels:

Need to Know
Crash and Burn
Point Blank
In Plain Sight
Eyes Only
Kiss and Tell
Blindsided
Gotcha!
Home Free
Déjà Vu
Cross Roads
Game Over
Deadly Deals
Vanishing Act
Razor Sharp
Under the Radar
Final Justice
Collateral Damage
Fast Track
Hokus Pokus
Hide and Seek
Free Fall
Lethal Justice
Sweet Revenge
The Jury
Vendetta
Payback
Weekend Warriors

The Men of the Sisterhood
Novels:

Truth or Dare
High Stakes
Fast and Loose
Double Down

Books by Fern Michaels (Continued):

The Godmothers Series:

Getaway (E-Novella Exclusive)
Spirited Away (E-Novella Exclusive)
Hideaway (E-Novella Exclusive)
Classified
Breaking News
Deadline
Late Edition
Exclusive
The Scoop

E-Book Exclusives:

Desperate Measures
Seasons of Her Life
To Have and to Hold
Serendipity
Captive Innocence
Captive Embraces
Captive Passions
Captive Secrets
Captive Splendors
Cinders to Satin

For All Their Lives
Texas Heat
Texas Rich
Texas Fury
Texas Sunrise

Anthologies:

Mistletoe Magic
Winter Wishes
The Most Wonderful Time
When the Snow Falls
Secret Santa
A Winter Wonderland
I'll Be Home for Christmas
Making Spirits Bright
Holiday Magic
Snow Angels
Silver Bells
Comfort and Joy
Sugar and Spice
Let It Snow
A Gift of Joy
Five Golden Rings
Deck the Halls
Jingle All the Way

FERN MICHAELS

THE
GODMOTHERS

Classified

KENSINGTON PUBLISHING CORP.
www.kensingtonbooks.com

KENSINGTON BOOKS are published by

Kensington Publishing Corp.
119 West 40th Street
New York, NY 10018

Copyright © 2013 by MRK Productions
Fern Michaels is a Registered Trademark of First Draft, Inc.

All Kensington titles, imprints, and distributed lines are available at special quantity discounts for bulk purchases for sales promotion, premiums, fund-raising, educational, or institutional use.

Special book excerpts or customized printings can also be created to fit specific needs. For details, write or phone the office of the Kensington Sales Manager: Kensington Publishing Corp., 119 West 40th Street, New York, NY 10018. Attn. Sales Department. Phone: 1-800-221-2647.

Kensington and the K logo Reg. U.S. Pat. & TM Off.

First Kensington Hardcover Edition: June 2013

ISBN-13: 978-1-4967-1302-5
ISBN-10: 1-4967-1302-8
First Kensington Trade Paperback Printing: August 2018

eISBN-13: 978-0-7582-9163-9
eISBN-10: 0-7582-9163-9

10 9 8 7 6 5 4 3

Printed in the United States of America

Prologue

Having tossed and turned for the past hour, Abby finally rolled over and looked at the alarm clock. It was 3:00 AM, the witching hour. Chris had fallen asleep on the sofa downstairs in the formal dining room. She didn't have the heart to wake him. She knew by the time he walked upstairs and showered, he would be wide-awake, and it would take hours for him to get back to sleep. He'd spent fourteen hours today stripping the wood floor in the dining room—backbreaking and exhausting work. He was sitting on the sofa when Abby went to the kitchen for ice tea. When she returned, Chris was sound asleep. She covered him with a light throw and decided to go upstairs alone.

Unable to sleep without Chris by her side, she switched the lamp on. A swatch of fabrics for the new drapes she wanted to order was lying on the night table. She picked it up, felt the different textures, examined the colors, feeling unsure. While she didn't want something dark and heavy, she didn't want something so light you could see through it. What she needed was something in between, yet something that stayed true to the Clay Plantation decor. Her mother had advised her and had spent many, many hours with her, going over the long history of the plantation, for she, too, had lived here for a short period of time when she was married to Garland, Chris's father. There were old pictures of the many rooms, but they were so faded she could not even begin to guess what kind of fabric had been used to decorate them. One thing Abby knew for sure, she had to get rid of the heavy dark green velvet drapes. They reminded her of *The Carol Burnett Show* parody scene of Margaret Mitchell's *Gone With the Wind,* which she'd watched late one night on TV. Carol Burnett, playing Scarlett O'Hara, had ripped the heavy drapes from the window and worn them as her new dress, hoping to impress Rhett Butler, who had just returned from fighting in the Civil War. Abby had laughed until she cried, but the drapes had to go. They were just plain ugly.

Not seeing any fabric or color that caught her eye, she found the remote and channel surfed for ten minutes. When none of the television programs captured her attention, she turned the TV off. She flipped through the latest edition of *The Informer.* Josh was doing an excellent job, but the stories didn't capture her attention, as they once had. Frankly, she thought they were silly and a waste of time. Why the sudden change of heart? She'd almost died because of that paper and that total idiot, Rodwell Archibald Godfrey—behind his back, they referred to him as Rag. He'd kidnapped her, locked her in a tiny closet, tied to a chair, while he waited for his ransom money to be delivered. As it turned out, her mother was the owner of *The Informer,* something that was unknown to her at the time. Clearly, Rag was also unaware of that minor factoid. It had been a horrifying experience for everyone, as well as one of the principal reasons she and Chris had moved to Charleston.

Now, for the past month, she'd been having trouble sleeping, only to be completely wiped out during the day. She thought of going downstairs to the kitchen to warm up a glass of milk, but she didn't want to risk waking Chris. He'd worked so hard, and their new venture required his legal skills, making sure all their documents and contracts were legal. But he continued to tell her he wanted to be a farmer, and she now believed him. She remembered his telling her this when they had lived in Los Angeles, but she hadn't believed him then. Of course, they had only been friends at the time. And he was her stepbrother, but not in a gross way. Her mother and Garland were married for a short period of time; Chris had been away at college; she'd been a teenager, spending time with her girlfriends, shopping, going to the movies, gabbing. Before she knew it, Garland had passed away. She and her mother, whom everyone called Toots, had moved into the house, which her mother would share many years later with Abby's three godmothers.

Finally, Abby started to get drowsy, and she turned out the light and curled up beneath the sheets. She drifted off to sleep quickly.

Octavia knew her time was coming soon, but prayed she would have a few more weeks left before she had to tell Mr. Clayton. He'd been sending for her since she'd been thirteen years old. She's tired, so tired, and it ain't even half day gone. Her belly hurts, an' her feets swollen, but she cain't stop 'cause there's so much work to do. She hates workin' in the big house. Ever' day she tries to upset the Missus in hopes she'd send her back to the field with her momma and sisters, but she says she be a "special" girl, and Octavia doesn't know what she mean by that. She dropped a fancy china plate yesterday, an' the Missus just tell her to clean up the mess, but Octavia might only be fourteen and three months, but she know the Missus knows she's with child. She seen her lookin' at her belly, she watches her, an' Octavia is scared, but not so scared that she's gonna stop tryin' to get back to her home with Momma. The little cabin ain't too big, but it be better than some other plantations have. They got real wooden plank floors, an' their house is made of the same bricks Mr. Clayton's got. They got a real fireplace, too. The beds is straw, an' the coverin's plenty soft, 'cause Momma cleaned them an' rinsed them in hot water, an' she put dried magnolias in the straw so's they'd smell good, too. Her back is hurtin' real bad, and she knows this ain't suppose to happen now. Her belly ain't big enough yet. How she wishes she could slip away to see Momma. She'd know what was ailin' her, an' what to do.

Octavia is gonna go see her momma tonight. After the Missus and Mr. Clayton go to sleep, she'll slip out through the kitchen door. Soon as she finishes her duties, she'll go. She hopes Mr. Clayton doesn't want to visit her tonight. She hates him. He crawls on top of her like she's an animal. Them sounds he make scare her, too. His breath is hot, and smells of tobacco. No, he'd been to see her last night. Maybe Telly would get a visit tonight. Telly was only twelve and four months. Octavia felt sorry for her, but she couldn't stop Mr. Clayton from crawlin' on top o' her any more than she could stop him from crawlin' on herself. She prays every night that he would die. She knows it's wrong to pray for bad things, but Mr. Clayton is a mean, bad man. He likes to use the whip on the men workin' in the fields. Her daddy had thick, ropy scars on his back and arms from Mr. Clayton's whip. Momma would cry when she see them. She'd rub lard on his wounds an' make a poultice that stunk to high heaven, but Daddy said it helped the cuts heal faster. Octavia knows as soon as he be healed, Mr. Clayton will rip him open again. And Mr. Clayton will laugh. She hates him, an' she hates the baby in her belly. A sharp pain rips through her back. She grabs the kitchen chair to keep from keelin' over. She takes a deep breath, an' the pain eases up. As soon as the pain's gone, she turns to head upstairs to turn down the beds, an' another pain hits her in the belly. She falls to her knees, pressing her hands against her, thinkin' this will stop the pain. Sharp searing pain in her back comes again. Tears fill her eyes, an' she bites the sides of her mouth to keep from screamin' out.

In the midst of her pain, she calls out, "Momma, I need you. Please, Momma, help me." Takin' a deep breath, she lets it out slowly, thinkin' her pain's all gone, when she feels another pain, this one worse than ever. She wants to push hard like she has to go to the bathroom, but she cain't. Rolling on her back, she puts both legs against the chair legs. She don't care no more. She pushes and screams. An' she pushes again. This time she feels like her woman part is tearin' in half. She screams again, not carin' if Mr. Clayton or the Missus hears her. She really hates him now and begs God to make him dead right now! She prays for his death and prays for her own as she gets hit with another sharp pain, hot like a kitchen knife got stuck in her belly. She bears down again, this time so hard she feels the veins in her head an' neck gettin' so big.

Another push, an' she feels something warm and damp between her legs. She tries to push herself up with her elbows so she can see. Another pain, and she screams and screams and screams. Again, she feels something warm and wet between her legs, something heavy. Her body gots sweat ever' place. She tries to push herself up, when she hears a soft sound, like a baby cryin'. She struggles to see what lies between her legs an' sees a baby, but it ain't right. It's got an arm missin'.

"The devil!" she cries out. She'd just given birth to Mr. Clayton's devil.

No!!!

Abby bolted upright in the bed. Trembling, she turned the light on. Chris ran into the room. "Are you okay?" He cradled her in his arms. "I heard you screaming."

"Oh, Chris, I had a terrible nightmare. My God, it

seemed so real." Abby pushed herself up in the bed and leaned against the headboard.

Chris cradled her against his chest. "Want to tell me about it?"

Abby took a deep breath. "There was this girl, a young girl. She was . . . she was a slave. In the dream, she was scared and so alone. She kept calling for her mother. It was so sad."

She stopped. Something in the dream was so familiar, tugging at the back of her mind, but she couldn't place exactly what it was. "She was having a baby! Alone. She was all alone! Chris, there is something in the dream that I should know, something I've actually seen, but I can't pull it up." Abby wrapped her arm around Chris's waist. "Sorry I woke you."

"Hey, I'm glad you did. That sofa is not meant to sleep on. Why didn't you wake me up?"

"You looked exhausted, and I knew that if I woke you, once you showered, you'd be wide-awake, so I let you sleep."

"And here you are in bed without me for the first time since we've been married, and you had a nightmare. What does that tell you?"

"Not to go to bed without you?"

"Yep. Now, since I'm up anyway, I'm going to take a shower. You want to join me?" Chris nuzzled her ear.

She gave a half laugh. "Not now, sorry." She glanced at the bedside clock. It was almost five o'clock. "I tell you what. Why don't you get your shower, and while you're doing that, I can make us some breakfast. I won't be able to go back to sleep anyway. If I get tired during the day, I'll have a nap."

Chris kissed her cheek and ruffled her hair. "You've got yourself a deal, Mrs. Clay."

As soon as Chris said "Mrs. Clay," she stopped mid-thought. "Chris, wait. Listen, I know this is . . . strange, but has this place always been called Clay Plantation?"

Standing at the chest of drawers, Chris pulled a pair of boxers out of the top drawer. "Good question. Why would you ask something like that?"

She didn't know, but she somehow knew it was important for her to find out. It was the dream. The man in the dream. The man the young woman hated, the man she wanted to die. "Just tell me, has the plantation always been referred to as the Clay Plantation?"

"To the best of my knowledge, it has, but then again, it's been around a few hundred years. It's possible that it had a different name at some point before the Clays owned it. Is it important?"

Abby's reporter instincts were at play. Instincts she'd scoffed at earlier. "I'm not sure. It's something in the dream. I don't know."

"Well, don't worry your pretty little head off. Now, woman, get your little rear end downstairs and fix that breakfast you promised me."

Abby grabbed her robe off the foot of the bed, careful not to wake Chester, who was still sound asleep at the foot of the bed. "Some guard dog you are," she said as she walked out of the room.

Downstairs in the kitchen, Abby started a pot of coffee. Her mind kept straying back to her dream, and it was silly. *Damn, Abby, it was simply a dream. Weird? Yes. Strange? Yes.* She opened the refrigerator. "What to make?" she asked herself aloud.

"Ruff!" Chester gave his low-sounding morning growl.

"You want some grub, old boy?"

Chester walked over and stood by his dog bowl. Abby had chicken breasts left over. She chopped half of one, threw it in the microwave for a few seconds to get the chill off, then scooped the chunks of chicken into his bowl. Mavis had started doing this for Coco and Frankie. Chester had been over a few times and received the same meal. Now Abby had to bribe him with chicken breasts just to get him to eat his dog food. "You are so spoiled," Abby said, leaning over and rubbing him between the ears.

She grabbed a carton of eggs, a chunk of bacon, and a can of buttermilk biscuits out of the refrigerator. Usually, she loved the smell of coffee, but for some reason it gagged her now. She would swear she smelled a chemical smell coming from the pot. She lifted the carafe up to her nose. "Yuck." She took a chamomile tea bag out of the canister, filled a mug with water, and popped it in the microwave. She usually loved her coffee, but not today. She felt shitty, like she was coming down with the flu. The last thing she needed now. With all that she and Chris had going on, she didn't have time to get sick.

Hurrying now, she removed a skillet from the cupboard, turned on the stove, and tossed several strips of bacon in as soon as the skillet was hot. She cracked half-a-dozen eggs into a bowl, added a splash of milk, and then, with a wire whisk, beat the mixture until the yolks were no longer in evidence. She'd seen this technique used on some cooking show, with the chef saying that the eggs would be much fluffier. It worked, so she'd been using it ever since. She heated another skillet, dropping in a tiny bit of butter. She stared as it sizzled and turned a creamy light brown. She poured the egg mixture into the skillet, then remembered the biscuits. "Oh, the hell with it. We can have toast." She took the can of biscuits and put them back in the fridge.

Chester ran through the doggie door, scaring her. "Darn, boy, you scared the bejeezers out of me." She hadn't even heard him go out.

"Hey, I thought you'd have the table all set with the fine china and cloth napkins. What's this?" Chris asked. He came up behind her, wrapping his arms around her waist.

"You smell good. And you're lucky I'm making your

breakfast. Don't get used to it, either, because I promise not to make this a habit. If my memory serves me correctly, you used to exist on mint chocolate-chip ice cream."

Chris kissed her head, then poured a cup of coffee for himself. "You're not having your coffee?"

"It smells weird to me. I'm having tea." She removed her mug from the microwave and dropped the tea bag in the hot water. "Does it taste okay?"

Chris took a sip. "Excellent."

"You can't smell that chemical smell? Like iron or something?" Abby asked as she stirred the eggs, then removed the bacon and placed it on a paper towel to drain.

"You're imagining things, Abs. This is perfectly fine. If it weren't, I wouldn't drink it."

She just nodded and set about finishing breakfast. She took two slices of wheat bread, put them in the toaster, then removed the eggs from the pan. She dabbed at the bacon with another paper towel, put four slices on Chris's plate, together with most of the eggs, just as the toast popped up. "Good timing, if I say so myself."

Abby put Chris's plate in front of him. "Remember, do not get used to this."

She took her mug of tea to the table and sat across from him. Chris dug into the food like he hadn't eaten in weeks. She smiled. She loved this man.

"How come you're not having anything?" he asked between bites. "You think the food smells weird, too?"

"No, I'm not hungry. Must be coming down with the flu or something. I can't seem to shake this."

"You need to rest."

"Yeah, well, tell that to . . ." She wanted to say "that poor girl in my dream," but she didn't. Still, she couldn't shake the dream. There was something about the man in the dream. The girl kept calling him something. . . . *Mr. Clayton!* She'd called him Mr. Clayton in the dream.

"Chris, are you sure this place didn't go by another name?" she asked again.

"Not that I can remember. When you live in one of these old places as a kid, it's almost an embarrassment. I remember thinking, when I was a kid, why couldn't I live in one of those McMansions that all my friends lived in? Of course, I was too stupid to realize the history, and too young to appreciate it. Why don't you ask your mother? She lived here, too. She might know."

Abby brightened. Of course. Why hadn't she thought of that? "You're a genius. Thanks." She took her tea into the living room. Her mother was an early riser. She glanced at the big grandfather clock. It was ten to six. Her mother was up. She grabbed the portable phone and took it back into the kitchen. They were going to get a phone installed in the kitchen, if it was the last thing she did. The house was old, but there had been many updates throughout the years. Unfortunately, a phone jack was not one of them.

She sat back down at the table. Chris took his plate, rinsed it, then put it in the dishwasher. He refilled his cup and came back to the table. "You going to call Tootsie?"

"Yes." She punched in her mother's number.

"Abby Simpson-Clay, what are you doing up so early?" her mother asked. No "hello."

Caller ID is killing the pranksters, Abby thought.

"Well, I just finished making breakfast for my adoring husband. I couldn't sleep, so I got up early, and Chris was up, so here we are. Mom, listen, I know this is going to sound odd, but do you recall the Clay Plantation being called something else? I'm talking way back in the day, when those slave quarters were in use."

"Let me think a minute. Hmm, I don't really know. I have some of Garland's papers stored away in a box somewhere. Seems like there were several documents that were connected to the plantation. Why do you want to know? You're not thinking of changing the name, are you?"

"No, nothing like that." Abby wasn't sure if she wanted to tell her mother about the dream just yet. It kept clinging to her; it was as though she were supposed to remember something from the dream for a reason. She just didn't know what it was.

"I can look for that box, if it will help."

"Thanks, Mom. Would you mind if Chester and I came over and looked through it with you? He's needing a doggie love fix anyway. And I'm sure Coco and Frankie could use a Chester fix."

"Come on over. We're on our third pot of coffee. I'll make a fresh pot for you."

"No, Mom, really, I'm drinking tea today. I think I have a bug, and coffee isn't agreeing with me right now. I'll be over in half an hour."

"Okay, dear."

"So, what did Tootsie have to say?"

"She didn't know, but she has a box of your dad's things at her house. She said she thought there might be some papers in there connected to the plantation. I'm going to take a look and see if there is anything in there. Chester, do you want to take an early-morning walk to see Coco?" Hearing the magic word *Coco,* the shepherd rushed out through the doggie door.

"I take it that means yes," Abby said. "You want to come with us?"

"No, I better pass. I'm expecting an early phone call. You go on, tell everyone 'hi' for me. I'll see you when you return."

Abby wrapped her arms around him, then stood on her tiptoes in order to reach his mouth. She planted a sloppy kiss on his lips. "I've got to dress now, Mr. Clay. I told Mother I'd be there in thirty minutes. She probably started a stopwatch the second I hung up the phone."

"Go on, woman, I'll be here waiting with bated breath."

Abby raced upstairs and grabbed a pair of yoga pants and a T-shirt. She crammed her feet into her sneakers. In the master bath, she washed her face and brushed her teeth. She looked at the mass of curls and balled her hair into a knot, securing it with a couple of bobby pins.

She raced down the stairs and out the back door. Chester was waiting at the gate. If she hurried, her mother's house was a ten-minute walk. She needed the exercise. Her clothes were starting to feel a bit too tight. *It's all this Southern cooking,* she thought.

Chester raced ahead, then stopped, waiting for her to catch up with him. "Smartest dog in the world, aren't you?"

Ten minutes later, she was at her mother's house. She tapped on the back door so as not to startle her or whoever was in the kitchen at this hour.

"Abby, Chester, I'm glad you came over. I needed a daughter fix."

Chester saw Coco and Frankie in their corner and took off. "He's happy, that's for sure. He needed a Coco fix, too. Did you find the box?"

"Right there." Toots pointed to a large plastic carton. "Some of those documents are very old. You should probably take them and have them preserved. The historical society will help you with it."

Abby dragged the box over to the table. Sitting in the chair, she removed the lid on the box. A musty odor assaulted her, and it was all she could do to keep from throwing up. Damn, she really hated feeling bad. She started removing papers, careful not to tear them. The documents were old and yellowed, stiff with age. Abby dug through the box and stopped when she pulled out a thick volume labeled THE CLAYTON PLANTATION.

"Oh, my God, Mom, now I know what's been bothering me about the dream I had this morning! Yes, that's what woke me up. There was this girl—she was young, in her early teens. In my dream, she was a slave, and there was something so familiar about the dream. You know, sort of like déjà vu? It's really been bothering me ever since. It was like there was something I was supposed to know, and now I think I remember. In the dream, there was a small brick house. It's where the girl lived before she was moved to the big house. It was one of the buildings at the plantation—I know it was. And in the dream, the girl kept saying something about a Mr. Clayton. She was pregnant, and the baby was his. Oh, my God, Mother, the dream was a nightmare."

Amazed at the significance of her dream, she said, "I know that what I dreamed really happened. I don't know how I know this, but I just do. Maybe I'm psychic, too!"

Octavia pulled her hand away, frightened when she felt another gush of somethin' warm comin' from her woman parts. She clenched her teeth and felt a crampin' sensation in her belly. Then, as fast as the pain came, it stopped an' was just a dull ache, like she got when she ate too many peaches. Fearin' Mr. Clayton an' the Missus had heard her hollerin', she knew she had to act fast. Not wantin' to, but knowin' she had no other choice, she pushed herself up into a sittin' position. The thing was still attached to her, an' she remembered Momma sayin' somethin' 'bout this. She couldn't remember what her momma called it, but she knew she had to cut the thing loose from her. The kitchen was dark, but Octavia didn't mind; she was glad for the darkness. She didn't wanna see that thing in the light. Workin' in the kitchen, she knew her way around with her eyes shut. She remembered usin' the butcher knife just this mornin' when she'd shown Telly how to cut up a chicken. Next to the pump on the choppin' block. All she had to do was slide across the pine floor with the thing stuck to her; then she could reach the knife.

Not knowin' how she was gonna get across the floor

with that devil thing from Mr. Clayton's crawlin' atop her, Octavia gathered the warm bundle in her skirt an' wrapped the thing up. It was whimperin', an' she felt sad, but she had to cut it away an' get to Momma's. With one hand holdin' the thing, she used the other to push across the floor. She felt another gush of hot liquid spill from her insides an' knew somethin' was wrong.

When she reached the choppin' block, she used her free hand to feel for the butcher knife. Careful, she ran her slim honey-colored hand along the edge of the choppin' block, then felt the heavy wooden handle of the knife. With her fingers, she grabbed the knife an' held it tight in her shakin' hand. In the darkness, she could see the heavy steel blade as moonlight glistened through the big kitchen window. The thing made a sound again, an' Octavia thought it sounded like a wounded polecat.

Her hands were shakin' as she unfolded her bloodied dress. The Missus would lash her, for sure, when she saw it. As her belly grew, her housedresses had squeezed her so tight, she was sure they'd strangle her. That's when the Missus gave her that bolt of cloth, told her to sew a new dress. An' she had, an' now it was ruined. Octavia smelled the coppery smell of her own blood, felt the stickiness thickenin' on her skin. The thing cried out again, only this time it wasn't a meow like a kitten or a strange sound, like the ones she made when Mr. Clayton clamped his hand over her mouth when he crawled on top o' her. This was a real cry, like a baby, like her little brother, Abraham. She remembered her momma birthin' him. She been scared for her momma when she heard her moanin' an' screamin'. Like her, she stopped, an' then the cryin' started. Now Octavia felt tired an' weak, like all she wanted to do was rest, jus' for a minute. She closed her eyes, driftin' off, rememberin' when she was jus' a girl. . . .

She jerked up, the knife still in her hand, the thing still nestled between her legs on her bloody dress. Before she blacked out again, she touched the thing, found the slimy snakelike part that grew out of its tiny belly. Without another thought, she took hold of the sliminess, an' quickly she hacked through the piece of snake. Frightened, she dropped the knife on the floor, the noise soundin' like glass shatterin'. Scared Mr. Clayton or the Missus would come down into the kitchen an' find her like this, she wrapped the baby in her bloody dress. With blood seepin' outta her an' drippin' down her legs, she raced out the back door.

The night air smacked her in the face. It was hot an' humid; flies swarmed around the bucket of chicken guts she'd set out for the hogs. Shoeless, her feet hit the dried grass, sounding like snapping peas as each foot bore down on the hard grass. Octavia ran as fast as she'd ever run before, both arms gripping the thing as tight as she could. She ran so fast that she could hardly breathe. Beads of sweat dripped in her eyes, burning. She blinked, not caring that she couldn't see, not caring that her side hurt so badly she wanted to scream like a wounded animal. All she could think of was Momma. When she got to Momma's, she would know what to do with this thing. Then maybe the Missus would see how bad she was, how she hated workin' in the big house, and then she would send her back to the cabin to work with Momma an' help her take care of the others. Then she wouldn't have to let Mr. Clayton crawl on her. She had a quick thought about poor little Telly, but she couldn't help her now. She'd have to get out like she was, but Octavia hoped Telly didn't have to have a baby with Mr. Clayton.

She didn't know how long she'd been runnin', when she saw her home, her momma's cabin, ahead. Dawn was just beginnin' to break; the men would be in the fields anytime now. She couldn't let them see her, or else the overseer would force the men to have her. She'd seen this once before, an' her momma said never let the overseer see you alone. He was meaner than Mr. Clayton; he never said nothin' nice to the men slaves, just to the Missus. She stopped to catch her breath and saw she still held the thing in her arms. Drawin' in as much air as she could, she ran faster now, spurred by the sight of the cabin, knowin' that hope lay behind those walls.

Holdin' the thing with one hand, she banged on the door. "Momma," she called out in a loud whisper. "It's me, Momma, please open the door."

Before Octavia could raise her one free hand to pound on the door again, it opened. "Octavia? What you be doin' here? The Mister find you here, he whip you!" Her momma was scared, she knew, but she didn't have no place else to go.

"Momma, this . . . I have this." She unwrapped the infant from her bloodied dress an' shoved it toward her momma. "I got this, an' it ain't right!"

Her momma took the baby an' wrapped it in a kitchen rag. "Octavia! My Lord, you has a baby! This yourn?"

She nodded. She didn't have to explain it to her momma 'cause she knew about Mr. Clayton. She be the one to tell her what might happen if'n she get sent to the big house to work. No, Momma knew.

"This baby ain't breathin'! Lord, chile, what you do to him?" her momma asked.

Octavia felt a fear like nothin' she'd ever known in her life. "Momma! I jus' bring him to you. You see he ain't right? He only gots one arm. He be the devil."

"Shhh, chile, you hush now. You go wash yourself. Get a clean dress. You needs to rest, but go now. . . . I'll take care of this." Her momma looked at Octavia, an' she knew what they were doin' would never be talked about ever again. Nodding, she took the bucket of water her momma always kept by the stove, to keep it warm, an' a rag. She stripped her dress off, hopin' no one would be up an' about to see her. Her little brother was still sleepin' on the straw bed in the corner; her daddy was out in the fields

already. She felt weak an' sore. Her feets was blistering up, but she had to do what Momma said, an' fast. Momma always knew what to do.

She dipped the rag into the pail of warm well water, then wrung the rag out, lettin' the water trickle down her body. The blood had crusted. Octavia found Momma's lye soap an' ran the sweet-smellin' soap over her tender body. Momma had the sweetest lye soap. After she collected the dried ashes, she always crushed her dried magnolias in before she added the fat an' put the soaps into the wooden molds. The Missus liked Momma's soaps, too. Octavia was glad she didn't have to think about anything more 'cept for cleanin' herself. She used the rag to scrub away the dried blood, then rinsed with a clean rag. She scrubbed again, jus' 'cause she had never felt so dirty in her life. She rinsed again; then with a fresh kitchen towel, she dried herself. When she saw blood on the towel, she screamed, "Momma!"

Her momma came back inside. "Shhh, I tell you to be quiet, chile!"

"Look, Momma, they's more blood!" She shoved the kitchen towel in her mother's hand.

"This be your woman time comin' back. Women bleeds after birthin'. Ain't no need to be scared. Grab a clean towel an' hold it between your legs."

Octavia did as her momma said; then she slipped the clean housedress over her. It was loose but clean. "Now, girl, I want you to listen up, an' what we says here cain't never be says again. You understan', chile?"

Octavia nodded.

"That poor little chile ain't right. He cain't breathe when he's born. Right, chile?"

"Yes, Momma."

"He's better off, you got that? He'd be kilt when they see him missin' an arm. Now we gonna put this in the book. It'll make it right."

"What book, Momma?"

Her Momma went to the corner of their cabin an' pulled up a piece of the wooden floor. Reachin' down below, she pulled out something covered in leather.

"Momma?"

"Shhh, you ain't ever seen this girl, you hear?"

Octavia nodded.

Her momma took a large leather volume an' opened it carefully. They was letters on the front of the book, but she didn't know what they say. Her momma took a piece of a bird feather an' a glass bottle of ink an' dipped the feather into the ink. "This is the book of life an' death, Octavia. I been writin' in it all my life. I's learned to read an' write when the old Mr. Clayton's Missus was here. She teached me to read an' write. She tell me to always write down what's most sacred."

She watched her momma as she made her letters in the book.

"What you sayin', Momma?"

"A minute, chile, an' I'll read to you."

Her momma wrote in the big leather book for a few more minutes; then she put the ink an' feather in the opening under the floor. She blew on the letters; then she put the book back in the dark ground.

"I gots all the names wrote here, all them borned an' died. I write you son's day of birth an' day of death. I call him John Thomas Clayton, you Octavia Charlotte Clayton an' Mr. Charles Garland Clayton. Now, you never speak this day again, you hear? The Missus gone come fo' you soon, an' you jus' say you scared 'cause your baby dead when he camed out. Missus don't want no one-arm baby to care fo'. Now you jus' rest until the Missus gets here."

Octavia knew that Momma would take care of her, she always had.

Chapter 1

"Simpson . . . No, I meant *Clay*," Abby said more to herself than to the FedEx guy who waited as she signed for the delivery. He raised his brow in question.

"I'm recently married," she explained. Well, not *that* recently. They'd just celebrated their first wedding anniversary last month.

"Congratulations," the FedEx guy said before taking his computerized clipboard from her before jogging back to his delivery truck.

Must have a lot of deliveries, Abby thought as she struggled to drag the large box inside the front corridor of her new digs, though one could hardly call this twelve-thousand-square-foot mansion "digs." The old plantation home had been in Chris's family for over two hundred years. Her mother had lived here briefly when she was married to Garland, Chris's father, who was her mother's fourth husband, Abby believed, but she hardly remembered the plantation. She'd been in her first year of high school when they had moved here and had spent more time hanging out with her girlfriends than she had at home. Garland Clay hadn't lived very long after marrying her mother—poor old soul—but he'd been a kind and decent stepfather. Her mother said that he was her second favorite out of her eight husbands—the first, of course, being Abby's father,

John Simpson. Abby didn't really have too many memories of him. He'd been killed in a car crash when she was five. Her mom had hired Bernice as an assistant/housekeeper/babysitter, and later the two women had become the best of friends. They'd moved from New Jersey to Charleston. Abby had spent most of her life in the South, save for the few years she'd spent living in Los Angeles. She still had her little ranch house in Brentwood, though she'd recently rented it out to a young couple who'd just had a baby. A little boy, if her memory served her right.

Her life had been running at maximum velocity since she and Chris married last April. After being kidnapped by Rag, Rodwell Archibald Godfrey, the former owner of, and her boss at, *The Informer,* Abby's passion for tabloid news had fizzled like stale ginger ale when she became the news herself. Though she still had a hand in the inner workings of the paper, Abby's heart wasn't in the business anymore. Not just because she knew her mother had secretly purchased the paper, when Abby told her they were about to go under. No, it was more than that: The chase. The interviews. And, even more than anything, the shallowness of what she actually wrote about had jumped up and kicked her between the eyes. It wasn't important. Any way you looked at it, it was simply silly trivia. It just didn't matter in the grand scheme of things, such as hunger, war, and natural disasters. Entertainment it was, but Abby had to admit—though she would never voice the thoughts out loud, especially to her mother, whose love of the tabloids hadn't decreased one bit since her abduction—most of it was exaggerated. Half-truths, actors' and actresses' lives pumped up to appear as though they were the chosen ones. Life was perfect if you were lucky enough, smart enough, and had the talent to achieve the glorified interpretation of what it was like to live the life of a celebrity in Hollywood. When speaking to or writing about an actor or actress, Abby always had to remind herself to be politically correct when using those words, as they were gender specific. According to her writings, and those of a hundred others, to have the opportunity to glimpse the life of a celebrity from the inside was quite exhilarating, and those who were granted an inside peek were also privileged. She'd had that attitude from the time she was a little girl, no doubt something inherited from her mother. Not any longer. Though writing was in her blood, and the desire to continue to do so would always be a part of her, she didn't care about Hollywood and all the glitz and glamour. Those few hours spent locked away in that awful, hot, dark closet had opened her eyes. She'd made a promise to herself then. If she survived, she was going to take life more seriously. And she had, she thought as she pushed and shoved the heavy box down the long corridor that led to the kitchen. For the past six months, much to her mother and godmothers' delight, she'd spent every waking moment decorating and refurnishing the Clay Plantation. Inside the heavy box was an antique oak bench from a church in southern Georgia, which dated back to the early nineteenth century. Her mother had insisted she purchase it for the kitchen; Toots told Abby that someday she would have children, and this bench would be the most perfect place for them to sit if they were being punished. Abby had laughed, but secretly, she agreed. She imagined a tow-headed little boy, with scraped knees and soulful blue eyes, begging her just to let him play one more round of Mario Brothers before he went to bed. And maybe a little girl with wispy curls and pillowy cheeks sticking her tongue out when she thought her mother wasn't looking.

Shit!

"The heat is getting to me," she said to herself as she ripped the packing tape off the top of the box. Hundreds of Styrofoam pieces shaped like peanuts scattered across the newly shellacked oak floor. She heard Chester, her dog-child, who just so happened to be a German shepherd, making his entrance as his nails clicked against the floor. He trotted across the large room to see what all the commotion was about.

"Ruff!" Chester barked softly. Abby knew this as his "I'm just curious" bark.

She reached across the bench she'd hefted out of its carton to scratch Chester between the ears. "According to Mom, this thing here"—she knocked on the bench for emphasis—"is going to be something of a discipline seat."

The big shepherd tilted his head to the left, contemplating her words as though they were pearls of wisdom fallen from the heavens.

"I don't get it, either, but it is what it is," Abby said as she continued to remove bits and pieces of plastic wrap and little balls of Styrofoam from the antique bench. She did get it, she thought, but she wasn't quite ready to say the words out loud. She needed to give them time to percolate in her brain, then bubble and simmer a bit before she actually said them out loud. And to Chris, she couldn't forget him. He was her husband. Just the thought of him made her grin from ear to ear. Her fondest wish had come true, and here she was actually living smack-dab in the middle of what she once thought to be an impossible dream. She and Chris had married, and their life, so far, had been one helluva blast. Though she sometimes missed Los Angeles and the excitement, it never lasted long enough to have an effect on her. Her life in Charleston was as close to perfect as one could get. At least she thought so.

"Ruff, ruff!"

Apparently, Chester agreed. "It's a cool place to be, Chester."

Again, the dog barked, in complete agreement.

Chester now possessed acres and acres of land to run on, and zillions of squirrels to chase. Plus, who knew what lurked beneath the dark water of the pond just south of the main house? Abby still had a hard time referring to her house as the *main* house. It dredged up memories of times that were best forgotten. Yes, this was a plantation home, she knew, but she hated to think of it as a place that had once housed slaves. No way, not now. A dozen small buildings that once housed the many slaves and their families were situated where you couldn't actually view them from the main house, but Abby knew they were there. Chris didn't like them, either, but he wouldn't tear them down, because they were part of his historic home. Together, they hoped to put the buildings to good use.

She and Chris had discussed it at great length, and both agreed they wanted to help those in need. With the $10 million she'd received from her mother as a wedding gift, plus the monumental inheritance Chris had received when they married, they had way more than enough funds to work with. Chris took care of the documentation they needed to establish a nonprofit foundation. All they needed now were volunteers, and they could begin. She planned to get her mother and the three g's to the table and share the idea with them. Of course, her mother would start asking 10 zillion questions about her and Chris's plans for a family, and she would tell her they had all the time in the world to start a family. Well, maybe not *all* the time in the world. She wasn't getting any younger.

Abby grinned. Why did her thoughts continue to stray down this path? It must be the bench and her mother's suggestion, she thought, as she continued to ball up the plastic wrap and toss it aside.

Being only children themselves, both she and Chris wanted a large family, but neither had pinned down a certain time. Abby figured, if it happened, fine; if not, then that was fine, too. Frankly, she thought at her age she'd probably have to go the in vitro route, and she would if it were needed. But until then, she planned to enjoy the privileges of married life. Often and heartily. She shivered at the thought.

Chris was all she'd ever dreamed of, and then some. Sometimes she still felt like this was a dream and she would wake up, back in Brentwood, with Chester nuzzling her neck. The image brought forth a toothy grin. Yeah, Chester would always be her main man. He'd practically saved her life; and for that, she loved him even more. The big dog had become quite attached to Chris in the past few months. There were many mornings when Abby awakened, only to find she'd been deserted by her hubby and her best friend. *My boys,* she thought as she wiggled the bench over to a large rug.

Once she had the bench properly positioned on the rug, she pulled the rug slowly to the kitchen, careful not to tip the bench on its side. Once she had it in place, she took her iPhone from her pocket and snapped a quick picture, sending it to her mother's cell phone. Her mother was a pro when it came to decorating, and she truly appreciated all of her suggestions.

Seconds later she heard a ping coming from her cell phone. Her mother. The message:

Perfect. Needs occupants.

Abby grinned. Since she and Chris had gotten married, her mother and godmothers never missed an opportunity to let her know they would love a grandchild. Abby texted back: In due time.

Her mother's response: Only takes nine months.

She quickly replied: I'll tell Chris. We so enjoy the practice!!! That was sure to keep her mother quiet for a few minutes.

Chris needs to spend more time with you, Toots texted back.

Abby's fingers raced across the touch screen: Enough, Mom. I mean it. She added three smiley faces, just so her mother would know her text message wasn't meant to be sharp. Actually, Abby didn't mind her mother's constant urging, but it just seemed like that's all she and the three g's talked about since she and Chris got married. Well, that and the redecorating, plus Sophie and Goebel's plans for the future, Ida's conceit, Mavis's love life, and Bernice's main man, Robert, who was obsessed with finding new recipes. Her mother was careful to keep her and Phil's relationship to herself, telling them it was no one's business. They had all agreed to leave it alone for the time being.

Chester chose that very moment to jump on his hind legs and scratch at the back door. "Hey, pal, what's this? You've got that fancy doggie door Chris installed if you need to go out."

Curious to see what Chester was so anxious about, she peered through the small pane of glass above the door.

What she saw caused her to laugh out loud.

Chapter 2

"I'm assuming she thinks I'm at home," Toots said to Mavis. Each held a small dog in her arms. Mavis held her beloved Coco, a demanding Chihuahua who insisted on being treated as though she were a member of the royal family. Toots had a death grip on Frankie, the adorable dachshund Phil Becker had rescued from her former neighbor, the now-deceased Mrs. Patterson.

She had an agreement with Dr. Phil Becker, whom she'd met at the hospital when he'd saved Bernice's life. While he was at work, saving lives as a top-notch cardiac surgeon, Toots insisted he drop Frankie off at her place. She feared that the little hound, who had had major back surgery last year, would try leaping on and off the furniture if he was left unattended. Now Coco and Frankie were practically inseparable, and Toots and the good doctor, too. He'd told her of his future plans last night, and she'd been in a mental frenzy since. She needed something to take her mind off him, and seeing her daughter always cheered her up.

With a rare free afternoon, Mavis decided to accompany her on a spontaneous visit to Abby's. Now that Abby was just a few blocks away, Toots and the three g's saw Abby all the time, much more than when they were all living in Los Angeles. Since Abby had returned to Charleston, Chester had gotten used to seeing Coco. When a few days went by without a visit, Abby told them, Chester acted depressed if he didn't see Coco, his "doggie love," as they now referred to her.

"So much for a surprise visit," Toots said when she spied Chester and Abby peering out the window of the back door.

"You should have told her you were practically in her backyard when you were sending her all those text messages," Mavis informed her.

Toots rolled her eyes. "You're no fun since you've turned into a skinny, successful entrepreneur," Toots shot back, smiling.

Five years ago, Mavis had been a heart attack waiting to happen. More than a hundred pounds overweight, she spent most of her days in her little Maine cottage in front of the television, with ice cream and potato chips for company. Toots had sent Mavis, Sophie, and Ida, her three dearest friends, airline tickets to Charleston right after her eighth husband Leland's funeral—rather, *event*—as she referred to the funerals of all her husbands. They'd made the trip, and life had been one great big whirlwind ever since.

Toots remembered picking Mavis up at the airport in Charleston and barely recognizing her. Being the take-charge person she was, Toots immediately insisted Mavis visit her longtime physician and friend, Dr. Pauley, for a complete checkup. Toots had told her she had best get a handle on her health now, before it was too late. It didn't hurt that she'd added that if Mavis wanted to live long enough to see her goddaughter marry and have a family of her own, then she'd best get her act together ASAP.

Mavis took her advice to heart. She shed her bad habits like dirty clothes, and lost more than a hundred pounds. Now Mavis was an inspiration to all of them, though Toots was not going to tell her this again. She was becoming almost as conceited as Ida. Secretly, Toots was extremely proud of her, and on occasion told her so. Mavis was the Goody Two-shoes in the group, and it was difficult to say anything negative about her now that she'd changed her wicked eating habits. She wasn't like Sophie, who, like herself, chain-smoked and cussed at every opportunity, or like Ida, who was just a plain uptight old bitch and full-time slut. No, Mavis was good and decent. Not to say Ida and Sophie weren't, but Toots could bad-mouth them without feeling the least bit guilty. Mavis simply inspired goodness in all those around her.

Before they even made it to the back door, Abby released Chester, who sprinted toward them like an athlete running in a marathon. He stopped as soon as he saw Coco and Frankie. Frankie wiggled free from Toots's grasp, and Coco practically flew to the ground. The three canines licked and sniffed before deciding it was okay to follow the humans inside.

"See what I mean?" Abby said as she stood aside, allowing them to enter. "When he sees Coco, he goes nuts. And Frankie, too. I'm surprised Chester isn't jealous of the little wiener. I think they're both head over heels in love."

Coco growled as though she knew they were discussing her love life.

"She loves Chester, too," Mavis said matter-of-factly, as though they were discussing humans. "I believe Frankie qualifies as her BFF," Mavis added.

They laughed as they discussed the animals who were like family to all of them.

"That's cool. Right, Frankie?" Abby said as she closed the back door.

The little doxie gave a low, manly growl.

"They really do understand me. I swear they're more intelligent than some of the people I know!"

"Like Ida?" Toots teased.

"Mom! You should be ashamed of yourself. Ida is a highly intelligent woman, not to mention she's quite an astute businesswoman." Abby motioned for them to sit. She'd made a pitcher of sweet tea earlier. "Jamie brought some of her pralines over yesterday. How many do you want?" Abby asked as she filled three tall glasses with ice cubes before pouring the chilled sweet tea over the top. She added lemon and a sprig of mint to each glass; then she piled a dinner plate high with pralines. Between her and her mother, she knew they'd make a nice dent in Jamie's specialty. Mavis wouldn't dare touch one, but that was okay with Abby. She and Chris would have the leftovers for dessert. Or dinner, whichever came first. She laughed out loud as she placed the glasses on the table.

"I don't think I've ever seen you this happy," Toots said to her daughter. "Marriage suits you."

"No, Mom, it's Chris that 'suits' me. He is so"—she looked away from her mother, a dreamy gaze filling her bright blue eyes—"perfect. Or at least the closest to perfect I'll ever find."

"That makes me so happy, dear," Mavis said. "I know what it's like to have a man light up your life, fill you with such joy that words can't describe the feeling." Mavis took a sip of her tea. "Herbert and I were like that, you know? At least the first few years. The sparkle doesn't wear off if you keep it polished." Mavis cast her eyes downward, a slight smile on her face. "If you know what I mean."

"Mavis, she's a grown woman. Of course, she knows what you're referring to. A good sex life makes for a happy marriage."

Abby's blue eyes rounded. "Poor mom. I guess that's why you've walked down the aisle so many times, huh? You liked all the good sex. Maybe too much, since all of your hubbies kicked the bucket."

"Abby Simpson-Clay, that's a mean thing to say!" Toots admonished her daughter, though she did so with a grin. "It seems like I jinx all the men I've married." Little did they know—this was now a secret fear she carried around.

"Maybe all that hot sex was too much for them," Abby added.

"You two are getting to be as bad as Sophie, all this sex talk," Mavis said, though she, too, had a smile as wide as the moon on her sweet face.

"Have you noticed how she's been kind of mum on the topic the last few months?" Toots questioned, then answered herself. "I think it's because she and Goebel are going at it hot and heavy, and she doesn't want us to know."

"Well, they are engaged," Mavis reminded her.

"Yes, and I, for one, am very happy for her. After Walter, that old bastardly drunkard, she deserves a man who appreciates her and treats her like a lady." Toots paused, then added, "Even though she doesn't act like a lady."

"And you're one to talk," Abby remarked; then she seemed to rethink what she'd just said. "I don't mean to imply that you're not a lady, Mom, just that . . . you know what I mean. I guess what I want to say is, you're one cool . . . chick!" Abby giggled like a kid.

"Well, then, coming from 'one cool chick' to another, I'll take that as a compliment," Toots replied.

"Good. So now that we've agreed you're a 'cool chick,' how are things going between you and Phil? I saw the two of you smooching the other night when you thought I was visiting Jamie at the guesthouse," Abby teased. "Actually, we both watched. Phil must be a good kisser, huh? And before you tell me you're just friends, well, *friends* don't kiss that way."

Toots felt her face flush. "It's none of your business, Abby. And we are good friends. Nothing more."

Mavis looked at Abby, brows raised. "That means there is something going on, or more than she wants the rest of us to know. Remember, she said there would never be another after Leland? Number nine was *not* going to happen."

Toots flipped her middle finger at Mavis, her usual answer when she didn't want to talk or when the topic under discussion wasn't to her liking.

"Mom, come on, tell us," Abby encouraged. "I see the way the two of you look at each other. You certainly can't deny that there's more than a bit of chemistry there. Remember, I'm a married woman myself. I know what lust is all about."

"And love, I hope," Toots added, before taking a long gulp of ice tea.

"Mother!" Abby said.

Toots took a deep breath and rubbed her finger along the bottom of her glass, where condensation had formed. Indecisive, she wasn't sure how to say what she wanted to say. What *needed* to be said. It was just so embarrassing.

Concern etched Mavis's brow. "Toots, dear, you're not sick or anything, are you?"

Toots was quick to raise her hand, motioning her hand left and right. "No, no. It's nothing like that," she responded, but she thought it might be easier than what she'd been struggling with since Phil revealed his big life plan.

"Then what is it?" Abby asked. "I don't like all this mysterious stuff when we're talking about family."

"She's right, Toots. If you have something you want to talk about, you can tell us. Like Abby said, we're family."

Toots nodded. "Promise me, you'll both keep this to yourselves until I make a decision?"

Abby and Mavis both nodded their agreement.

Sighing heavily, as though she had the weight of the world on her shoulders, Toots said, "I suppose it has to come out sooner or later."

Chapter 3

"Mom, you're scaring me," Abby said, her blue eyes widening with concern.

Toots took another sip of her tea. "It's nothing for anyone to be worried about."

"Then you should simply tell us, Toots. Don't keep us in suspense," Mavis said, then reached for her friend's hand. "It can't be that bad."

Though she was reluctant to reveal her inner dilemma, she knew she had to tell someone what she'd been going through—if for nothing more than to let someone else share her embarrassment, and possibly help her make a decision. Another deep sigh. "Phil wants to take things to"—she made air quotes as she spoke—" 'the next level.' He's retiring this year and wants to go to Myrtle Beach and write that medical drama he's been talking about. He's asked me to come along." There, that was out. Now if she could just bring herself to tell the rest of what had been bothering her, she might be forced to acknowledge what she hadn't been ready or willing to acknowledge until she absolutely had to.

Abby refilled their glasses; then she sat next to her mother. "That's it?"

Toots nodded, took another drink of tea, anything to

stall the inevitable. "With my past, don't you think that's enough?"

"I don't see that your past has anything to do with your future with Phil," Abby stated.

Toots's voice wavered when she said, "I've been around the block. Eight times. That doesn't bode well for Phil."

"Mom, you didn't kill the men you married. They all died of natural causes. If Phil wants to go to 'the next level,' whatever that means these days, then I say, go for it."

Toots hadn't even thought of *that*, but still she needed to explain something she hadn't yet explained. "It's not that, Abby. Of course, I am sorry for all of them. I am aware that I had nothing to do with the timing of their deaths. If that were the case, then your father would still be alive, and we wouldn't be having this conversation."

"Then, please, don't keep us in suspense any longer," Mavis said. "I worry."

Toots knew when enough was enough. She'd stalled as long as possible. Taking a deep breath, she lowered her voice as though the words she was about to deliver would be less embarrassing. "I know it's been over a year since I met Phil." She paused to look at Abby and Mavis. When she saw she had their undivided attention, she continued, but spoke in a normal tone. "We haven't gone to 'the next level' in our relationship." She stopped, unsure how to word what she had to say.

"You haven't slept with him? Is that what you're trying to tell us? He wants to, and you're skeptical?" Abby asked, seemingly unfazed at her mother's seeming inability to form the words.

"Yes, but there's more."

"Spit it out, Mom! For God's sake, it's not like you're Miss Polly Purebred."

When Toots tried to speak, her voice wavered. *This is not good,* she thought, for she was rarely tongue-tied or at a loss for words. *This shit is downright embarrassing,* she thought. "If you weren't a married woman, I would send you straight to your room without your supper."

"Toots, we know whatever it is you're trying to say is difficult. It's me, Tootsie, and my dearest goddaughter, your only child. There is no reason for you not to tell us something that is apparently very important to you," Mavis coaxed. "We're not going to judge you. Right, Abby?"

"Of course not."

Taking yet another deep breath, Toots knew it was now or never. "I haven't told Phil how many times I've been married. As far as he knows, he thinks it's only been a couple of times. Abby's father and then . . . one other."

Exasperated, Abby said, "Mother! How could you not tell him? You've been a couple for a long time. And what I want to know more than anything, why haven't you slept with him? As I said, it's not like you're Polly Purebred. You're still young enough to have a sex drive! Geez, Mom."

An uncomfortable lull of silence fell over the kitchen, broken only by the sounds made by the three dogs as they growled at one another, communicating in some sort of dog-speak that only they understood.

"Phil has never been married. With my record, I'm afraid that once he finds out, it will all be over. That's one of the reasons why I haven't slept with him. I don't want him to think I'm . . . easy. You know, a slut like Ida." She didn't want to reveal her fear that if she and Phil took their relationship further, he might die. No, she would keep that to herself.

There, it was out, and she did not feel one bit better. As a matter of fact, she felt worse for discussing the details of her private life with Abby. Mavis, well, that was different.

Abby reached for another praline and took a bite; then she gave her mother the evil eye. "You have to tell him. If you're really serious about him, honesty is the best policy.

I believe you're the one who taught me that, too. I guess this is a case of needing to practice what you preach."

"That's just it. I don't know if I have the right to be 're-ally serious' with any man at this stage of my life." Her eyes pooled with unshed tears. "This is so . . . unlike me!"

Maybe she was in the beginning stages of Alzheimer's, something she thought more often than she cared to admit, but only when she was fearful or in the midst of a life-altering decision. Sophie would call her a "wuss," and she'd be right on the money. She wanted to say, "The hell with it, just live in the moment," but she also felt as if she'd misled Phil. Once he learned she'd been around the block eight times, she just knew he wouldn't want any-thing to do with her.

And, really, could she blame him? If he'd had eight sig-nificant others, she would drop him like a hot potato. What was making this decision so hard was that she had real feelings for him. Maybe just a pure case of mature, aging-adult kind of love? The companionship kind of love where you were content to hold hands and watch reruns of *The Golden Girls*.

No, no, no! If this was going to work, she had to be honest, and she had to start by being honest with herself. She did not feel like a mature old woman with calf love for a man she only saw during meals and movie night at the senior center. No, her feelings were wild, exhilarating, ex-citing, the way she'd felt about John all those years ago when she was young and ripe for new love. The time she and Phil spent together just got better and better; it had to be the real deal. The butterflies in her stomach had not lessened one little bit, but maybe that was because she'd put off sleeping with him. What if she slept with him, and all of the lovey-dovey, I'm-on-top-of-the-world feelings disappeared? She was damned either way.

Abby placed her hand on top of hers, leaning across the

table. "Mom, stop being so hard on yourself. I wouldn't have wanted our life to be any other way than it was. I loved all those stepdads, except for Leland, whom I only met once, but can't you see? These life experiences have made you the woman you are today. If Phil Becker can't appreciate you for the woman you are, then he's not the man we think he is. Right, Mavis?" Abby asked.

Mavis's eyes darted from left to right; then she directed her verdant gaze directly at Toots. "Abby is right, Toots. You have nothing to be ashamed of. You've led a remarkable life. Look at me! Why, had you not sent for me, I would probably be up there"—with her index finger she pointed straight up, and they both knew what she meant— "with Herbert, and frankly, I loved Herbert with all my heart and soul, but I am not ready to give up on love. We're not that old. Wade teases me all the time, tells me my eyes are as bright as a ten-year-old's."

"He's right. They are, but you're high on life, Mavis. You've led a very normal life. You don't have all the baggage to carry around that I do."

"If I were Sophie, I would tell you, 'I'm gonna smack you in the face.' But I am not Sophie, though I would have to agree with her if she were listening to this conversation right now . . . but she isn't and I am. So . . . I did have a lot of baggage, Toots. Just a different kind. All those years I wasted, stuffing my face while spending all that time in front of the television. I'm so grateful to be alive, to be able to feel 'high on life.' If it weren't for you, and if I was still among the living, I would be in my little cottage in Maine, gorging on potato chips and ice cream. You touch everyone you come in contact with, Toots. Why can't you see what an amazing woman you are? So what if you've married a lot of men?" Mavis insisted. "They were men you cared for, so there should be no shame in that."

Toots knuckled the tears, which now flowed freely. Abby grabbed a stack of paper napkins off the counter and placed them in front of her mother. Toots dabbed at her eyes. "I don't deserve either one of you."

"Mom, stop it right now! I don't know what's crawled into your undies today, but whatever it is, it can't be that bad. This isn't like you. Like Sophie always says, 'Spit it out.' "

"Phil wants me to go with him when he retires, and I'm terrified if I say yes, I'll jinx him. All the men I've married seem to kick off as soon as I say, 'I do.' " So much for keeping her fears to herself.

"Has Phil asked you to marry him? Is that what you're trying to tell us?" Abby asked.

"No, of course not. I haven't even been intimate with him. Why would he want to marry me, without . . . well, you know what I mean." Toots blew her nose with another napkin.

Abby came around the table and sat next to her. She placed an arm on her mother's shoulder, and Toots squeezed her hand.

"Mom, you know what I think?"

Sniffing, she gave a halfhearted smile. "If I don't, you'll tell me anyway, so go ahead. What do you think?"

Chapter 4

"I think you need a project. Something to immerse yourself in. Other than helping me redecorate this place." Abby waved her free arm in a semicircle. "You haven't started any new projects, something you can really sink your teeth into."

"My gosh, Abby, after all those trips to Wilmington to tape for The Home Shopping Club, plus trying to look after Bernice without her knowing I'm actually looking after her, I haven't had much free time. What time I've had, I've spent with Phil."

"I know, Mom. But you're the kind of woman who thrives when you're busy, involved."

Abby was right. Since she'd returned to Charleston after the kidnapping fiasco, Toots hadn't really tackled a new project. Yes, she had the bakery, but Jamie and Lucy didn't need her help. If anything, it was better that she remain as far away as possible from The Sweetest Things, or she would wind up looking like a barn. Every time she stopped in the bakery, she left with ten pounds of pralines. If she kept that up, they'd soon be attached to her hips.

At that moment, the dogs started to bark hysterically. "I'll go see what's up with that trio," Mavis said, excusing herself.

"She's giving us some mother/daughter alone time," Toots said. "I'm all ears."

Abby laughed. "I know what she's doing."

Toots blew her nose on the last of the napkins.

Glad for the reprieve from her depressing thoughts, she smiled at her daughter, thinking, *"Fake it and you'll make it. An insincere grin is not a sin,"* her own mother's favorite words when Toots had been unhappy as a kid. They were words of wisdom, Toots realized.

"You know that Chris and I have more money than we know what to do with, right?"

Toots lifted a brow. "I suppose."

"Mother, you know we do! Now, listen, because what I am about to tell you is big. At least we, Chris and I, would like to think so. I want you to listen and don't interrupt me with a million questions that I probably won't be able to answer."

"Abby, you are a true brat, but I love you anyway. Now hurry," Toots said. "I am dying for a cigarette."

"You're gonna die *because* of those nasty things if you don't give them up."

"Sophie and I are down to five cigarettes per day," Toots informed Abby.

"And here I thought you'd all but quit."

"Abby, I know it's a nasty habit, but it is what it is. I have cut down, and maybe I'll give them up entirely. And, yes, I know I've said that before, but now isn't the time. I have a personal crisis and need the crutch."

"You can wait five more minutes to hear what I have to say," Abby insisted.

"Of course, I can." Toots looked at her watch. "Time's ticking away."

Abby rolled her eyes, smiling. "All those buildings that were once used as slave quarters, the ones by the pond, you know how much I dislike them."

Toots nodded.

"I'm aware of the historical value, but who says we can't put them to good use? Okay, here's the deal. Chris and I have set up a nonprofit organization called Dogs Displaced by Disaster. Whenever there's a natural disaster, there are always thousands of animals who are left homeless. What Chris and I want to do is find them, and bring them here to DDD. That's what we're calling our organization."

"Abby, that's a fantastic idea! Why didn't you tell me?"

"I'm telling you now. I didn't want to say anything until I was one hundred percent sure we could do this. I'm not talking about just stray dogs in the Charleston area. I'm talking all animals who are displaced by one disaster or another. Horses, cows, pigs, the whole nine yards. You know, Chris said he always wanted to be a farmer. This is as close to farming as it gets. I know you and Mavis will climb on board, pitch in whenever our services are needed. We planned to ask Phil about his doctor friend in Florida, the one who saved Frankie. We'll need all kinds of volunteers, from specialized vets to someone willing to clean up after the animals. Then we'll find good homes for them or return them to their original owners, only they'll be in tip-top condition. So"—Abby paused—"what do you say? Are you in or not?"

Returning to the kitchen, Mavis was just in time to ask, "In what?"

Toots whirled around, her issues with Phil temporarily forgotten. "Mavis, you are gonna love this. Go on, Abby, fill her in."

Toots and Mavis spent the next hour going over the details with Abby. When they'd covered all the basics, Toots had another idea. "So if we're going to be caring for these animals, twenty-four/seven, why not push the envelope a bit further?" Toots stood and picked up Frankie, who'd relocated to a place by her feet. Mavis scooped up Coco, and Chester inched up next to her.

"I can't believe you're doing this. You know I always wanted to do something special for animals. I do send a hefty check to the ASPCA every month, but this is different." Mavis glowed with excitement. "We can all help out, Abby. I'm sure Sophie and Ida will want in on this, too."

Toots grinned. "Sophie, for sure. Ida? Somehow I can't picture her slopping the hogs, but she continues to surprise me." Toots's eyes sparkled, and she knew it. She loved it when a new idea sparked her imagination. "Now, as I said, we might as well go all the way. Once in a while, Jamie bakes doggie treats for Coco and Frankie. They're actually pretty good." Toots laughed when she saw the look of horror on her daughter's face. "They're all natural, Abby. Jamie needed a human taste tester, and I was there. Anyway, we could have a canine café or something like that. A place to bring the animals when they're able to get out and about. Sort of like reintroducing them to the world."

Abby appeared to be in deep thought. Mavis vigorously rubbed Coco between the ears. Chester lay beneath the table, licking his paws.

"That's not a bad idea, Mom. Though we'd have to set limits on what size animals could visit the . . . café. I can't see horses and cows parading down the street, searching for a bale of hay or whatever."

They all laughed.

"Of course, we'd have to put restrictions on the types of animals, the city has all kinds of codes we'll have to work through, but I don't see that as a problem."

"I will tell Chris you're all in. He's going to be so excited when he hears your idea, Mom. Or would you rather I not tell him?"

Toots waved her free hand around. "No, no. Go ahead

and tell him. That way he can get started on whatever paperwork we're going to need. First we'll need to find a suitable building, something that's off the main streets where all the tourists go. We can't use the same building as the bakery. Besides, Jamie has most of the space rented out. The horse-and-carriage tours could scare a skittish animal, and we don't want that. I've got a few places in mind, but I'll have to call Henry. With all those real-estate agents coming and going at the bank, he's probably got inside information on real estate that someone wants to get rid of quickly." Toots was so focused on her new project, she almost forgot about her predicament with Phil. Almost.

Abby was right, though. She needed to get involved in a new project.

Taking a deep breath, Toots squared her shoulders and tucked Frankie close to her chest. "I'm going home to think this through. I am so excited, Abby. This is a really good thing to do. You're a good egg, Abby Simpson-Clay. A very good egg."

Abby followed her mother and godmother out the back door. "That's because I was raised by one hot chick!"

They all burst out laughing.

Toots gave her daughter a hug, Frankie gave her several doggie kisses; then Mavis and Coco repeated the actions.

"Mom!" Abby called out as soon as Toots had turned her back. "I haven't forgotten what we talked about. Just do it. You only live once."

Toots paused to hear Abby's words and couldn't help but smile. She'd screwed up a lot in her lifetime, but one thing she had not screwed up—she'd raised a remarkable young woman.

"Thank you, Abby. I'll certainly think about it."

Before Abby could say another word, Toots raced down the pathway leading to the main road. Once she saw it was safe, she put Frankie down and clipped on his leash. Mavis did the same with Coco, even though Coco constantly tugged and pulled at her leash. She wanted the world to know she was queen and did not need restraints of any kind. Mavis maintained a firm grip on her, though.

"I know you don't want to talk about it, but this is probably the only private time we'll have for a while. I promise to keep whatever you say between the two of us."

Though it was late April, Toots felt chilled as the afternoon breeze lifted the hair on the back of her neck. The air still held a slight chill, and she suddenly wished for a sweater as she walked alongside Mavis.

Clear skies, trees burgeoning with newly green growth, springtime in Charleston was Toots's favorite time of the year. Her azaleas were in full bloom and the night-blooming jasmine was just beginning to bud. As they walked, Toots couldn't help but notice that the side of the road was covered with yellow jessamine, its bright green foliage and deliciously fragrant flowers shaped like little yellow funnels. Its sweet, fruity scent wafted in the breeze. She loosened her grip on Frankie's leash, suddenly glad simply to be alive to enjoy nature and its divine delights.

"It doesn't get much better than this, does it?" Toots asked Mavis.

"It's quiet. We need quiet in our lives. The world is always in a hurry, but to answer your question, you're right. It doesn't get much better than this. Makes me homesick for Maine. I take it this means you don't want to discuss your relationship with Phil?" she concluded. Coco continued to trot alongside Mavis as though she were a breed of royalty, her little black nose held high in the air.

Taking a deep breath of the cool air, Toots held it in as long as she could, then exhaled. "Mavis, I feel like such a fake. To be frank, I think I'd rather lose Phil than have him think of me as a liar. I hate dishonesty." Fumbling in one of her pockets, Toots removed her cigarettes and lit up. She hated to taint the pure air, but screw it. She needed something to calm her nerves.

"You're not a dishonest person. You don't need me to tell you that. Just because you haven't revealed your past to Phil doesn't mean you've intentionally tried to deceive him. It's just one of those things that you'd rather not talk about in the beginnings of a new relationship, that's all. You're worrying over something that hasn't even happened and most likely won't."

"You're a good soul, Mavis. When did you become so wise?" Toots asked before taking a big puff of her cigarette.

Mavis blushed. "Oh, I'm not so wise, just getting older. Though I must admit, I didn't have as much fun when I was young as I'm having now. Of course, times were different then."

Toots nodded, lost in thoughts of her own youth. What if John had lived? She often went through that "what-if" scenario in her mind, all to no avail, as she could barely recall John's face without looking at a photograph. When they'd first met, she'd never thought in a million years that she would forget a single line, a single crease, on John's handsome face. Sadly, it had happened, and now it was hard to even imagine their life together. Though she'd married seven times since then, her heart had never felt as light and free as it had when she'd first met John Simpson all those years ago. That is, until now.

Here she was, pushing seventy, and she'd fallen madly in love with Dr. Phil Becker. She hadn't slept with him or married him. *Wonders never cease,* she thought. As much as it hurt to admit, Toots would have to give him up. Her luck with men—or, rather, their lack of luck with *her*—*really* did stop with Leland. It had to.

"We were ornery as hell back in the day," Toots said wistfully, then added, "Shit, Mavis, we're still the same girls we were back then. We've simply refined our ornery ways."

"Yes, I would say so," Mavis acquiesced.

They both cackled as they reached the gates to Toots's beautiful Southern estate. Toots mentally removed herself from her reverie, and knew it was time to get real, make a decision.

She had to tell Phil it was over between the two of them. If not, he would die.

Chapter 5

As Toots and Mavis rounded the sharp twist in the drive leading to the house, they were greeted by three police cruisers, their red and blue lights flashing against the lush gardens, making the bold colors appear wild and unnatural.

"What the f—?" Toots shouted. She scooped Frankie up and ran as fast as she could. Mavis followed suit. *Something must have happened to Bernice! Oh no, not now.* She was not ready to lose her. *Hell no,* she inwardly screamed.

"Something's happened!" Mavis shouted the obvious.

Racing to the steps leading inside, Toots pushed the door aside. The murmur of voices led her to the kitchen.

Seated around her kitchen table were four men and two women she did not know. Half of them wore dark suits; the other half wore the police officer's standard uniform.

Toots let Frankie loose and stepped into the room. "Would someone tell me what's going on? Where is Bernice? I want to know, now!"

"Oh, for cryin' out loud, I'm in the pantry looking for something to serve these officers."

Relieved to hear that Bernice was her usual bitchy self, Toots's heartbeat returned to something close to normal, but only a little bit. It wasn't like she came home every day to a houseful of blue suits. "Someone want to tell me exactly what's going on?"

The back door to the kitchen opened. Sophie, followed by Goebel, entered; both wore somber expressions.

"If someone doesn't tell me what's going on, I'm not going to be held responsible for my actions! Now, damn it, why in the hell are these . . . strangers sitting in my kitchen?" Toots knew she sounded a bit hysterical, but at that moment, she just didn't care.

"Sophie?" she asked, turning to her longtime friend. "Are you in some sort of trouble?"

"Shut the frig up, Toots. No, I'm not in trouble, but you may be," she said as she stood at the head of the table. She gave Toots a wink, letting her know she wasn't completely serious. Still, Toots knew there was more of the brown stuff headed her way.

Goebel, ever the gentleman, spoke. "Toots, two kids have disappeared, a brother and sister. The place they were last seen was The Sweetest Things. The officers want to speak to all of us. Jamie and Lucy are on their way."

It took several seconds for Toots to gather herself. Taking a deep breath, she exhaled and reached for a cigarette, then thought better of it and put her pack of cigarettes on the counter. "I don't . . . I don't know what to say! Dear God, this is horrible!"

At her words, one of the men seated at the table stood. He wore a dark charcoal suit, a collared white shirt, and a royal blue tie, with a ship emblazoned in gold in its center. He had close-cropped brown hair and clear gray eyes. He was all business as he held out his hand to her. "I'm Detective William Howard."

Toots wished she'd had a few minutes to make herself half-assed presentable, but she hadn't. She shook hands with him. His grip firm, his gaze direct—Toots liked him immediately. "Teresa Loudenberry."

"Ms. Loudenberry," Detective Howard spoke kindly,

his voice that of a genteel Southern man, quite the opposite of what you'd expect. "Early this afternoon, Jeremy Dunlop and his sister, Kristen, were seen leaving the aforementioned bakery."

He is all business, Toots thought, but she kept it to herself. This wasn't time for any smart remarks. "Were they alone?"

"Yes. Jeremy is twelve and Kristen is nine. Their parents are visiting relatives in Charleston. Apparently, they were touring some of the local sights on the waterfront. The parents stopped for a coffee break at The Daily Grind, which is just down the street from the bakery. The kids asked their parents if they could go to the bakery. Of course, being as it was only a few doors down, they let them. They waited for half an hour, then got distracted while they were talking with another couple, who'd been on a tour with them. Another hour passed, and they went to the bakery, searching for the kids. According to the parents, that was the last time they were seen."

"I don't know what I can do to help, but just say the word and consider it done," Toots said, a wave of sadness overcoming her. *Those poor little kids . . . and the parents. They must be going through hell right now.* She recalled when that scummy bastard, Rodwell Archibald Godfrey, kidnapped Abby last spring. She'd wanted to strangle the life right out of him. Luckily, she'd had a happy ending. Toots hoped like hell these parents got their happy ending, too.

Detective Howard nodded, shook hands with Goebel, then Sophie, as they stood next to Toots.

"You're Sophia Manchester," the detective acknowledged as Sophie took his hand.

"The one and only. Now, tell me, what can I do?" Sophie asked.

Okay, now this was making a bit of sense to her, Toots thought.

"As you know, when a child disappears, the first forty-eight hours are the most critical. We've asked your employees to close the bakery and leave the premises. Two of our best bloodhounds are there as we speak. Mrs. Manchester, the parents know of your . . . success in locating missing people. Once the children's parents learned that you had relocated to Charleston, they asked us to contact you. They've given me some personal possessions that belong to Jeremy and Kristen. If that's how you work." He stopped, then directed his gaze back to Toots.

"The girl"—he removed a black leather notebook from inside his jacket, flipped through several pages—"Jamie says she remembers the kids because she gave them an extra praline. She told us the kids were extremely polite, and she'd said this to Lucy as soon as they left the bakery. Now, my questions to you . . . What do you know about Jamie Cooper and Lucy Rice? How long have you known them? Where did you meet them? We need some connection, and we're not coming up with anything."

Toots felt a moment of anger; then she regretted it. These people didn't know Jamie or Lucy. It was simply part of their interrogation process, or whatever they called it. "You're not coming up with anything because Jamie and Lucy have absolutely nothing to do with those children's disappearing. I've known Jamie for three years. And Lucy, about two years now. I met Jamie when she first opened her bakery, which was later shut down due to bad publicity."

Toots wasn't going to mention the superstitions that were running rampant that day. Some guy, heavy and out of shape, had stood in line waiting to purchase some of Jamie's cupcakes. He'd died of a heart attack while standing in line. Nor was she going to mention the haunting at the bakery. If he accepted Sophie as a psychic, then that was enough for now. She didn't need to add any more suspicion to an already disastrous case.

A sharp knock on the kitchen door was followed by Jamie and Lucy, both still wearing their pink-and-red aprons. "Toots! Oh, my gosh! Those kids. I swear I . . ." She stopped when she saw all of the police officers in the kitchen. "Have you found them? The dogs went wild as soon as they entered the store."

Mavis, ever the nurturer, came into the kitchen and took Jamie in her arms. "It's all right, sweetie. We know you didn't have anything to do with their disappearance." As soon as the words were out of Mavis's mouth, Jamie pushed out of her embrace, astonishment causing her face to turn as white as the flour she used.

With a hand over her mouth, and an index finger pointed to no one in particular, Jamie finally got her bearings. When she spoke, they all had to strain to hear what she was saying. "You think I had something to do with those kids disappearing?"

The other officers had remained silent the entire time. The two women, one in plainclothes attire, the other wearing the traditional cop uniform, walked over to stand beside Detective Howard. "This is Officer Dawn Furdell and Detective Shannon O'Banyon. Officer Furdell responded to the call. Shannon heads up our Missing Child Unit."

Jamie nodded, "Uh, okay."

Detective Shannon O'Banyon exemplified her Irish name. Rusty hair cut into a neat pageboy; clear green eyes oozing sincerity; a smattering of freckles across her pale face, which gave off an air of confidence, with a quiet authority. "I know this isn't easy for you, but if you could tell me what you told Officer Furdell."

Jamie made a halfhearted attempt to smile at the officer she'd met earlier, but she failed. Tears ran down her cheeks. Toots grabbed a kitchen towel and handed it to Jamie.

It took her a few seconds to compose herself. Detective

O'Banyon waited patiently, as though they had all the time in the world; in reality, every minute counted.

Jamie sniffed, blotted her eyes, then proceeded to repeat what she knew. "As I said, it was a bit after lunchtime. We always have a lull then. Lucy and I took a break, as we'd been swamped all day. We were sitting at one of the tables, having lunch, when the two kids came in. You could tell they were excited when they looked in the display cases and saw them filled with all the goodies. I got up and went behind the counter and asked them if I could help them. They took a couple of minutes to decide. Then both of them asked for a bubble-gum-flavored cupcake. It was the flavor of the day. We do that sometimes," Jamie added, even though this information was of no importance. "They paid for their cupcakes, then stood in the store and ate them. They thanked me and told me they were the best they'd ever had in their lives. Lucy and I laughed. That's when I offered them a praline. They said they didn't have any more money, but I told them it was on the house. They finished their pralines, and after thanking me again, they left. That's all I can tell you. They were nice kids, very polite. They used several napkins and were very careful not to get crumbs on the floor or themselves. Usually, kids just plow right into whatever they're eating, not caring one way or another about making a mess."

Detective O'Banyon smiled. "That would be my two. Twins. Boys, they're seven. When they have food in their hands, they leave a trail."

Toots listened to the exchange between Jamie and the detective, thinking of Hansel and Gretel. If only Jeremy and Kristen had been messy and left a trail of cupcake crumbs behind, maybe they wouldn't be here now discussing a parent's worst nightmare.

"Did you notice anyone lingering about the bakery that day? Before they came in? After they left?" Detective O'Banyon asked.

Jamie shook her head. "Like I said, we were slammed, and I didn't really pay that much attention. It's just Lucy and me. We fill orders, work the register, and run back and forth to the kitchen when we run out of whatever is selling the most."

Detective O'Banyon took notes as she spoke. "Thanks, now, uh"—she hurried through her notes again—"Lucy, could you tell me what you told Officer Furdell?"

Lucy, who'd been hired after Bernice's heart surgery, had been quiet the entire time. She'd worked with Jamie in the bakery at Publix. Jamie and Toots took exactly two minutes to hire her; or, rather, Jamie had, as Toots had been out of town at the time. Lucy was a few years older than Jamie, and was far more experienced when it came to decorating the cupcakes, cakes, and anything that required something extra. A bit on the quiet side, Lucy stood shyly by Jamie as she recalled the events of the day. "Like Jamie said, the kids were friendly and polite. Once they finished their pralines, they said good-bye and left."

O'Banyon jotted something down; then she addressed the officers, who remained seated at the table. "Okay, you all have heard as much as you need to. Go ahead and return to your assignments." The unnamed police officers left without sampling the box of stale Fig Newtons Bernice held in her hand.

Toots trailed behind Detective O'Banyon and Officer Furdell as they followed the other officers to their vehicles. The four police officers made fast work of getting inside the two cruisers parked directly in front of her house. With only one left, Toots was surprised when she saw headlights heading toward the house. Not completely dark, with sunset minutes away, she thought of the missing children and prayed wherever they were, they were safe and warm. The vehicle coming toward the house was a long, sleek black limousine.

"Shit! It's Ida," she said out loud.

Ida had spent the past three days in Wilmington, North Carolina, where The Home Shopping Club recorded its programs. She'd had such overwhelming success with her new line of skin-care products that she was now featured at least once a month to update the world on what was new at Seasons, Beauty at Every Age. So successful, Ida had even been featured on *The Today Show.* Toots was beyond thrilled for her, but the notoriety simply fed Ida's already giant-sized ego. Ida removed something, Toots assumed it was cash, from her Chanel bag, placed it in the driver's hand, said a few words, then walked up the stairs to the veranda, where Toots, Officer Furdell, and Detective O'Banyon were waiting.

"I passed two police cruisers on my way in. What in the world has happened now?" Ida asked. As usual, she was dressed impeccably. Wearing cream slacks with a matching silk shirt, low heels, which Toots knew were exclusively made by hand for that particular outfit, and carrying the Chanel handbag, Ida looked as though she'd stepped right off the runway. Her silver-blond hair was now cut short in the back, and the sides were cut at a sharp angle. She looked sleek and sexy, and she knew it.

"Nice to see you, too," Toots smirked; then she remembered now wasn't the time for her or any of them to start their usual smart-ass banter.

Once the introductions were made, Toots suggested they all go back inside. Bernice had brewed a pot of that new Kopi Luwak coffee, for which she paid almost two hundred dollars a pound.

Sophie and Goebel were putting cups and saucers on the table. Bernice poured the coffee into a carafe, placing it in the center of the table, with a small pitcher of cream and a bowl of sugar. Jamie came through the back door with a box of baked goods from The Sweetest Things, which she had at the guesthouse. Lucy took the box of pastries and put them on a dinner plate. Though it wasn't a formal occasion, Bernice used Toots's good crystal dessert plates. *What the hell,* Toots thought. *You only live once.*

"Detective, Officer, please sit and have some coffee. It's the best money can buy," Toots said, for lack of anything else to say.

"Thanks, that does smell good," Detective O'Banyon said, then poured herself a cup before taking a seat at the head of the table. Officer Furdell filled a cup and sat next to her superior, with another little black notebook placed in front of her.

Toots and Mavis scurried around the kitchen for napkins, while Sophie and Goebel made themselves comfortable. Bernice was busy looking out the back door for Robert, their neighbor. His brother, Wade, was out of town on business, and that left a bereft Mavis waiting anxiously for his return.

They took a couple of minutes to gather themselves; then Detective O'Banyon prepared to remove two items from a small leather pouch, which appeared out of nowhere. Before removing the contents, she took a pair of latex gloves from her back pocket and snapped them on.

All eyes were focused on her and the contents of the bag. Carefully she pulled out a worn stuffed rabbit, which looked as though it had seen far better days. A dirty white, the fur was all but gone. One bright blue eye and one black eye. Someone had sewn the blue eye on because it looked new and didn't match the original eye. Limp ears hung on either side of the mismatched eyes. With care, she placed the bunny on the table. Next she took a Nintendo Game Boy out of the bag and placed it beside the stuffed animal.

"The parents told us that Kristen takes this old bunny with her everywhere they go, because she can't get to sleep without it. Like most twelve-year-old boys, Jeremy doesn't travel far without this electronic gadget, either." Detective O'Banyon looked at Sophie, skepticism hardening her features. "So, is this something you can . . . will pull up images with, or whatever it is you do?" Her voice was not kind as she spoke.

For the first time since she'd returned from Abby's and met Shannon O'Banyon, Toots saw her other side and knew why she'd made detective. She was by the book, no bullshit. And Toots was sure she thought Sophie's abilities nothing more than a great big pile of it.

Sophie, being Sophie, was quick to cut the detective off. "First of all, let's make one thing clear. I don't give a big rat's ass if you believe in what I do or not. Second, I did not come to you volunteering my services. The parents of these poor children asked you to contact me—which you have done. And third, I don't perform on command. I'll take the items now. And I am not doing this for you. I will do what I can for those kids and their parents. But I won't do anything here in front of you. I need to be alone. And I make no promises, either."

Toots had never heard Sophie tell anyone this before and wondered if that was a bad omen already.

She needed to work her magic and do it fast. It was dark outside, the kids would probably be scared and hungry, and who knew what had befallen them?

"Sophie, take their things to my room. I'll make sure you're not disturbed," Toots said, loud and clear.

Chapter 6

Sophie took the worn-out stuffed animal and Game Boy upstairs to Toots's room. Taking a deep breath, she sat on the edge of the bed and did her best to clear her mind of all negative thoughts, especially those she had let loose downstairs in the kitchen. Inhaling deeply through her nose, she held it; then she slowly released her breath through her mouth. She did that a few more times until she could feel the negative energy leave her body.

She took both objects, holding the rabbit in her right hand and the Game Boy in her left. She waited for an image, a feeling to come over her, but nothing happened. Sophie hadn't practiced clairsentience, the power to use one's psychic abilities by sense of touch. Though she'd had many physical reactions using this method in the past, her abilities to pull up real-time images had never been tested. She knew what the parents expected of her, and she was going to do her best to help them locate their children.

Sophie put the bunny and the Game Boy in the center of Toots's bed; then she turned her back to them. She walked across the room and peered outside. Twilight gave the gardens below a surreal appearance, as though a gauzelike haze blanketed the surroundings. Focusing on the giant oak trees that canopied the path in front of the house, Sophie did her best to clear her mind to open it for a message of any kind—an image, a feeling, anything that would help in the search—but she continued to come up empty. Impatient with herself, she took the rabbit and the Game Boy off the bed and held them against her heart. Eyes closed, Sophie suddenly felt a jolt, as though she'd placed her hand in an electrical outlet. Startled, she opened her eyes. Expecting to see the bedroom, Sophie's heart raced. Blinking rapidly to dispel the image didn't work. A deep breath. *So this* is *clairsentience!*

The detective downstairs hadn't mentioned what the children looked like, or what they were wearing when they disappeared. Now she knew why.

With her eyes wide open, Sophie watched the scenario take place as though she were watching a film.

A young boy who appeared right on the precipice of reaching his early teens had an arm around a small girl. He wore a dark blue shirt with a cartoon character on it. The little girl wore a pink skirt and a top with a kitty on it. Her long brown hair was plastered to her cheeks from crying.
Back to the boy.

Sophie could hear his thoughts, see his face as clearly as if he had been standing right in front of her.

His eyes were glazed over with tears, but he wouldn't cry. He didn't want to scare Kristen any more than she was already. He was going to be in so much trouble when his parents found him. If they found him. He'd just helped that old man, or that's what he thought. He stank of alcohol and urine. Jeremy felt sorry for him. His mom and dad told him and Kristen about the homeless, but they'd never really seen a real-live homeless person until now. As soon as they left the bakery, the old man had asked for their help. They followed him for a few blocks away from the coffee shop, where his parents were waiting, so he didn't think it was a big deal. Besides, he had an excellent memory. He rarely got lost.

The old man stopped in an alleyway and motioned for them to follow him down a steep set of steps that led them to a basement-like apartment. That was when Jeremy felt the first stirring of fear. The old man turned into a monster then. He'd slammed the heavy door, then locked it. Then Jeremy knew this was what his parents had warned him about. Kristen started to cry, then wet herself; she was so frightened. Being the big brother, he knew it was up to him to protect his sister. "Shhh," he'd said to her as the man locked the dead bolts on the door. She nodded, but she continued to cry silent tears. Her bottom lip quivered, and Jeremy put his arm around her shoulders and pulled her as far away from the monster as it was possible to get. She, in turn, wrapped her free hand around his waist.

"What do you want from us?" Jeremy asked.

The old man laughed, revealing decayed teeth, with several missing. "It ain't me that wants anything from ya, kid. Just shut up and be quiet, and this'll be over real quick-like."

Jeremy's pulse increased. He knew the old man was crazy when he started laughing hysterically. He took a cell phone from a small table, punched in a number, and said, "I've got two of 'em."

"What are you going to do to us?" Jeremy shouted, not caring if anyone heard him. He wanted someone to hear him! Raising his voice as loud as he could, he yelled, "Look, you dirty old bastard, you better let us go or . . . or my dad'll kill you!"

Sophie's vision instantly cleared. She was back in Toots's bedroom. She'd had her first clairsentience vision. Knowing time was running out for those two kids, Sophie practically flew down the steps to the kitchen.

"Okay, someone write this down or record what I'm about to tell you."

Officer Furdell removed a slender voice recorder from one of the many items attached to her police-issued belt.

"The kids left the bakery just as Jamie and Lucy said they did. A few yards away, they were approached by an old man. He reeked of alcohol. He told them he needed their help. They followed him to an alley. The alley is only a few blocks away from the coffee shop, where the parents were. They went down a set of steep stairs. It's a basement apartment. One room. Filthy. It has one small window, but it's covered with something to block out the light." Sophie paused, trying to recall what else she'd seen in the apartment.

"Mrs. Manchester, Charleston has hundreds of filthy basements that serve as apartments. Is there anything more specific? Did you *see the children*? Something that can validate what you've said," Detective O'Banyon asked.

Sophie shot Toots their secret evil-eye look, but she didn't comment. Now wasn't the time. Later, when the kids were safe and sound, then she was going to blast this redheaded bitch. Even more than she already had.

"Yes. The boy is tall and thin, with dark hair. He's just beginning to get peach fuzz above his lip. He's trying to protect the little girl. Her hair is long and brown. She was crying. Her hair was plastered to her cheeks."

Detective O'Banyon took a deep breath; then she looked at her watch. "Is that it? Can you tell me anything significant? An address, a sign, anything other than this generic crap."

Toots took a step toward the detective, then saw the look on Sophie's face. She stopped dead in her tracks.

"The boy had on a navy blue T-shirt with a goofy-looking cartoon bird on it. I'm not familiar with cartoons. He had on khaki cargo shorts with deep pockets on either side. He wore a pair of black Crocs. The girl wore a pink skirt with a Hello Kitty top. She wore Crocs, too. Hers were bright green with . . . with little pins placed on them." Sophie paused, eyeing the detective. "One other thing—Kristen wet herself. She does this when she's frightened. Is that *significant* enough for you, Detective O'Banyon?"

The detective quickly scanned her notes. "I don't know what to say, other than I owe you a huge apology. You've described Jeremy's shirt. It's not a cartoon. It's a game. *Angry Birds.* You'll find all versions of it on his Game Boy, according to the parents. Kristen wore the skirt with her favorite Hello Kitty shirt." The detective looked as though she'd been blown away, Toots thought, and in a sense she had. Not many psychics were as good as Sophie.

"Well, don't just stand there and stare at me like I'm an alien. Get the hell off your ass and go find those kids. We're running out of time. Whoever took them is moving them to another location. Or do I have to prove that, too?" Sophie shouted, not caring if she pissed off the cops.

"No. I do have one question. Would you do me the honor of riding in the patrol car with me? I think I might know this place."

"Why me?" Sophie challenged. "Afraid you won't be able to find them on your own?"

"Look, I'm sorry I doubted you. Ride with me and I'll tell you my reasons. Or not. It's up to you. As you said, we're running out of time."

Goebel spoke up. "Go on, Sophie. We'll be here waiting when you get back."

"Okay, let's go. And you'd better turn the siren on or drive as fast as you can, because some sick son of a bitch is on his way to pick up those children. If he gets to them before the cops do . . ." Sophie stopped talking.

Toots watched her. Sophie was having a vision.

"Those kids will never be found alive if we don't find them within the next hour. Now let's get the hell out of here!" Sophie shouted as she raced for the front door.

Chapter 7

Toots's house phone rang. She almost jumped out of her skin. The day had been quite strange, and she was on edge.

"Hello?"

"Mom, it's me. There are police cruisers leaving your place. I saw them when I let Chester out. Is everything okay?"

"Abby, it's a zoo around here. Yes, we are all fine, but there are a couple of missing kids. They were last seen leaving The Sweetest Things, and, well, you can only imagine the rest."

"You're kidding! No, you wouldn't do that," Abby said. "Can you tell me the details?"

"I'd prefer to wait until there is some good news. The cops came here to question me, sort of. They thought Jamie or Lucy might've seen something, but they didn't. The parents are here visiting, and somehow they knew about Sophie and her abilities. A detective ran her through the mill, and Sophie is now with said detective trying to help locate the kids before it's too late."

"I thought you were going to wait for the good news!"

"Oh, Abby, you know I can't keep things like this to myself, especially after what you went through last spring."

"Chris and I are coming over. Be there in ten," Abby said before hanging up.

Two seconds later, Toots whirled around when she heard a tapping on the back door. Bernice almost broke her neck getting to the door. It was Robert, her paramour from next door.

Bernice lit up like a full moon. "Come in, Robert. We've just made a pot of that coffee you like so much."

Toots couldn't help but overhear Bernice. That's why she was going through that two-hundred-dollar-per-pound stuff like water. Not that she cared, but it was just Robert. He was a good old guy and totally smitten with Bernice. They spent their days walking back and forth to visit each other. Bernice would bring a pie. Robert would bring a recipe he'd clipped from a magazine. Bernice would prepare whatever recipe he clipped and turn around and bring that to him. It was hard for either of them to remain still for longer than an hour. Toots was sure she knew why they were doing all this back-and-forth stuff, and soon she was going to tell Bernice. Well, hell, she was going to tell her now, while she had a minute before Abby and Chris arrived.

"Excuse me, Bernice, could you help me out?" Toots walked into the giant pantry.

"What do you want? I'm warming up an apple pastry for Robert. His sugar is low."

Toots rolled her eyes. Robert's sugar was fine. The old dude was as fit as a fiddle.

"You both need to stop this back-and-forth shit, Bernice. It's driving us crazy. That damn screen door gets slammed a hundred times a day. Now I want you to listen to what I am about to tell you. Then I want you to serve Robert his pastry before he keels over. You two need to screw, just do it and get it over with. I'll bet the bank Robert's as virile as a teenager. He has to be. Either that, or he's preparing for the Senior Olympics with all this damned walking. Now, do you get where I'm coming from, Bernice? And don't tell me Dr. Becker won't allow you to be sexually active, because he says it's perfectly fine with him." Toots stopped to catch her breath.

"Then he's been discussing my medical status with you? I swear I will turn that man in to the American Medical Association."

"Bernice, you signed over power of attorney to me last year when you had your surgery, so it wouldn't mean jack shit to the AMA. Now, why don't you run out there, shake that skinny little ass of yours while you serve Robert, then take him to bed. I know for a fact that Wade is out of town because Mavis has been tagging along with me all day."

Bernice, being Bernice, rolled her eyes, mouthed "F off," then shot Toots the bird before stepping out of the pantry. Toots burst out laughing.

"Mom, is that you?" Abby called out.

Damn, caught again. "Uh, yes, Abby, come in. I'm looking for some . . . artificial sweetener."

Abby peered around the door. "Mom, you are not looking for artificial sweetener. You wouldn't use that fake stuff if your life depended on it."

"Yes, you're right. I just needed an excuse to hang in here an extra minute. It's been an extremely long and tiring day. Come on, let's have some coffee, and I'll fill you in on what's happening."

Chris was already helping himself to a variety of the pastries from the plate in the center of the table. Goebel had made another pot of coffee. Ida went upstairs to change and missed most of the excitement. Toots guessed she had a million e-mails to take care of. Running a successful business was not all fun and games. Toots knew it to be a fact.

Mavis sat quietly at the table and slowly sipped her coffee. Bernice was practically salivating over Robert as she served his pastry. Goebel and Chris were at the opposite end of the table, speaking in low tones.

"Toots, this hasn't been a good day. Goebel filled me in on what's happening. I hope they find those kids before anything bad happens to them," Chris said between bites.

"I do, too." Toots had been there, done that, and certainly didn't want to go there ever again. Plus, she had that instance when Chris went missing, only to be found and accused of abducting Laura Leigh, that airheaded actress who was now getting $15 million a pop for all those ludicrous vampire films that were all the rage.

"They'll find them," Goebel said. "Sophie's with the detectives now. I think she was holding something back when she told that cop what she'd seen in her vision. I would bet anything Sophie knows exactly where to find those kids."

"Good, I hope you're right," Abby said. She poured herself a cup of coffee, took a sip, and wrinkled her nose. "Mom, is this that Dollar Store stuff you've been putting in the Kopi Luwak coffee tin?"

"You cheap old hag," Bernice said without missing a beat. "I thought I recognized this crap."

Now that the cops were out of her house, Toots freely waved her middle finger about. "I have not bought coffee from the Dollar Store since I was married to Leland. That cheap son of a bitch actually liked it. So, Abby, to answer your question, no, I have not switched the good stuff with the bad. Here, let me have a taste."

Toots took a drink of Abby's coffee. "It tastes perfectly fine to me. Maybe you need more sugar. Here"—Toots added two hefty spoons of sugar to the cup—"try this."

Abby took a large gulp of the sweetened coffee. Her eyes were as big as saucers when she said, "Move!" She raced around the corner to the downstairs bathroom.

Ten minutes later, pale and trembling, Abby returned to

the kitchen. "I wouldn't drink that coffee if I were any of you. It's bad. I think I was just poisoned."

At the mention of the word *poison,* Ida, who'd slipped downstairs without making a sound, was instantly alert. "What are you talking about?"

"Mom's Kopi Luwak coffee, the stuff she gets in Indonesia. Don't drink it," Abby cautioned.

Ida took a sip. "Abby, hon, there is nothing wrong with this coffee. Trust me, if it's laced with anything, I would be the first to pick up on it. Remember, Thomas was poisoned."

"If my recollection is correct, you wouldn't let us forget, Ms. Clorox Queen. You thought everything you touched would poison you," Toots said. They'd all been to hell and back when Ida had OCD. She'd been pitiful, but recovered quickly when her new doctor paid extra attention to her. But that was in the past; and like she always said, "The past is prologue."

Ida gave her the single-digit salute as she drank her coffee, and read through what appeared to be a new stack of fan letters. "I'm not that way now, Toots, so hush. I have fans to respond to, not to mention a million requests to buy me out."

She probably did, Toots guessed. They'd all lost easily ten to fifteen years when they started using her new line of skin care for Seasons. Abby was using it now, and she glowed like a spring blossom.

"I wouldn't sell yet. You're having too much fun," Toots said.

Ida looked up from her paperwork. "I most certainly don't plan to, at least not anytime soon. I'm actually enjoying this, and not just the publicity. I like helping ugly people."

Coffee spewed from Toots's mouth like a geyser. "Damn, Ida, you're starting to sound more like me each day. I must be rubbing off on you."

Ida smirked. "Could be. Now one can only hope my classy ways will do likewise to you."

"You two, stop it," Mavis said. "Now isn't the time to act like"—she wanted to say "children," but thought better of it—"two idiots," she finished.

"Mavis is right. Now isn't the time, so you just wait. When the time is right, I am going to really let you have it for that comment, Miss Classy Ass," Toots said, but there was no real venom in her words. She was saying the words just to hear herself. Took her mind off those kids who were lost.

She prayed Sophie's vision was spot-on this time, because the lives of those two children just might depend on it.

Chapter 8

As the police car sped along, Sophie looked down a second time to make sure her seat belt was fastened properly. She was having second thoughts about getting into the police cruiser with Detective O'Banyon, but she reminded herself that time was of the essence.

They sped through the side streets near Charleston's waterfront. She could barely read the signs as they whizzed by at full cop speed: KING STREET, CALHOUN STREET, MEETING STREET. Left, right, left. Sophie was totally ready to lose it, when Detective O'Banyon suddenly slammed on the brakes and practically did a one-eighty before coming to a complete stop on East Bay Street.

"Follow me," the detective said.

Sophie bit back a nasty comment, which was hanging on the tip of her tongue. She simply did as she was told, because just then it was all she could do to keep Toots's expensive coffee down after the harrowing ride. *The kids, Sophie. Focus on the kids.*

Taking a deep breath, Sophie trailed Detective O'Banyon. The redheaded cop removed a radio from her hip and spoke into it. All Sophie could make out was static, but she knew they were in the right location, that the kids were very close by. Actually, she could feel them, their fear, their sense of doom.

"Stop!" Sophie called out.

Detective O'Banyon and several more police officers turned to look at her. Not giving a flying frig what they thought, she said, "They are here. We are practically standing on them."

The other officers looked to the detective for further explanation. She held her hand palm up, indicating for them to be quiet. "Just listen to what she's saying," she admonished, then turned her full attention on Sophie.

Sophie took a deep breath and called up every psychic power she had. Closing her eyes, she waited for an image. When nothing happened, she opened her eyes and gasped.

Not wanting to lose whatever connection she had, she began to walk quickly away from the water. Then she started to run.

"Hurry!" she shouted out. Hopefully, they'd follow her, because they did not have a single extra minute to spare. As quick as the vision overtook her, it was gone. Now all she could see were dark alleys and the tall, stately mansions that shadowed them.

"Shit! Come on, come on," Sophie said out loud. She tried closing her eyes and opening them, anything to bring back the vision she'd just experienced. Sophie took a deep breath and felt her heart pound so hard against her chest that she thought it would explode.

The officers caught up with her. Gasping for breath, she pointed to the alley to her left. Before she knew it, the vision had overtaken her again. She turned in the direction her index finger pointed. Sophie didn't dare stop, because it was almost over.

At the end of the alleyway, Sophie turned around, her finger held out in front of her as if it were a Geiger counter. "Here!" she said in a loud whisper.

The cops and Detective O'Banyon circled her.

"Down there," she said, pointing to a set of steps that otherwise would've gone unnoticed. They were surrounded by banged-up metal trash cans and several dark green bags filled with God only knew what. There was barely enough room for the police officers to descend the steep flight of stairs single file.

Sophie knew that her work was finished. She saw her surroundings clearly and hoped like hell she was right. If she wasn't, those kids were as good as dead. She'd seen it and knew it was up to her to lead the officers to them. She just prayed she'd hit the mark. Now was the time to trust her talent, not doubt it, she thought as she watched the cops move silently down the steps.

Chilled by the cool night air, Sophie crossed her arms over her chest, wishing she had on long sleeves instead of the sleeveless shell she wore. Goose bumps dotted up and down her arms.

Below her, the cops shouted in harsh whispers, but she couldn't make out what they were saying. Detective O'Banyon left her standing alone as she followed the blue suits downstairs. Curious, Sophie took a few steps forward, careful not to step on the garbage scattered at the top of the landing. Assaulted by the pungent odor of urine, mixed with enough alcohol to gag a maggot, Sophie looked down the staircase. The officers flanking the entrance had their weapons drawn, ready to aim at the front door. Detective O'Banyon knocked loudly on the metal door.

"Come out with your hands up now!"

Just like in the movies, Sophie thought, then mentally kicked herself for the comparison. There were children's lives at stake.

"I know who you are. Now come out peacefully, or we're coming in!" the detective shouted again, only this time they got a response.

"We're in here! Help! They have another door! Hurry!" the kid screamed. The next second, all Sophie could hear was the sound of the metal door being kicked open, bodies slapping against one another, and a sorrowful "Oh, shit," probably from the kidnapping pervert. Detective O'Banyon raced up the stairs, followed by two officers, each carrying one of the missing kids.

The kids were placed in a patrol car, and Detective O'Banyon spoke into her cell phone. No more than five minutes passed before she walked over to where Sophie stood.

Running a hand through her thick auburn hair, the woman, not the cop, spoke. "Thank you. And I am so damned sorry I doubted your abilities. These kids have you to thank for saving their lives. I've called the parents. They're waiting down at the station. When I told them how—or, rather, who helped to locate the kids, she insisted on thanking you personally. I told her I would relay the message, but it's really up to you. If you'd rather not meet them, I'll have one of the officers drive you home."

Sophie gushed with pride. "Are you out of your mind? No way do I want to go home! I want to see those kids and their parents. I want to make damn sure this has a happy ending." Speaking of happy endings, she needed to call Goebel and Toots. "Mind if I use your cell?"

The detective handed it to her. "It's all yours."

Sophie made fast work out of calling Goebel, who relayed the message to Toots, who then told the others that the kids were safe. Then they all decided they would go down to the station to meet the family and give Sophie a ride home. "And don't forget to bring the little girl's bunny and that game. I left them in Toots's room," Sophie added before hanging up.

Car doors slammed, and tires squealed, as the other officers left the scene. Sophie wanted to see the sick son of a bitch who had taken the kids. "Is he still in there?" she asked, indicating the basement apartment below.

"Yes, and I need to go. You wanna come with me?"

Sophie couldn't believe her ears. Detective O'Banyon was actually inviting her to sit in on an interrogation.

"We wouldn't be here now if you hadn't led us to the kids. Again, I'm sorry I was so rude earlier. I was in a similar situation once. A psychic swore he knew where a missing young girl was. He said all I had to do was listen. I did, and the girl was found murdered two days later. It wasn't a happy ending. That's why I'm such a skeptic. But you are the real deal. Again, I am so sorry for doubting you. You saved those kids' lives."

"Enough, already. Apology accepted. Truthfully, most people feel the way you do, especially in this kind of instance, when it's a life-or-death issue." Sophie suddenly realized she was crying. Tears as fat as raindrops fell from her eyes. Relief, these were plainly tears of relief. She hadn't been 100 percent sure about this newfangled talent, and now it hit her. If she'd been wrong, those two kids would have died. She offered up a quick prayer, thankful the kids were safe, and more thankful than ever for the gift that had been bestowed upon her.

"Come on. Just stay in the corner and be quiet. If this is what I think it is, then you've brought down one of the largest child-pornography rings in the state."

"Really?" Sophie said, stunned. She hadn't given the first thought to anything more than finding the kids. Why were they taken? Well, that hadn't entered the picture at all. And she knew she wasn't supposed to know the "whys" of everything. What she knew had to be enough.

Downstairs, the smell of urine nearly took Sophie's breath away. Odors that she didn't want to put a name to assaulted her senses. Once again, she resisted the urge to upchuck. It wouldn't have mattered down there, she thought. Hell, it might actually have been better than what she was smelling.

Careful not to touch anything, Sophie stood close to the door while Detective O'Banyon and two other plainclothes detectives talked among themselves before turning to the old man.

"I got my rights, and I ain't sayin' a goddamn word until I get me a lawyer. I know my rights, by God!" he declared.

Sophie could smell his sour breath across the room, because the entire apartment wasn't much larger than a small bedroom.

"Yeah, you've got rights, Clyde. And if you're smart, you'll tell me where the kids were to be taken. And who ordered this, Clyde? If you don't spill, I can sit here all night long. I've got all the time in the world. But you might want to think about delaying this any longer than you have to. Whoever you're working for will leave town the minute you make that call. It's completely up to you." The detective crossed her arms over her chest and walked around the filthy apartment like she was perusing a model home.

"How'd you know my name?" the sour-smelling old man asked.

"Clyde Baines. Everyone in law enforcement knows your name. You've got a rap sheet as long as the Edisto River. Lewd and lascivious. Possession. The list of felonies goes on and on, old pal. You can either spit out the name of the person who was to receive those kids, or we can sit here in this nasty fucking shit hole all night. What do ya say, old man?"

Detective O'Banyon is not playing nice with this perp, Sophie thought, *and she shouldn't. Sick old bastard kidnapping kids right in broad daylight.*

"Where you plan on takin' me?" he asked. " 'Cause I got rights, and I know what they are."

"So you keep reminding me. Look, Clyde, let's just cut through the bullshit. It doesn't matter where I take you now. You're still going to end up spending the rest of your life in a nice, clean prison with the big boys. I hear they don't take too well to pedophiles, that sort of thing—unless they're into that, too—but most of the sick bastards are placed in a cell all by their lonesome, so some big, bad murderer doesn't slice their useless ass to ribbons." The detective walked away from the scumbag and gave Sophie a big grin.

"So, what's it gonna be, Clyde, my man? Him or you? I've decided I don't have all the time in the world, you worthless fuck. I am giving you exactly thirty seconds to spill that name."

Detective O'Banyon began to count out loud. "One, two, three . . ."

When she reached twenty-nine, the old man spoke up. "Okay, goddamn it, but I want a smoke first."

"Clyde, you're really not in any position to negotiate." She turned to the officer at the door. "Get him a cigarette, will you, Harry?"

Sophie whipped a package of Marlboros out of her pocket, lit up, and watched the old man stare at her. "I'll die before I share my smokes with you, you dirty old pervert!" said Sophie.

Detective O'Banyon laughed. "See, Clyde? People don't like you. Now, are you gonna give me a name or am I gonna have to rough you up a bit?"

Sophie wasn't sure she'd heard correctly and didn't care. This was better than TV. This was the real deal. With a new respect for Detective O'Banyon, she took a long drag from her cigarette and blew the smoke in Clyde Baines's direction.

The taller of the two plainclothes officers returned from wherever he had gone and stuck a lit cigarette between Clyde Baines's smelly lips. Baines took a long drag, making the end of the cigarette glow like a fireball. Sophie watched as he fumbled with the smoke. With his arms handcuffed behind him, she could see what a difficult time he was having. He took another long puff and pushed the cigarette out of his mouth with his tongue, being careful to lean forward when he did so that the cigarette wouldn't land on his pant leg.

Detective O'Banyon stomped on the cigarette. "Okay, Clyde. My patience is almost gone. You got your smoke. Now it's your turn to give up that name."

The old man smiled at the detective. "You still ain't told me where you're gonna take me. That's part of the deal."

Sophie knew the detective had reached her boiling point when she leaned eyeball-to-eyeball with Baines and said, "Okay, you smelly fuck, your chance is gone."

She walked away, then quickly turned around. Before Sophie knew what was happening, the detective hauled off and slapped Clyde Baines squarely in the face.

He sputtered, "You fuckin' bitch! I'll have your ass for police brutality!"

"And who do you suppose will believe you? The chief? I don't think so. The state's attorney? I don't think so," she singsonged. "Now I am pissed, and I'm tired. I've got two boys at home. . . ." Detective O'Banyon stopped short.

Baines began to laugh; then he doubled over, laughing, spittle flying from his foul mouth. "Damn woman! If I'd-a known you had a couple-a young'uns, I'd gone after them, too." He continued to laugh and taunt the detective.

Sophie couldn't stand it anymore. She didn't care who saw her. She took a few short steps over to the single chair, where Clyde Baines sat. Before she could stop herself, she spit directly in his face.

Chapter 9

Toots, Ida, and Mavis crammed themselves into the backseat of Toots's Lincoln Town Car while Goebel, Robert, and Bernice crawled into the front, raising the center armrest/storage compartment to make room to seat three, however uncomfortably. Jamie and Lucy opted out, telling the others that they'd stay with the animals. Chris and Abby returned to their house, though Abby asked Toots to call as soon as they had news of the children. "Good or bad," she'd added.

"I can't believe what Sophie did," Robert said. "She sure isn't what she appears."

"And what would that be?" Ida asked haughtily.

The older man chuckled. "I thought she was kinda nuts when I first met her, but now I know better. She's like that old Miss Cleo, huh?" He laughed again.

"Robert, whatever you do, never say that in front of Sophie. Miss Cleo is a total fake. Sophie hates those so-called psychics who lie to people, give them false hope, and take their money. So never, ever compare her to that fraud, or she's liable to place some kind of hex on you," Toots offered from the backseat, but poor old Robert couldn't see the huge grin that split her face.

"Are you telling me she can cast a spell or something?

Like those women with the voodoo dolls I see down there at Market Street?"

"Robert, dear, you've got it all twisted up in a knot. She's just messing with your head," Bernice explained, giving Toots a dirty look. "We all agree Sophie has a very unique set of skills."

No one had told Robert or Wade everything that went on in the house next door. At the moment, Toots figured that was a good thing. Wade and Mavis were content to talk about dead people, while Bernice and Robert kept the recipe thing going. Someone would have to give them a bit more insight into Sophie and her skills as soon as the current mess with the kids' kidnapping and rescue was put to rest.

Goebel, at the wheel, chose that moment to comment. "Indeed she does, Bernice. Yes, indeed." He wore a grin as wide as the vehicle they drove.

"Oh, please don't paint that nasty picture of that woman in my head," Ida shot out. "It's all I can do to imagine she's even having sex."

"Who said anything about sex?" Toots asked. "Ida, are you getting weird on me again? I know it's been a while since you've bedded some unfortunate soul, but please."

"I was only saying what Goebel was thinking. Right, Goebel?" Ida teased. To this day, Sophie swore that Ida had a crush on Goebel. Toots believed she was right.

"Well, I'm not sure what you thought I was thinking, so I'd be hard put to agree to something that I'm so unsure of."

"Please, Goebel. Listen to yourself. You're starting to sound exactly like my attorney, and you would not believe the way in which he is able to use words that, when push comes to shove, don't really mean anything. Why, I thought you were smarter than that," Ida continued to tease.

The silly banter went back and forth until they reached

the police station in downtown Charleston. Now it was time to get the real scoop, time to face the music.

Goebel found a parking spot for visitors only. As they emerged from the Lincoln, a group of photographers surrounded them in the parking lot. Klieg lights were positioned around the front of the police station, and a podium stood at the top of the stairs leading inside to police headquarters.

Oh, shit, Toots thought. *It's press time.* Time for Sophie to show her face, reveal to the community where her real talents lay, if they didn't know already.

A crowd of reporters huddled around the foot of the steps. Toots watched as the camera people searched for the best angle, while others shouted out commands. Cables were coiled around the steps like black snakes. Microphones from all the local stations were jammed together at the podium, and Toots was sure she saw Nancy Grace from HLN skirting around the perimeter of the building. If so, whoever took those kids would have hell to pay, once the cable star broke the news.

The hubbub of television reporters rehearsed their intros, making sure there wasn't a single hair out of place; the women powdered their noses and reapplied their lipstick. It reminded Toots of Los Angeles, all the cameras, lights, throngs of people waiting at a movie premiere. As much as she loved her Malibu beach house, right now she was content to stay in Charleston for as long as she wanted. With Abby and Chris at the plantation, right around the corner, being home in Charleston was a trillion times better. She made a mental note when she got home to call Abby and see if she was feeling better.

A tall police officer, who couldn't have been a day over twenty-one, directed the throngs of people away from the podium. Everyone did as instructed, which put Toots and her crew a couple of hundred feet away, but that didn't matter, since they weren't really there to hear the news. They were already aware of the outcome; the staging of the announcement was just for the general public. They had come to take Sophie home, and, of course, they wanted to meet the parents and see the kids Sophie had saved, but those were things that would come later. As of this moment, they were simply gawkers, like the rest of the onlookers gathered away from the base of the steps. The drone of low voices reminded Toots of high-school basketball games, when they'd all sit in the bleachers, slowly start to stomp their feet, then chant until the team hit the court. Though this was much more serious, she couldn't help but smile at the memory of the four old friends at high-school basketball games.

A hush fell over the crowd as the glass doors opened. Ryan Lowande had served as Charleston's police chief for the past twelve years. A distinguished officer in the U.S. Air Force, as were his father and grandfather before him, Chief Lowande took his duties seriously. His commitment to the people of Charleston County was: public trust, high standards for those who served with him, and relationships with community groups in order to help deter crime of every kind. Toots made a hefty donation to their budget for the K-9 Unit, noted as one of the best in the country. She used to volunteer and work with the dogs when Abby was in school, but now she left it to those specifically trained for that sort of work. Her donations hadn't stopped and wouldn't. She had a stipulation in her will that would take care of the K-9 Unit as long as it existed.

Chief Lowande fit the picture of a chief of police. He was tall and broad-shouldered, with the kind of silvery gray hair that would only look good on a man, and had the clearest blue eyes. Eyes, Toots knew, that didn't miss a beat. He cleared his throat; then he tapped at the jumble of microphones in front of him. "I'm going to make a statement. Then I'll answer a few questions."

He removed a slip of paper from his crisp blue jacket, along with a pair of reading glasses. Taking a deep breath, Chief Lowande read from the paper.

" 'Tonight I am proud to announce that we've captured the leader of one of the largest child-pornography rings in the state of South Carolina and now have him and several others in custody. This has been an ongoing investigation, and we will continue to search out and make arrests as warranted. Because this is still under investigation, there are details I can't give out at this time, but we will make them public as soon as we are in a position to do so.' " He looked at the large crowd gathered around him. "I'll take your questions now."

Several reporters shouted out questions, each trying to speak over the other, and it was nothing more than a shouting match. Chief Lowande immediately took control of the situation. "Please, one at a time. Maria Marttila from WTAT, Fox 24, go ahead." The chief had picked one of the top news anchors in the city. Gutsy and unafraid, Maria had won numerous awards for her investigative reporting. Toots wondered how she would have fared at *The Informer.*

"My source tells me you were tipped off by a psychic. Can you confirm this?"

The crowd went crazy. Chief Lowande smiled and held both hands out in front of him to indicate he needed silence. "You must have many sources, Maria," the chief stated. "The South Carolina Law Enforcement Division, along with the Charleston County Sheriff's Office, have been working together on this operation for several months. We're proud to say that because of months of undercover work and the help of a well-known woman whose psychic abilities led us to the location where two young children were being kept, while waiting to be transported, we're confident this ring is closed. Since the kids are minors, I won't be releasing any information about who they are, but I can tell you that both children were extremely brave and were not physically harmed."

"How old are they?" shouted one blond reporter.

"Are the parents willing to be interviewed?" John Moxley, evening news anchor from WCIV, Channel 4, shouted, holding his minirecorder high in the air, even though his station's news van was covering the event live.

"I am not releasing the names of the parents at this time. If they wish to speak to you at a later date, then I am sure they will contact you," Chief Lowande explained.

"So you're not really telling us anything?" came a voice from the crowd.

"Only that tonight's arrests were instrumental in bringing down one of the largest child-pornography rings in the state. Now I'll let you question the real hero of the hour."

Chief Lowande stepped aside, making room for the crowd of policemen and policewomen surrounding Sophie as she walked over to the podium. The microphones were lowered for her before she stepped up to the podium.

A high-pitched squeal emanated from the speakers. Everyone placed their hands over their ears until some techie fixed the sound.

Toots wondered if Sophie had orchestrated that herself. Her talent was growing by leaps and bounds. Maybe she'd be able to move things around with her mind before all of this was over. She'd come a long way from Madam Butterfly's in New York. Toots was so proud of her friends. If pride were money, she would be the richest woman to ever live.

More high-pitched noise; then Sophie's sultry voice filled the cool night air. Toots observed her. Hot damn, she was a knockout! Sophie's sculpted beauty was made to be admired, and Ida's concoction only made her look even better.

"I just want to thank the officers who took me seriously enough to follow my instructions. Without their hard work, none of us would be here now, nor would those children, who were taken against their will. The kids are fine, and let me tell you this, they're two of the bravest souls I have ever seen. I know you all have questions, but before you ask, I'm on the same page with the chief." Sophie shot Chief Lowande her best smile. "So nothing about the children, other than that they're safe. And brave."

Toots caught Sophie's gaze over the many heads in the crowd. She gave her the thumbs-up sign; then Sophie directed her attention to a young female reporter who wasn't well known.

"Hi, uh . . . yes." The reporter appeared flustered, surprised when Sophie chose her over the many high-ranking news anchors. "I'm Sally Owens with the *Charleston County Courier,*" the reporter stated as protocol dictated. "Can you tell me how you knew where the children were? What kind of vision led to their discovery?"

Sophie nodded. "First, let me correct you. I didn't have a vision." It was then that Sophie spied Goebel in the crowd. She blew him a kiss. She was on top of the world now and wanted the world to know that she, too, had a significant other. He blew her a kiss, acknowledging hers. She simply grinned and continued to answer the young reporter as all eyes were focused on her. She had the crowd's undivided attention as she told her version of events leading up to the discovery of the kids.

"This is a first for me. I was given some personal items belonging to the children. I held them, and prayed for guidance. They call this kind of 'vision' "—she made air quotes with her hands—" 'clairsentience.' Clairsentience is the ability to receive an image from the item owned by the person. Personally, I think Detective O'Banyon already had a good idea who had taken the children. It was simply a matter of finding their exact location. I followed my instincts, and the children led me to the place where they were being held." Sophie paused to glance out over the crowd. It had doubled in the past ten minutes.

"Miss Sophie," came a voice that almost everyone was familiar with. "May I ask you a question?" The one-and-only Nancy Grace herself, former Atlanta prosecutor and participant on *Dancing with the Stars,* minus the twins, shoved her way to the front of the crowd. She didn't bother to wait for Sophie's answer. "Weren't you the psychic that found Laura Leigh last year?"

From the expression on her face, if you knew Sophie, you knew she was caught off guard by the well-known anchor.

"Yes, but that isn't what I'm here to share with the good people of Charleston."

"Would it be true to say you are tops in your field of locating missing persons?" Nancy Grace asked, then added, "Dead or alive?"

Sophie took a deep breath, not wanting the crowd to see she was pissed at this line of questioning. "And I have always found them alive. I hope that answers your question, Ms. Grace."

Toots listened to the beginning of what might've become the battle of the bitches, had Chief Lowande not stepped forward. "That's all we're going to discuss now. Note that several suspects have been arrested after a lengthy investigation that remains ongoing. The police department will keep the media updated on tonight's arrest. For now, I just want to thank Sophia Manchester and say how pleased I am that her God-given abilities helped us to find those children."

Nancy Grace and her team disappeared in the crowd.

The mob of people booed and aahed, none of which mattered to Sophie. She stepped away from the podium, heading inside where the grateful parents were waiting to speak with her.

Inside, away from the mob, Sophie dialed Toots's cell. "There's a side entrance you can use. Just be careful and make sure that Nancy Grace isn't on your tail." Sophie gave Toots directions to the private entrance; then she raced down a flight of steps to greet her.

"What the heck?" Sophie asked as Toots was followed in by Goebel, Mavis, Ida, Bernice, and Robert. "Looks like a family reunion."

"Now, before you cast a spell on me or whatever it is you do, I just want to say that I'm not afraid of you," Robert stated as though he were up against an armed robber with a sawed-off shotgun rather than Sophia Manchester.

"Robert, that is good to know. I didn't realize I was so frightening to you, but keep your eyes open because sometimes I've been known to do things I can't control."

Robert's face turned ten shades of white. His eyes were as big around as the moon. He looked to Bernice.

"Sophie, if you cause this man to have a heart attack, I swear I will kick your ass myself. Now tell him you're not serious. Right now," Bernice demanded.

Toots bit the insides of her mouth to keep from laughing.

"Robert, I'm just joking." Sophie turned to Bernice. "Satisfied?"

Bernice rolled her eyes, then stood next to Robert linking her arm through his as though she were offering some kind of protection against Sophie's psychic threats.

Chief Lowande chose that moment to make his presence known. "If you all are ready, the family is waiting." He gave them all a once-over sweep, then said, "Follow me."

The Dunlop family, along with a crew of law enforcement officers from every branch, waited in a conference room. When the kids saw Sophie, their eyes lit up like sparklers on the Fourth of July.

Sophie made her way across the small expanse and wrapped both children in a giant bear hug. She had tears in her eyes, but they were happy tears. No one said anything while Sophie held the kids in her embrace. As soon as she released them, the mother and father both wrapped her in their arms.

Evelyn and Buddy Dunlop were in their early forties. Both lean, with athletic builds, the couple looked exhausted, but their smiles could've lit up the Christmas tree in Rockefeller Center. Toots observed the pair. Given what they'd been through, and having been through this with Abby, she thought they looked pretty darn good.

"I can't tell you how grateful we are," Evelyn Dunlop said. "What can I do to repay you? There must be something." Evelyn Dunlop's brown eyes were filled with happy tears.

"Never, Evelyn. This is what I do. It's what I *am*. But my friends are dying to meet you and the kids."

Sophie introduced the Dunlop family to Toots first, then Goebel. "Abby, who's not here, is Toots's daughter, and Mavis and Ida and I are Abby's godmothers. And, of course, Bernice here with her . . ." She was going to say "bed partner," but she remembered there were children in the room. And she did not have a clue whether Bernice and Robert had made it official by doing the deed, and didn't care. ". . . good friend, Robert. He and his brother are our very friendly next-door neighbors."

After they were introduced, they talked for a while. When Jeremy and Kristen started yawning, Toots was the first to say, "These kids need their rest."

After another round of saying "thank you," hugs, and promises to stay in touch, they returned to their homes, each thankful that they had been there to witness a happy ending.

Chapter 10

Phil Becker dialed Toots's telephone number for the fifth time in the past two hours. Finding it highly unusual that no one was around to pick up the phone at such a late hour, he quickly dressed and headed across town.

Twenty minutes later, he was at the entrance to the colossal Southern home. Seeing that the gates were open, he pulled inside, without bothering to stop and close them, which was his normal practice. The situation was not totally unusual, given the women who made this their home. He punched down on the accelerator, causing the car to fishtail. "Shit," he said out loud. Then he thought he'd better slow down, or he'd be returning to the hospital as a patient. Tapping the brakes as he approached the main house, Phil grinned. A light emanating from the windows in the old mansion let him know someone was up and about. When he saw Toots's Lincoln parked in the drive, he knew something was up. She loved that old car and always made sure to keep it garaged when she wasn't driving. She'd often told him she preferred driving the Lincoln over the Land Rover, except when she was in California, where her little red Thunderbird was the vehicle of choice.

He parked behind her. As was his habit, he left his keys in the ignition, just in case he was called to the hospital. Years of late-night calls and lost car keys had forced him to do this, even though he knew there was a chance a car thief could drive off without any warning. Just a chance he took; and if his car was ripped off, he would have no one to blame but poor memory and sheer stupidity on his part.

Normally, he would walk right into the house, unannounced, but something told him to knock this time. He tapped on the door frame and heard a voice from downstairs call, "Come in!"

Voices and the heavenly scent of coffee led him to the kitchen. When he entered, everyone seated at the table stopped talking, focusing their attention on him. "What?" he asked. "Do I have a horn growing out of my head or what?"

Sensing a reluctance among the group gathered around the large dining table, he asked, "What's wrong?"

Goebel spoke up. "I take it you haven't been watching the eleven o'clock news," he stated.

"No, I was home catching up on paperwork. Why? Did I miss something important?"

Staring at Toots, who remained seated at the head of the table, Phil raised an eyebrow in her direction. Something was going on. It was a rare moment to find the girls so quiet.

Unable to keep silent any longer, despite her earlier misgivings concerning her relationship with Phil, Toots couldn't help but perk up when she saw him. "Two children disappeared today. They were last seen at the bakery." Toots paused, taking a deep breath. "They questioned us, wanted to know how well I knew Jamie and Lucy."

Intrigued, Phil helped himself to a cup of coffee, then leaned against the counter. "Have they found them?"

"Yes, thank God," Toots said, then gave him a brief rundown. "We just finished watching the eleven o'clock news."

"This is good, then, right?" Phil asked.

Toots looked at Phil. "It is. For the family. Sophie actually found them by using her psychic abilities. It's all over the news now. I've had to unplug the phone because the media hounds are out, and they want an exclusive with Sophie. I know it's crazy coming from me, of all people, but I do wish they would stop right now and go find something else to write about. This isn't stuff for . . . *The Informer.*"

"Oh, crap, Toots, we're not in LA. This is big news here," Sophie said, then stood up. "I'm going outside. You coming?" she asked Toots as she took the package of cigarettes next to her cup of coffee.

Phil just shook his head and gave a little grin. "Go on, I know you're just dying to smoke."

"I just want a puff or two. Goebel, explain to him how this unfolded," Toots said on her way out the door.

Once they were outside, where no one could overhear them, Sophie instantly picked up on Toots's inner conflict before she even had a chance to mention it. "You can't stop seeing Phil," Sophie said as soon as they had a few drags from their smokes. "He's your 'the one,' like Goebel's mine."

Dumbfounded, Toots turned to her friend. "What the frig are you talking about?"

"Oh, stop acting like you don't know what I know. I'm psychic, remember? Plus, you're my best friend in the world—though don't tell that to Mavis, because I told her that, and asked her not to tell you, which is beside the point because you haven't been acting like yourself all day. I'm not so engrossed in tonight's events that I can't tell you're not yourself. So you either tell me, or I'll find out by some other means."

Toots rolled her eyes, even though she knew Sophie couldn't see her in the darkness. "You really are a nosy bitch, but since you claim to be my best friend, at least for today—and if you'll promise to keep this between the two of us until I've reached a decision—I suppose it's okay for me to tell you what's going on." She inhaled another gust of grayish white smoke from her cigarette, holding it deep in her lungs. Then she exhaled, and one giant huff came from her mouth like an angry storm cloud.

"I'm listening," Sophie said.

"There really isn't much to tell. I had an epiphany of sorts today when Mavis and I stopped by Abby's." She took a deep breath, thinking it wasn't going to be as easy as she thought to say the words out loud to Sophie, because then it would make this real. Plus, Sophie wouldn't stop pestering her until she'd forced Toots to examine her situation from every possible angle. Perhaps that was precisely what she needed. "Phil's talked about retiring, moving to Myrtle Beach, and writing that novel he's always wanted to write. Then, boom, out of nowhere, he told me he wanted to take our relationship to 'the next level.' I haven't told Phil everything about my past. I . . ." Toots paused, searching for the right word. "It's been over a year, Soph. What will he think of me when he finds out I've been married eight times? And what's even worse, and scares me more, every man I marry dies. Don't you find that strange? Too strange to chalk up to coincidence." There, the words were out again. She felt crummier every time she spoke them.

Sophie drew on her cigarette, then crushed it out in the old coffee can they kept filled with sand just for that purpose. "How long have we known one another, Toots?"

Again, Toots rolled her eyes despite the fact that Sophie couldn't see her childish action. Somehow, it made her feel good to do that, so she rolled her eyes again. "Since seventh grade. I believe we were twelve, thirteen. What does that have to do with anything?"

"We don't keep secrets from each other."

"And your point?" Toots asked.

"That's why our friendship has lasted all these years.

We don't keep secrets, at least none that are really important. Like none of us really cared when we found out that
Ida had her privates waxed. Those aren't the kind of
things I'm talking about. Little everyday stuff doesn't count.
But, Toots"—Sophie lowered her voice—"you can't keep
this kind of stuff from Phil. I can't believe he hasn't heard
any jabs coming from any of us. It's not like we don't tease
you about your past, though not quite as much as we've
teased Ida. You have to tell him, Toots. I know you're
head over heels in love with the guy. He's an honorable
man. You owe him the truth."

"You're right, but after a year, it's not going to be easy,"
Toots agreed. "I'm thinking it might be best to end this
now. I know it's wrong, but, shit, Sophie, Phil will think I
am nothing more than a lying slut. Like Ida," Toots added,
grinning.

"Okay. End it. But what are you going to tell Phil when
he asks why? Have you thought of that?"

Toots shook her head. "No." And she didn't want to,
but if she planned on saving his life, she'd have to, and
simply suffer the consequences. This was her choice; though
she had to admit, she hadn't intentionally set out to deceive Phil. It just never seemed to be the right time. Now
that Phil wanted to take their relationship up a level, there
was not a shred of doubt that it was the right time. But her
heart fluttered at the thought. Sophie was right. Phil was
her "the one," and she'd totally screwed herself for not being totally honest with him. And why was her conscience
eating away at her now? After she had experienced eight
marriages, one would think sliding into a romantic relationship would be as easy as pie for her, whatever the hell
that meant. Why now?

"Someone always told me the truth stands. Always. I
think that someone was you, Toots. Take your own advice. Tell Phil the truth. Give the guy some credit. Most
likely, he won't give a flying frig about your past. As we al-

ways say, 'The past is prologue.' Let Phil have a say in this decision. It's the right thing to do, and you know it full well."

"Yes, but I don't always do the right thing," Toots added glumly.

"Stop feeling sorry for yourself! There are a million women out there who would give their middle fingers and then some to be in your shoes."

Again, Sophie was right, but it didn't help to make Toots feel any better about herself. And if she felt like pond slime, surely Phil was bound to feel the same way, too.

"I doubt that very much," Toots replied.

Sophie lit a cigarette, passed it to Toots, then lit another for herself. "Look, we can't sit out here all night and decide what you should or shouldn't do. You know deep down that you should tell Phil the truth. If he doesn't want to continue in the relationship, then he's not the man we think he is. Has it ever occurred to you that he may have things in his past that he hasn't told you about?"

"He's not that kind of man," Toots said. "He's told me just about all there is to tell. Hell, he spent most of his life in school, then in private practice. I don't think he's had much free time to do anything that would even be considered a secret."

"Yeah, but do you know this for sure? Are you one hundred percent sure?"

The words *never say never* came to mind. And honestly, she was not 100 percent sure of anything, except her love for Abby and Chris. *That,* she knew to be real and honest. Toots lived in the real world. And in that world, one could never be completely sure about *everything.*

"Do you know something I don't? Because if you do, you'd better tell me before I make a total and complete idiot out of myself."

All at once, Sophie stood up and opened the screen

door. "This isn't up to me. You're on your own this time." The screen door creaked as Sophie closed it behind her.

Toots planted the last of her cigarette in the can of sand, tucked a few loose strands of hair back into her topknot, and opened the back door. She would tell Phil about her past. Then, if he decided he didn't want to continue their relationship, she would accept it as her fate. However, tonight wasn't going to be the night she revealed her deep, dark secrets. Too much had happened, and besides, she was tired, too tired to care one way or another. Surely, one more day couldn't make a difference.

Toots stood in the doorway observing the comings and goings in her kitchen.

Bernice was making yet another pot of coffee. Robert's chin rested on his chest, a slight snore coming from his mouth. Ida had apparently called it a night, as she was nowhere to be seen. Mavis was rinsing out their coffee cups, readying for round two of the coffee klatch. Sophie and Goebel were making doe eyes at one another in the hallway. Toots wondered if he was going to spend the night tonight. Sophie tried to act like Miss Innocent, but Toots knew that Goebel often slept over. She didn't mind; they were all adults. As a matter of fact, she found herself relaxing at the thought of having a male presence in the house, something she never would've thought possible in those weeks after Leland's death. She'd been so relieved to be on her own, free again, that the mere thought of another man had raised her blood pressure so high, she thought her head would explode. Time had softened her hard edges, and Phil had certainly played a role in it, too. Taking a deep breath, she stepped into the pantry, needing a minute to compose herself. Her eyes were wet with tears at the thought of what she had to tell Phil.

She was straightening the cans on the shelf, when she felt a hand on her shoulder. "Oh!" she said when she saw it was Phil. "You scared the shit out of me! Don't do that again!" Toots said a bit too harshly.

He turned her around so that she faced him. "It's not too often I find you alone," he said; then he placed a kiss on the top of her messy hair. "And it's late, too."

Knowing he wanted her to invite him to stay over, she couldn't help but laugh. He'd been trying this for the past few months, telling her it was high time he got lucky.

"All the more reason for you to go home. Don't you have to be at the hospital early tomorrow morning?" Toots asked, trying to avoid any form of intimacy, no matter how brief.

"No," he said, and nibbled at her neck.

Toots felt goose bumps prickle down her spine. Before things went any further, Toots pushed Phil away, giving a wry laugh. "Bernice will have another heart attack if she sees us in here." She grabbed a can of corn and placed it beside a can of tuna, anything to keep her hands busy, away from him. "Let's have another cup of coffee."

Reluctantly, Phil followed her out of the pantry closet to the kitchen.

"Did I ever tell you that I think you drink way too much coffee?" he asked as he followed her to the table.

"Yes, and I believe I told you on more than one occasion to kiss my ass," Toots reminded him, then wished she'd said something else.

"I do remember that, and I want to, but somehow we always end up"—he pointed to the table—"there. Drinking coffee."

Robert chose that moment to jerk awake. "What? Where am . . . Oh," he said, taking in his surroundings, then taking his napkin and wiping his mouth. "Where's Bernice?"

"I'm here, sugar," she called out. "I just made another fresh pot of coffee. You want another cup before you call it a night?"

"See?" Phil said, his grin a mile wide.

Toots shrugged. "What can I say? We all like our coffee, and the caffeine has no effect on any of us."

"This is the last pot of the night," Bernice said as she poured another cup for Robert without waiting for his answer. She filled her cup and sat down beside him. "I do not like having my cardiologist watch me drink coffee and stay up half the night. I am supposed to be taking care of myself," Bernice said when Phil took the chair across from hers.

Phil took the cup Toots placed in front of him and sipped at the hot brew. "You can drink coffee and stay up all night, Bernice, as long as you're exercising and eating the right foods. Remember, I'm not here as your physician. I'm here to hang with Toots."

She couldn't help but smile at Phil. Damn, but he was so handsome! Sophie was absolutely right. He was her "the one," and she knew it. All the more reason to keep from taking their relationship to "the next level." Tears threatened to spill as Toots suddenly visualized her life without Phil. Damn! She was turning into Ida. Couldn't live without a man. Then she remembered what had happened to all of her eight husbands; and though it hurt like hell, she knew she was doing what was best for Phil. Sadly, even though she knew she was doing him a favor, she dreaded the days ahead without him. It wouldn't be like widowhood. This was different. Becoming a widow was final, no second chances, the end. For the first time in her life, Toots was going to let a man go without his taking a trip to a funeral parlor.

Because it was the right thing to do.

Chapter 11

It had been over a week since Jeremy and Kristen Dunlop were taken and returned to their family; yet the local news stations continued to report on the story. The leader of the largest child-pornography ring in the state turned out to be a prominent businessman. His family had gone into hiding, and he was in jail, awaiting a trial date.

Toots had decided to wait a few days before revealing her wicked past to Phil. They hadn't been alone since the night the kids were found because her dear friend Sophie, the ornery ass, was now in the initial stages of filming a reality special for a top-notch cable news station. When the cable station had heard about her success at locating the children, its producers had immediately started calling. Yesterday the film crew arrived at Toots's house to set up cameras and take location shots. Sophie and Goebel were both going to be featured, so they'd had to be there for still photos and interviews, which would air long before the special did. The executive producer, a young woman named Karen, who was around Abby's age, had referred to them as teasers. It had been a madhouse ever since Sophie agreed to allow them to film the two-hour special. Toots was okay with it; but when the crew actually arrived, she almost wished Sophie had said no to the producers.

Cables, lights, and microphones were in every room Sophie and Goebel would enter. Why they hadn't filmed at Psychic Investigators, Sophie and Goebel's company office in Charleston, which they'd opened six months ago, was a mystery.

Sophie made her first appearance in the kitchen at six o'clock this morning, when Toots, Bernice, and Mavis were enjoying their first cup of coffee for the day. Ida wouldn't come downstairs until she was in full makeup, which was fine with the rest of them. She wasn't a morning person.

The crew consisted of two cameramen, the executive producer, and two assistants. Five extra people to contend with at this early hour, Toots thought, as the crew came downstairs.

"Morning," said Eli, the head cameraman.

"Good morning, young man," Mavis said, as always her voice full of cheer, no matter what time of day.

Toots had told them they could stay at her house, and now she wished she had booked them into a hotel. She hated being polite this early in the day, so she simply nodded at Eli, refilled her cup, and went outside to smoke.

A few minutes later, Sophie joined her. "They're all up now. Damn, Toots, I didn't realize they'd be underfoot twenty-four/seven. This is too damned early." Sophie lit up, then said in a whisper, "I don't have a good feeling about this"—she tossed her free hand in front of her—"life-invading stuff. It kept me up all night."

"What do you mean?" Toots asked, her voice laced with tension. "This wasn't my idea."

"Doesn't matter. I just have a bad feeling. I can't put my finger on any one specific thing, but when my gut talks, I always listen. You know that feeling. You have it, too."

Toots nodded and crushed out her cigarette. "So this isn't one of your psychic things?"

Sophie shook her head. "I don't think so. It's not right, whatever it is. I don't know if I should tell Karen to pack up and go home, or just go with it." Karen, the executive producer, was all business.

"She's a ballbuster for sure. I almost feel sorry for her two assistants," Toots said. "But this is your gig, so you do what you feel is best, but it would not hurt my feelings one little bit if you told the crew to pack up and head back to New York. What does Goebel think?"

Sophie lit a second cigarette off the first one. She inhaled, then blew the smoke out of the side of her mouth. "He says he'll do whatever I think is best. Damn, they just got here. I would really hate to toss them out on their asses the first day of shooting. Do you think the assistants are lesbians? I've been watching them, and they can't keep their eyes off one another."

"It's none of our business if they are," Toots said. "But I don't think so. I think the blonde is new to the job and just follows the other around like a lost puppy. They haven't been here long enough for me to get a take on them. As I said, this is your gig. You have my house for one week, and not a minute longer, as I agreed. After that, it's going to be my gig and your ass."

Sophie was quiet, which was highly unusual, since her mouth usually ran nonstop. "Yeah, I know. Goebel put a bid in on that big old house down the road. You know the one that's older than dirt and painted purple?"

Toots smiled. "Yes, as a matter of fact, I do." No way was she going to tell Sophie or Goebel that she, Toots herself, was the owner of said house. She'd purchased it years before as another one of her decorating projects. The move to LA and taking over at *The Informer* had put that project on the back burner. Until now. She'd been home for a year. When Goebel mentioned something about the house a few weeks ago, she'd given him her real-estate agent's phone number and told him to call, and what to bid. If he played his cards right, the house would be his for a song.

"If he buys it, we're going to shack up. What do you think of that?" Sophie asked, glad to change the subject.

"You're asking me? If I was as smart as I thought I was, I would've shacked up with seven of my eight husbands. I sure as hell wouldn't be in the predicament I'm in now."

"You're not in a 'predicament' at all. You just think you are. I take it you haven't revealed the magic number to Phil?"

"I haven't had an opportunity. With all this hoopla, we haven't had a moment alone. I'm going to tell him, though. As soon as the production crew leaves, I'm kicking all of your asses out for the night. Then, when we're alone, I'll tell him. He's really retiring, Soph. At first, I thought he was just telling me that, but he isn't. He's cutting out new patients."

"Really? 'Cutting'?" Sophie teased.

"Oh, kiss my ass, you know what I mean. He's cutting back on new patients and sending his old patients to his partners. He is the oldest doctor in their practice. He really wants to write that medical thriller he's talked about. Told me it was time to start a new chapter in his life."

Sophie nodded in agreement. "You should be with him, Toots. Remember, none of us are getting any younger. We need to grab whatever happiness we can. Hell, we'll all be seventy this year!"

"Don't remind me. But, hey, we don't look that old—thanks to Ida's miracle cream."

"True, but you really need to tell Phil why you're not going with him," Sophie said, then stood up and turned around.

"Yes, she should tell me why she's not going," Phil said. He'd just arrived for the early-morning taping, thinking it would be a fun day spent with people he truly loved and cared for. Mostly Toots.

Toots whipped around so fast, she was sure she'd suffered whiplash. "What are you doing here?" she snapped before she could filter the words. She stood up, and Phil backed into the kitchen, allowing Toots and Sophie to step inside without crowding each other.

"I called earlier, but there wasn't any answer," Phil said, his expression stilled and serious.

Toots wondered how long he'd been standing at the door, but she wasn't about to ask. She prayed he hadn't heard her and Sophie's entire conversation. If so, then she would have no other choice but to tell him her sordid past.

Chapter 12

Apparently, not long enough, Toots thought, when he leaned over and placed a kiss on her cheek. She let out a breath, unaware she'd been holding it. Now wasn't the time. With all the comings and goings over the next week, she would do whatever she had to, just to make sure that she wasn't alone with Phil. At least long enough for her to give him a detailed account of her marital history. When the producers packed up, then she would invite Phil over for a nice intimate dinner. He knew she didn't cook, so they'd have to eat Froot Loops again. It wouldn't matter what they ate, she thought as she offered up a hesitant smile.

Grinning, Phil said to Toots, "You stink."

She laughed, then pointed to his head. "Your hair is so stiff it looks like you washed it in formaldehyde. I better ask Mavis or Ida if they're missing any."

"Hey, if I wanted the stuff, I could get it. Remember, I work in a hospital."

"True, but don't they keep inventory on that stuff?" She didn't really care, but it was conversation, and anything impersonal worked now.

"Yes, they do. They know where every last aspirin and Band-Aid goes."

Karen chose that moment to make her announcement. "We really want to get started, if all of you are ready. As I explained, I want this to be as close to Sophie's normal day as possible. So . . . if everyone is ready?" She let the question hang in the air.

Sophie swallowed the last of her coffee. "I am not. I'm waiting for . . . Ida. She has to do my face. I don't walk out the door without my face on. So as soon as she's downstairs, we can get started. I can't let the public see me like this."

Mavis choked on her coffee; Bernice rolled her eyes; Goebel chuckled. Toots knew that Sophie was stalling, but she wasn't exactly sure why. Yes, Sophie had said she had a weird feeling, but why not go on with the production? It would take her mind away from the negative vibes.

Toots poured herself another cup of coffee, adding three huge spoonfuls of sugar and lots of cream. "Don't say a word," she said before Phil admonished her for another bad habit.

He held his hands out in front of him. "I'm not saying a word."

"Phil, I need to speak to Sophie. Alone. Do you mind?"

Sophie cast her the evil-eye look, and Phil said, "Go ahead. I'm going to have a bowl of Froot Loops."

"Thanks."

Without another word, Toots grabbed Sophie's arm and practically dragged her upstairs to her bedroom, where the cameras were off-limits. "Tell me why you're stalling. You don't wear makeup every day any more than Phil does. What gives?"

Sophie sat down on the bed next to Toots. She'd dressed in forest green slacks and a matching silk blouse for the shoot. Her long hair was loose, settling on her shoulders. Gold hoops hung from her ears. A diamond necklace given to her for Christmas by Goebel glistened as the early-morning sun peeked through the bedroom windows.

"You never dress like this, Soph. I thought this was supposed to be a reality show."

Sophie took a deep breath. "Yeah, well, there is no way in hell I'm going on national television looking like a two-dollar tramp. I can't seem to shake this bad energy. I've had it ever since the crew arrived."

"Look, Sophie, even though your face is fairly well known from Ida's cosmetic line, it's normal to feel a bit nervous when you're about to make your television debut. Didn't they say that if this was successful, they wanted you and Goebel to sign on for a season of specials? I'd be feeling a bit off, too, if it were me," Toots said, hoping to reassure her suddenly skittish friend.

"Oh, shit, you know that doesn't bother me. I'm not the least bit camera shy. It's something more. I can't put my finger on it, and I feel as though I should be able to."

Though it had been a few weeks since they'd held a séance, Toots voiced her thoughts. "Maybe you need to read their cards. Have a séance while they're here. You might be able to tune in to what's bothering you. Maybe one of them has recently lost a family member, or a friend."

Sophie got off the bed and began pacing back and forth. "No, Toots. Trust me, I know those things. This is completely different. It's just—"

She didn't get a chance to finish her sentence because Goebel burst into the room. "It's that girl—something has happened to her!"

With Goebel in the lead, Sophie and Toots rushed downstairs to a scene none of them could have predicted in a million years.

Phil was checking Karen's vitals and speaking into the phone that Bernice held to his ear.

"Blood pressure is dropping," he told the person on the other line.

Toots knew that Phil carried the proverbial little black bag wherever he went, and today she was grateful.

"What happened?" Toots asked the blond assistant, who by now was crying. The other assistant, whose name she had never heard mentioned, answered, instead. "Karen said her head was hurting. Then she just kinda slid to the floor, and he called 911. I hope she's okay. I really, really need this job. My brother got me this job as a favor. I don't know what will happen to me now," the young woman said.

Toots wanted to smack her face, but refrained. Instead, she said, "How the hell can you be thinking of yourself at a time like this? This woman could be dying, for all we know!"

Goebel took charge. "Everyone, calm down. Girls, why don't you and the camera crew wait in the kitchen. There's coffee and pastries on the counter."

The four TV people did as advised. Goebel stooped beside Phil. "What's your professional opinion?"

Phil finished his conversation, and Bernice took the phone. Her face was as white as a ghost, and her hands trembled. "Dear Lord, what's next?" she asked of no one in particular, then headed for the kitchen, her hand placed over her heart like Redd Foxx's character used to do in his old sitcom from the seventies, *Sanford and Son.*

"I'm not sure," Phil said as he poked and prodded Karen, who lay unconscious on the floor.

Sophie stared at Karen; then she glanced at Toots. "This is what I've been talking about! I knew something was going to happen to her before it happened! If she dies—"

"She isn't going to die," Phil said in his doctor voice. "The paramedics are here."

They all heard the sirens in the background; and as luck would have it, the gates had remained open since Phil's earlier arrival.

In less than two minutes, the paramedics had Karen on a stretcher. One placed an oxygen mask on her, and another expertly placed an IV line in her vein within seconds.

They checked her vitals, then adjusted the stretcher so that it rose about three feet from the ground. All was done very quickly, in no more than two minutes, before they wheeled her to the ambulance.

Toots had lingered in the background, not daring to interfere, but she followed Phil, Goebel, and Sophie as they trailed the paramedics. "Phil, do you have any clue what happened?"

He wrapped his arm around her, pulling her close to him. "I'm guessing she might've had a stroke."

" 'A stroke'?" Sophie yelled, not caring one little bit who heard her. "That girl is too young to have a stroke! It's something else. . . . I just know it is," she added.

Toots wished Sophie could pinpoint exactly what had happened to Karen, since it would make things a lot easier, but she kept that to herself. Sophie was her own worst enemy right now. From past experiences, Toots knew she would never forgive herself for not preventing this.

The ambulance doors closed, and the siren started wailing a second time; then the paramedics raced down the drive to the main road.

They all clustered around the porch, none of them sure about anything at the moment. Toots, always first to initiate a plan in times of crisis, spoke up. "Let's go inside. We need to see to the film crew, let them know what's going on. None of them look a day over twenty, if you ask me."

All of them followed Toots, who came alive in these emergency situations.

In the kitchen, Bernice was practically beating Egg Beaters to death in a bowl, while Mavis had the toaster going at full throttle. Ida was sitting at the table, chatting with the crew. As usual, she looked like she'd stepped right out of a bandbox.

Toots poured herself another cup of coffee, laced it with sugar and cream, then sat at the head of the table. "As you all know, they've taken Karen to the hospital. We aren't sure what's happening, but one of you should call the studio and let them know what's going on. Also, do any of you know how to contact her family? I'm sure they would want to know what's happened."

Eli was the first to speak. "Karen lives alone in the city, and I'm not sure about her family. She's all business, never really talked to me about anything outside of work."

The assistant who was new to the job said, "I don't even know her last name."

"Wait a minute, all of you, before you continue," Toots said, her voice several octaves higher than normal. They all focused their attention on her. "Let's have a quick round-robin and tell me your names."

"Eli," he said, "And this is Jack, my assistant." He directed his gaze to the junior cameraman.

"I'm Haley" came from the blonde.

"My name is Serena Stillman," said the uncaring new girl.

Toots rubbed her hands together. "Okay, Eli, Jack, Haley, and Serena, it's obvious we're not going to film any more of this reality special until we get word on Karen's condition. So having said that, I'm going to pay for you all to stay at the Hampton Inn until you hear from your superiors. Dr. Becker will keep us informed on Karen's progress. Now," Toots asked, "do you all have any questions? Anything I should know?"

Serena spoke first, but she directed her question to Eli. "Are we being paid to sit here while Karen's lying around in the hospital?" The girl was all about herself. Again, Toots wanted to smack her in the face but didn't.

"Yes, I think so, kid. I wouldn't worry about it just yet. We need to find out what's happening with Karen. She is our immediate supervisor for this gig."

Jack and Haley chose to remain quiet.

Maybe they were smarter than Toots thought.

"Phil, can you make a phone call later to check on Karen?" Toots asked.

"Yes, I want to see her as soon as it's allowed," Sophie finally spoke. "I need to . . . Just let me know when I can see her."

Goebel placed a comforting arm around Sophie and ran his free hand up and down the length of her spine. She laid her head against his chest, her eyes closed. "I should've seen this."

The back door slammed shut, startling them all. Abby and Chris, with worried looks on their faces, stood in the center of the kitchen. "Mom! What is going on? I just saw an ambulance leave, and you're not answering your cell or the house phone, so we came over. Is everything okay?"

"The executive producer may have suffered a stroke. We're not sure yet," Toots said, her voice lowered.

"That's terrible! Phil?" Abby asked, turning to him for an answer.

Phil leaned against the counter, arms crossed over his chest, and one jeans-clad leg crossed over his ankle. "I can't be one hundred percent sure. Her vitals were decent. Not good, but I didn't see them as life-threatening. I'll give them time to admit her, and then I'll call and find out if they know anything more."

Abby nodded. "This is awful. I know how excited you and Goebel are. What's going to happen with the reality special?"

Eli spoke up. "We don't know yet."

"I'm Abby Clay. This is my husband, Chris." Her eyes lit up every time she said those five words. Eli quickly introduced Chris and Abby to the crew.

After the introductions were made, Bernice served them all what she called a proper breakfast. Robert showed up just as she'd served the last of the fake eggs. Wade came trudging in behind his brother, a look of concern on his face.

Mavis caught this immediately. "I'm so glad you're back, Wade." She looked at Robert. "Is everything okay?"

"Can we take a walk?" Wade whispered in her ear.

"Of course."

Wade and Mavis wandered out the back door, down the path that led to Jamie's cottage. "I'm worried about Robert. He isn't acting normal. Have you or Bernice noticed anything unusual about him since I've been gone?"

Mavis thought for a minute. "Other than his usual coming and going, you know how he and Bernice are with the recipes. Though, honestly, I haven't been paying a lot of attention to him. Things are unsettled around here now. Lots of good things about to happen, so . . ." She stopped talking. "No, I haven't noticed."

Wade took her hand. "Well, it's good to know you're here. Just in case."

They walked along in companionable silence until they reached the cottage; then they turned back, heading for the house. "Mavis, did you ever have a chance to think about my proposal?"

"Yes, I have. And my answer is yes." There! She'd made the decision, and now there was no going back.

She and Wade were going to become business partners. They were opening a brand-new funeral parlor together.

Chapter 13

Three hours later, they all waited anxiously while Phil called the hospital to check on Karen's status. While they waited, Sophie stared out the front window as though she were in a trance. Without warning, she spun around to face the group. "Phil, she has an aneurysm! They have to find it now before it's too late!"

Toots, Mavis, and Ida stared at her.

Phil whispered a few words into the phone before hanging up.

"Well?" Sophie asked. "Don't keep us in suspense. What did they say? Am I right?"

Phil took a deep breath. "I don't want to know how you do what you do, but to answer your question, yes. Karen has a brain aneurysm. She's going to be fine. As far as they can tell, anyway. There's a simple procedure they can do, a coiling. Kind of a mini-craniotomy, a small incision above the eyebrow, where they go in and clamp off the vessel. If they're able to do this, then she'll be out of the hospital in two or three days. I think you should really put those talents to good use, Sophie. Do you always know what ails a person before it even happens?"

"No. This is the first time for that, too. Seems that ever since we've been back in Charleston, I'm able to do and see things that I've never done before. Yes, I can call up the

dead, but seeing those kids through touch, and now this."
She spread her hands out in front of her. "I don't know
what this is, but I do wish I could've done something to
prevent this. I knew something was off, a strange feeling
unlike any I've had. And this is it."

"She'll be fine, Sophie. Trust me, this isn't the death sentence it was a few years ago. She's lucky she was here
when it happened."

Toots agreed. "Yes, she was. What are the odds of there
being a doctor in the house? The Big Man Upstairs must
be looking out for that girl."

"Goebel, I want to see her as soon as I can. Will you go
with me?" Sophie asked.

"Of course, I will, but in the meantime, you need to
relax a little. There is nothing you can do for the young
girl now, except pray."

"You're right, but it's hard knowing what I know after
the fact. I feel responsible, as though I should've been able
to prevent this, or at least . . ." Sophie threw her hands in
the air. "I don't know anything right now other than if I
don't get a cigarette, I'll die. Toots, you wanna huff with
me?"

"I thought you'd never ask. Excuse us, gentlemen," Toots
said. "Phil, have another cup of coffee. You look tired."

It was early afternoon by then, and the sun sparkled
above them, its warmth welcoming. Toots sat down on the
top step and lit two cigarettes, giving one to Sophie.

"Is there something you wanted to tell me, or did you
really just want to huff?"

"I just needed a smoke. Look at my hands." Sophie held
a shaking hand out for Toots's perusal.

"You're really nervous, aren't you?"

Sophie rolled her eyes. "Hell yes! If you want to know
the truth, this shit is scaring me, big-time. What if something is about to happen to one of us, and I could've pre-

vented it? And Abby? I don't think I like this part of having a sixth sense or whatever you want to call it. Psychic, my ass. If I were truly gifted, I would have known how to tune in to those bad vibes. Maybe I need to give this psychic investigation a rest for a while. I wish Madam Butterfly were alive. She'd know how to help me."

"You need to chill out. I think you and Goebel should go away for a few days. Relax. Get laid. Take your mind off this."

"You really need to screw Phil. You've been focusing on sex too much." Sophie blew a white cloud of smoke out of her nose.

"My situation with Phil isn't like yours and Goebel's. You don't have lies about almost your entire life between the two of you," Toots said.

"That's a crock of shit, and you know it. You haven't deliberately lied; you just haven't broached the subject," Sophie said. "Or have you?"

"Not in the way you think. Oh, we've talked about our youth, things we did and didn't do, that stuff. But as you know, I've never mentioned the marriages, and he's never asked. We're always on the go, doing something, or he's working. It just never seemed to come up."

"Then let it go. Tell him and get it the frig out of the way. I know you're head over heels in love with the guy. Who gives a good rat's ass if you've had a few husbands? Look at it this way. If the first one hadn't died, you'd still be married, right?"

Toots laughed. John Simpson was the love of her life, but Phil was coming in a close second, even ahead of Chris Clay's father, whom she had loved very much. "I suppose when you put it that way, it's not so bad, but then I ask myself, 'Why did they all kick the bucket?' I'm afraid I'm a jinx."

"Bullshit! There is no such thing as a jinx. Karma, yes,

and, Toots, remember, most of the men you married were a bit older than you, except for Garland, Chris's dad. You weren't in love with those men. You simply felt sorry for them because they were lonely. And so what if they were all oozing in the cash department. If they hadn't left you their fortunes, then you wouldn't be able to do all the good that you do. Think of that."

Toots grinned. "Yes, there is that. And speaking of good—and, no, I am not trying to change the subject—I am so excited about Abby and Chris's new project. Dogs Displaced by Disaster. Though Abby says they'll take in all animals. She's really onto something. I think I've already found a building for the canine café. At first, I thought about buying the bakery building from Jamie. Did you know her grandmother left that to her? I decided against it, though. That's all Jamie has left of her grandmother. That building and the property were in her family for more than a hundred years. When the real-estate market picks up, if she were to sell out, she'd be set for the rest of her life."

"Tell me you're going somewhere with this, or I'm going back inside. I want Ida to fix my face before I go to the hospital to see Karen."

Toots flipped her the bird.

"I'm talking about investing some of my many husbands'—may they rest in peace, except for Leland, the cheap bastard—I'm going to invest some of their money so I can open a café for dogs and cats. The Canine and Feline Café. I like that name, don't you? It's simple and straightforward."

"Yes, it's a good idea, but you'd need some rules."

"Such as?"

"I would think you would want to make sure the animals are clean. No fleas, parvo, all the bad stuff animals can have."

"You're right. I've already got that covered with the

health officials. Chris has really taken the bull by the horns on this deal. You know he always wanted to be a farmer? Now let's go inside before those two men of ours get suspicious and suspect us of something wicked and vile." Toots stood up and stretched. "Besides, Abby's here. I want to catch her up on everything."

Sophie followed Toots inside. As was becoming the norm, everyone gathered at the dining table. They'd had to bring chairs in from the veranda so there would be enough seating when the camera crew arrived. Maybe it was time to invest in a larger table. One that would seat at least twenty? Thirty? The next time she and Abby went antique shopping, she would look for a new dining-room set. For now, she needed to get the camera crew settled in at the Hampton Inn, at least until she and Sophie knew what their plans were.

Clearing her mind of all things negative, or as much as one could, given the circumstances, she rubbed her hands together and prepared to do what she did best. Make people happy.

"Mavis, would you and Wade mind driving the crew over to the hotel? We'll need two cars for this. You can take the Lincoln and the Range Rover."

"Of course, I can," Mavis said, turning to Wade. "Did you have anything planned?"

He glanced at Robert, who seemed perfectly content, sifting through the latest copy of *Martha Stewart Living*. "I'm not dead yet," Robert said. "Go on. I've got to run over to the house and get that copy of *Southern Living*. You have to know the laws of physics to understand these ridiculous recipes that felon publishes." Standing, he wobbled a bit, using the table to balance himself.

Bernice saw this and was quick to act. "I'm going with you. I want to see that new mattress you were telling me about." Bernice looked at Toots, giving her a wink.

Robert perked up. "We'll have the house to ourselves, too."

Toots chimed in. "Remember what we talked about, Bernice? Just do it, okay? It's good for your heart."

Bernice flipped her the bird. For a split second, the production crew appeared stunned; then they all laughed when both Toots and Sophie returned the gesture.

"If you're ready, we can go now and get back before the traffic gets too bad," Wade said to Mavis and the production crew.

"Would it be all right if we left our equipment here, until we know what we're going to do?" Eli asked.

"I don't see why not," Toots answered. "Let's hope Karen recovers quickly. Then you all can resume filming if . . . Oh, don't mind me." She was about to tell them that Sophie might not allow the production to continue after what happened with Karen, but then she thought better of it. This was Sophie and Goebel's gig. Not hers.

Fifteen minutes later, the house was empty except for Toots, Ida, Sophie, Phil, Goebel, and "the kids." Abby hated it when Toots referred to her and Chris as the kids, but they were kids to her, just adult-sized.

They spent the next few minutes catching up with each other; then Abby suddenly bolted for the bathroom.

Concerned, Toots followed her daughter. She heard the toilet flush, and then the water running. She tapped lightly on the door. "Abby, are you okay in there?"

The door opened. Abby's curly blond hair was sticking to her neck. Sweat beaded her forehead. "I've got a bug or something. I've been sick off and on ever since I drank that nasty coffee," Abby said as she walked down the hall and up the stairs to Toots's bedroom. "You don't mind if I lie down for a bit, do you? I'm a little light-headed."

"Of course not. Make yourself at home, sweetie. Is there anything I can get for you? Soup? Ginger ale maybe?"

Abby curled up on the bed, pulling the duvet over her

feet. "No thanks, Mom. If I had to eat anything right now, it would just make me sicker. Go on down and tell Chris about the tables you ordered for The Canine and Feline Café. He thinks I'm teasing him."

Toots smoothed Abby's hair back, surprised at how warm her skin felt. "Okay, but you call me or Chris if you need anything. If you don't start to feel better in another day or so, I think you should go see Dr. Pauley. You're like me—you rarely get sick."

"Sure, Mom, whatever you say," Abby whispered, then closed her eyes.

Unsettled, Toots left the room, quietly closing the door behind her.

Chapter 14

As Toots made her way downstairs, a quick and disturbing thought brought her to a complete stop before she reached the last step.

What if Abby is really ill? As in terminally ill?

"No," she said out loud, not caring if anyone heard her. Abby had been trying to do too much. The poor girl was physically exhausted. Restoring the Clay Plantation would exhaust an Olympian. Add the prep for the Dogs Displaced by Disaster, and it was no wonder Abby felt bad.

Negative thoughts breed negative actions, she reminded herself. She took a cleansing breath before joining the others gathered around the dining-room table.

Toots was surprised to see someone had returned the chairs to the veranda and stacked the camera equipment neatly in the corner. The cable wires were coiled on their spools and the lights pushed against the wall. Probably Goebel. The guy was a true gem. She hoped Sophie would marry this man, as he was a keeper.

Frankie and Coco frolicked with the new babies Abby had supplied them. Both dogs had been quiet today, as though they sensed something was off kilter. Toots thought that the two were smarter than some of the people she knew.

Squaring her shoulders back, reminding herself to keep positive, she entered the dining room. "Sophie, before you go visit Karen, would you mind reading for me?" Toots asked upon entering the dining room. She didn't want to tell anyone her thoughts about Abby, for fear that saying them out loud might make them real. Silly, yes, but she wasn't trusting her daughter's welfare to fate. She'd already jinxed eight men to their grave.

All eyes focused on Toots, but no one commented. A tense silence filled the room. Sophie spoke up. "I think it's a good idea if we go all the way and have a séance. I want to contact my spirit guide. I need some advice." Sophie glanced around the table, daring anyone to make a smart comment. She said this as though it were totally commonplace.

Ida, Chris, Goebel, and Phil all cast surprised looks at Sophie.

"Don't tell me you're chickening out. You've done this before," she said, stating what they all knew.

"I'm all for it," said Goebel. "Might just clear up all these negative vibes you've been having."

"If you're going to do this, at least that crew won't be here to witness it," Ida said, then added, "Even though that's why they're here in the first place."

"Just exactly what's that supposed to mean?" Sophie cracked.

Ida, as always the picture of perfection, gave up a wry smile. "Whatever you want it to mean."

"I can see you're back to your usual bitchy self."

"Stop it, you two, before I kick both of your asses," Toots admonished the two women, suddenly feeling more like herself because this was the norm for them. "You both still act like you're in the seventh grade. Now let's do this before Bernice and Robert return. He's already afraid that Sophie is going to cast some deep, dark evil spell on him. I'm not sure how he'd react if he stumbled upon us in the middle of a séance."

"If we don't get started soon, he'll find out. It won't take him and Bernice all day to scope out that new mattress. I hope he doesn't give Bernice another recipe for any more of that off-the-wall Indian shit she's been forcing us to eat."

"For once, I agree with you," Ida said. "I had enough Indian cuisine when I was with Dr. Sameer." Ida looked at Toots and Sophie, daring them to comment.

Toots rolled her eyes, and it felt damn good to do so. "I refuse to go there, Ida. I know what you're up to, and he was not a doctor. He was a fraud and a perverted panty sniffer."

Ida's beautifully made-up face turned crimson. No one had told Phil about Dr. Sameer's tastes in lingerie.

Sophie chuckled out loud until it turned into a genuine belly laugh. "Phil, aren't you just dying to know who Dr. Sameer is? Perhaps you've heard of him? He operates The Center for Mind and Body in Los Angeles, specializes in OCD."

Guessing there was more to the story than Ida wanted him to know, he shook his head. "I don't believe I've heard of him, but I'm in Charleston, not LA. We have a clique of doctors at the hospital who seem to know a bit of everything, so I can ask them if it's important."

"No!" Ida shouted, practically jumping out of her chair. "It's not important at all. Forget you ever heard the name." She stared at Sophie and Toots, her eyes glowing like two daggers. Sophie knew when she'd pushed Ida to the limit.

"Let's discuss something pleasant. Like dead people and guardian angels," Sophie declared, as if she hadn't partaken in the previous conversation. "We're still set up in the formal living room?" she called out as she retrieved the wineglasses and candles from the hutch in the kitchen.

"Of course," Toots said, following her. "Phil, you are going to join us, I hope?"

"Damn straight I'm joining you. I haven't had this much

fun since the last séance we had in LA, when you contacted Abby's father."

Toots recalled that day and never wanted to experience
anything like that ever again. Abby's life had been on the
line, and, thankfully, Sophie had used her superb skills to
contact John, and it'd worked. And it was the first time
she'd really kissed Phil. *Really kissed.* Just thinking of it
sent a delicious shiver down her spine.

Sophie hurried through the preparations. "The table-
cloth hasn't been washed, has it?" she asked Toots.

"No. I gave Bernice strict instructions that she was not
to wash any of the items we use during a séance, or, I told
her, we would kill her," Toots replied.

Goebel and Phil looked at one another, then at Toots.

"Phil, you don't ever want to get on the wrong side of
these old girls here," Goebel informed him, though he was
smiling.

"I think I've figured that out already."

They all took part in setting up the table for the séance.
Ida rimmed the wineglasses with salt and placed one on
each corner of the table. Salt was supposed to ward off any
evil spirits they didn't want to come through. Toots lit the
candles and placed a rocks glass in the center of the table.
Once everything was ready, Sophie indicated that they
should take their places at the table.

Sophie took the seat at the head of the table, with Toots
taking the seat to her right and Ida the seat on her left.
Goebel sat next to Toots because he knew Sophie wouldn't
like him sitting beside Ida, because she thought Ida had the
hots for him. She smiled when he sat down. Phil sat next
to Ida. The rule of thumb was that each of them should sit
at a corner representing a cardinal point of the compass.
Sophie had told them this was very important, and they always remembered when she said that because they all
knew this was in no way a joke. Sophie had proven herself
too many times.

With the heavy drapes tightly closed in the formal living room, and with only the candles for light, the atmosphere immediately became subdued, silent, except for the ticking of the grandfather clock. Sophie took a deep breath, closing her eyes for a moment. When she felt the calm, peaceful feeling telling her she was open to the spirit world, she raised her head and said in a low, sultry tone, "Let's all join hands." She reached for Toots's and Ida's hands. "As you all know, I like to say a prayer before we open the doors to the other side."

The setting was perfect to receive spirits, ghosts, or an entity of any kind, or to open one's mind to receive guidance.

Sophie closed her eyes and bowed her head. The rest of the group followed her lead.

"Please clear my mind of any remaining negative thoughts and energy so that I may receive guidance from those wiser than I." Sophie hadn't used this method of prayer before. She really wasn't here to communicate with the dead. She wanted to contact her guardian angel in hopes of receiving advice regarding Karen's health crisis. She also hoped to gain new insight into her latest ability to see through the eyes of another by touch.

A chill permeated the room, and the candles flickered. Sophie spoke in soft tones. "We have made contact with a spirit guide. Let us all place our fingertips on the glass to receive answers to any question asked." She stopped for a few seconds as the others touched the rocks glass. When they were all interlinked, each felt a small electric shock. Phil almost pulled his hand away, but Toots whispered, "Not yet." Sophie continued to call for guidance from her spirit guide. They all kept their heads lowered, waiting for her instruction, as this was different from the séances they were used to.

"Spirit guide, if you are here with us, can you communicate with us by guiding our fingertips to slide the glass we have placed in the center of our table?"

Ever so slowly, the rocks glass moved slightly to the right.

"If I am interpreting the movement correctly, can you move the glass to the right for yes, and to the left for no?"

They all watched as the glass slid to the right, the tips of their fingers feeling the magnetic-like pull as the spirit guide took control.

"Yes," Sophie said in a low voice.

"Today there was an incident that is causing great physical harm to a young woman." Sophie paused, unclear how to phrase a question that required more than an answer of yes or no. Knowing there really wasn't any other way to state her question, she decided to simply ask, and hope the answer was the one she wanted.

"Karen is in the hospital." Sophie sneaked a look at Toots, who gave her a slight nod, indicating she should continue. "Is she going to survive?"

All eyes focused on the glass and their fingertips. A few seconds passed. Nothing happened. Sophie waited another minute, which seemed like ten, then repeated her question. She'd learned that many times the spirit guide or guardian angel didn't always answer right away, and often one had to search for another form of communication. Repetition was supposed to work, too. She spoke out loud again. "Is Karen going to survive?"

Again, they focused on the glass in the center of the table. Suddenly the temperature in the room dropped several degrees. Unsure how to proceed, as this was a new experience for her, Sophie asked another question. "Is there a supernatural presence in the room with us? Another presence besides my spirit guide?" Sophie had yet to learn the name of her spirit guide. This wasn't unusual, since she was just now learning ways to tune in to her spirit guide. She was unsure if her guide was male or female.

The candles flickered, then smoldered. Silvery gray wisps of smoke billowed from the extinguished wicks. Several intakes of breath, then silence. Taking a deep breath, Sophie tried again. "If this is my spirit guide, would you please move the glass to the right?"

Straining to see in the darkness, they all focused on the glass. Still nothing.

Sophie was just about to give up when the room suddenly filled with an eerie, bluish light. "Shhh," she said to the others. The light swirled around; then it took the form of what appeared to be a woman dressed in clothing from another century. Glistening gold sparks shot out from the figure, allowing one to see the features of a woman. Her long hair, a golden brown, framed her face. Her eyes were an intense shade of blue, almost like a fluorescent blue that glowed as though a light shone through them. Her lips were rose red, her skin pale.

They stared at the figure, but no one spoke. Sophie focused her gaze on the woman figure, hoping to memorize every detail. As she stared at the apparition, she instantly knew who she was.

"You are my spirit guide," Sophie said.

The woman figure smiled and nodded, then spoke. "I am Joy."

Feeling creeped-out, but fascinated, Sophie swallowed, her throat as dry as the desert. "Joy. That's . . . a beautiful name."

Again, Joy, the spirit guide, smiled at her.

Unsure how to proceed, but needing answers, Sophie spoke. Her voice was raspy; her throat was so dry. "Will Karen survive?"

The spirit guide, Joy, smiled, and then nodded in the affirmative. Before Sophie had a chance to ask about her new abilities, the bluish haze disappeared, and Joy with it.

The candles lit up; the temperature returned to normal.

No one moved or said a word. Again, they were witness to an event—and if they were to tell anyone else about it, that person would almost certainly dispute the truth of what had been described. But they knew what they had seen, and that was all that mattered.

Chapter 15

When Sophie entered the ICU, she was expecting to see an unresponsive woman hooked up to all kinds of life-support machines. Instead, she saw a smiling Karen sipping from a plastic cup, which the nurse held for her.

Shock kept her lingering in the doorway. She blinked a few times, just to make sure she was really seeing Karen. This certainly was not the girl lurking at death's door as she had been earlier, that very morning. She needed to make sure she was not experiencing another clairsentience vision.

No, this was real.

Sophie tapped on the door frame to let Karen know she had a visitor.

Karen and the nurse turned. When Karen saw her, she smiled. "Sophie, what a surprise. I didn't think anyone would come."

Sophie felt a rush of pity for the young woman. "Well, think again. You've got a houseful of old women who are sending good vibes and prayers for your complete and speedy recovery. From what I can see, they're being answered."

Several monitors were attached to various parts of Karen's body. Beeps and gushes of air from the machines provided unnatural background noises, but Sophie was used to it. When Bernice had her heart surgery, she'd been connected to all kinds of machines. The noise became secondary after the initial shock. The nurse, a petite woman in her midthirties, with friendly eyes, bustled around the room. "Karen is our miracle patient. Dr. Waterman, her surgeon, says her case will go down in the books."

The surgery was textbook, according to Phil, who'd been notified by Dr. Waterman as soon as Karen was in the recovery room. They were able to make a small incision above her eyebrow and clamp off the offending blood vessel in order to do the coiling procedure. Phil was told she would make a full recovery. As soon as they heard the news, Sophie insisted Goebel take her to the hospital, once Karen was out of recovery and allowed to receive visitors.

Sophie grinned, knowing this to be a fact, but she was not going to say so in front of the nurse. "That's the best news I've heard all day."

"I'll leave you two alone for a few minutes," the nurse said, then hustled out of the room.

As soon as she left, Sophie moved to stand by Karen's bedside. Taking her hand, she said, "There is something I need to share with you. I don't want to upset you, but given that you're in the kind of business that you're in, I hope you're open to what I have to tell you."

Karen closed her eyes, then opened them. "After what I've been through today, it would have to be catastrophic to upset me."

Sophie couldn't imagine anything more "catastrophic" than a brain aneurysm. "I think there was a reason you were sent to Charleston to film me and Goebel." There, it was out; now she would give Karen a minute to absorb her words.

Karen gave up a halfhearted laugh. "And what would that be?"

"I know reality shows are all the rage these days. Add the psychic element, you're sure to gain an audience." She held up her hand. "Of course, you know this, or you wouldn't be here." Sophie took a deep breath. She didn't want to just spit out what she'd experienced, but really, she thought, there wasn't any other way. "After you were brought to the hospital, I had a séance of sorts." She paused, waiting for Karen's reaction. When she saw she had Karen's undivided attention, she continued to speak. "I wasn't completely honest with you this morning. I really don't have Ida do my makeup every day. All morning I had an odd feeling, unlike any I'd experienced. I couldn't place what it was, but I felt as though something bad was about to happen."

"You're psychic. Isn't this normal?"

Sophie took Karen's hand. "Not this. This was different. It frightened me because I couldn't chalk it up to a psychic prediction."

"So what do you think you were experiencing?" Karen asked her.

"This sounds strange, but I believe my spirit guide was trying to warn me." That sparked her attention.

"About?"

"You. This," Sophie said, nodding at the bandage on Karen's head.

"Nonsense. You couldn't have prevented this, Sophie. I've been suffering with terrible headaches for weeks. I should've gone to the doctor, but I was too busy working. The doctor told me I was lucky. I realize that now. My health has to come first."

"I'm glad you feel this way. I felt I needed to try to make contact with this guardian angel or spirit guide. Personally, I believe them to be one and the same. I held a séance, not the traditional speaking-to-the-dead kind, but I knew I had to try to make a connection to the negative feelings I'd had since your arrival. This is going to sound insane to you, but it is what it is. My spirit guide told me you would be just fine." There, she'd said it! Suddenly she felt light and joyful.

*Joy*ful!

Sophie had to acknowledge the connection to her spirit guide's name and the feeling attached to it just now.

It dawned on her that this was her spirit guide at work. Though Sophie herself was never in danger, she had unknowingly been given the responsibility of protecting Karen. It wasn't coincidence that she'd traveled all the way to Charleston to film a reality show. Nor was it coincidence that Dr. Phil Becker had been there. Sophie didn't recall Toots's mentioning anything to her about inviting Phil over while they were filming. No, this was divine intervention. Just to make sure, she planned to question Toots as soon as she returned.

Karen didn't say anything; she just nodded.

"You think this is a crock, right?" Sophie asked.

"No. I think you're one hundred percent right."

Surprised, Sophie had expected Karen to laugh at her spirit guide theory. "Why?" she had to ask.

Karen took a deep breath. "I probably shouldn't tell you this, but since I'm crediting you for saving my life, I'm going to anyway. When the network called and asked if you and Mr. Blevins wanted to film a reality special, they only called because their first choice, John Edward, had to cancel."

"See? Then that proves I'm right about all of this," Sophie said. Then she asked, "So, were you really going to air this special with me and Goebel?"

"Oh yes. It was and is the real deal. The network wanted that other psychic, but you were definitely their second choice. So, yes, they would've aired this. Eli is very capable of taking over for me. I'm not sure what the network wants to do at this point, so don't count yourselves out just yet."

Sophie knew that John Edward's schedule wasn't compatible with the network's because *she* had to protect Karen. It was as simple as that, if one believed in the spirit world.

The nurse stepped back into the room. "I'm sorry, but she's only allowed visitors for fifteen minutes until we move her out of ICU."

"That's fine. I think we've discussed enough, and I don't want to tire her out too much," Sophie said. She squeezed Karen's hand. "I'll be in touch."

"Thanks, Sophie. I owe you one."

Sophie offered a halfhearted wave, then stepped out of the room. Goebel was downstairs in the lobby, waiting for her.

Shit happens, she thought as she stepped inside the elevator. *Shit always happens.*

Chapter 16

"Then close the deal. Tell them I'll pay cash if it helps to move this along," Toots said to Henry Whitmore. "I want that property."

After viewing a handful of possible buildings for her new business venture, The Canine and Feline Café, Toots had finally found the perfect building with the perfect location. She'd spent the past three days doing nothing but viewing property. The minute she saw the building and the land on Byron Road, she knew it was the piece of property she'd been searching for. It was exactly what she had in mind. After seeing the property, Abby and Chris agreed. Now all she had to do was to get the Realtor to push the closing date up as fast as humanly possible.

With the Clay Plantation virtually set up for a variety of animals, a handful of newly hired personnel ready to start their new jobs, three top-notch veterinarians ready at a moment's notice, Toots wanted the café up and running so the animals would have a place to go, once they were rehabilitated. Phil had contacted Dr. Carnes, and she promised to make a trip to Charleston for the café's grand opening.

Toots gave herself six weeks max to finish the project.

Toots hung up the phone, checked her "shit-to-do" list, and made one more phone call to her personal Realtor.

"Alice, lower the price on 'the purple plantation.' I don't care how low you go, either. Just take the offer when he calls. Yes, I promise not to hold you responsible for the loss. He will be calling you within a week. Make sure we get this handled." She checked that off her list. More than ever, Toots wanted Sophie and Goebel to have what she nicknamed "the purple plantation" house. They were the love match of the century, and she didn't want to be too far from either of them. Goebel had become the brother she had never had.

Phil. She had to call him. It'd been two days since they last spoke. He'd called numerous times since, but she had avoided his phone calls. Not wanting to, but knowing it was the right thing to do, she dialed his number. He answered on the first ring.

"Toots! I was about to get in my car and drive over there. Where have you been? I've been worried to death about you," Phil said in one long breath.

It *was* kinda nice to have someone care about her that much. She would miss Phil, but she had her list, and this was the last call she had to make today. She might as well do it and get it over with. But after hearing Phil's voice, the concern he showed, she wasn't prepared to drop the ball yet.

"I've been trying to buy a piece of property for the café, taking care of Bernice, or trying to. Then, of course, Abby and Chris have needed my help with the dog project." She stopped. All she was doing was making childish excuses. She either told Phil about her past, or she did not. She opted to tell the truth.

"Phil, there is something I've been meaning to share with you, but I never seem to find the right time." This was not going to be easy; and for a second, she thought laying one's spouse to rest was a much easier task. Except for John and Garland—their *events* had been a great loss. Leland's *event* had been more of a relief than a time of sadness. She'd gone home, catered to those mourners who required it, grabbed her much-loved stack of tabloids, a bottle of wine, and gotten pleasantly drunk while reading in her Jacuzzi tub. She'd mourned for ten days, and moved on. And now, almost five years later, that part of her life was nothing more than a distant memory.

"Tell me now. I have all the time in the world. Today is the first official day of my retirement. I'm glad you called. I wanted to take you to dinner and celebrate. Sophie's psychic abilities must be rubbing off on you."

Shit, piss, damn! Now was not *the time!*

Not wanting to rain on his retirement parade—not to mention that she missed him like crazy—Toots again put off telling Phil what she'd wanted to for almost a month.

"That's wonderful! I would love to go out to celebrate with you," Toots said, and found that she was being totally honest and truly wanted to share this milestone with Phil.

"How about I pick you up at seven? Will that give you enough time to get ready?"

"I'll be waiting on the front porch," she said, a grin stretching so wide it made her face hurt.

Upstairs, she took a quick shower, applied her much-loved cream from Seasons, Ida's growing line of cosmetics, and twisted her hair up in a chignon. Then she added blush, smudged a bit of eyeliner on her lids, added a coat of mascara, and her new favorite black honey lipstick. She rubbed her lips together, then kissed a tissue to remove the excess lip gloss. Looking in the mirror, she realized that she didn't look her age anymore! Damn, but Ida was changing her life in a good way. Still, no way in hell would she tell her so, at least not now.

In her closet, she found a pale green sheath dress she'd bought on sale at a little boutique in California. The dress fit perfectly, clinging in all the right places without being tight. She hated it when women crammed themselves into dresses two sizes too small. Green being one of the colors that went with her auburn hair, she located a pair of pale green strapless heels that matched the dress perfectly. *Damn, when you're good, you're good,* she thought as she slipped on the shoes. She saw green of every shade in her closet. It truly was *her* color, though Sophie looked fabulous in the dark forest greens she wore.

She spun around in front of the mirror. Seeing that this was as good as it got, she hurried downstairs to take care of the pooches before leaving. Mavis and Wade were in Charlotte, attending a convention for the owners of funeral parlors, so she'd volunteered to care for Coco, since Frankie was really her dog now. He spent more time with her than with Phil; but lately that was her own doing, for she'd not bothered to answer his calls. Briefly she had a thought: What if Phil took Frankie away from her when she broke it off with him? She'd become so attached to the little wiener dog that she had started letting him sleep at the foot of her bed.

The dogs were lounging under the kitchen table, their favorite place when the kitchen was empty. Bernice was at Robert's, no doubt searching for recipes. Sophie and Goebel had been called out on their first big psychic investigation job. It was for a young couple who had just purchased an older home and thought it was haunted. Ida had returned to Wilmington to record another segment for The Home Shopping Club, and was due back later in the evening. She'd send her a text message letting her know she had the house to herself, at least for a while.

Toots found the poached chicken, which Mavis had prepared for the dogs, in the refrigerator, along with instructions on how long to heat it in the microwave. "You two are treated like children," Toots commented as she placed the bowl of chicken in the microwave for ten seconds— *Just to take the chill off,* the note read. She laughed. They were all madly in love, except for Ida, and their careers had blossomed and taken them all places they would never have imagined in a million years. Life was good, except for the lie she carried with her.

Toots scooped the warm chicken into separate bowls for the dogs; then she rinsed and refilled their water bowls. When they were finished, she opened the back door in the kitchen. Both dogs raced out so fast, Toots thought they might actually take off and fly away.

"Three minutes, you two," she said, closing the screen. She'd let them sniff, do their business, then give them their nightly treat. By then, it would be time for Phil to pick her up.

Ten minutes later, with the dogs settled for the evening, Toots stepped out onto the veranda. Pleasantly warm, the humidity zilch, Toots thought it was a totally perfect evening. Her night-blooming jasmine scented the warm evening air; the azaleas were in full bloom, their array of colors a burst of brilliance against the deep green shrubbery. She gazed down the winding path, still in awe of the majestic oak trees that bowed over the road leading to the house. This was home. She inhaled the fresh scent of newly mowed grass, courtesy of Goebel, who had developed a new passion for gardening. Just wait until they get "the purple plantation," she thought. There were so many wildflowers, shrubbery that dated back to when the house was built, and the giant angel oak trees. He would have plenty to keep him busy. Toots couldn't wait to view his handiwork. Of course, all of this wouldn't take place if he didn't buy the house. Hell, she thought about giving it to them for a wedding gift, even though they hadn't really set a date. They simply said they were engaged, and for now that was enough.

Headlights coming down the drive brought her back to the present. She followed the lights around the curve; and when the car came into view, she realized she'd made a mistake. It was not Phil. While she did not know much about cars, she knew enough to know the purplish red sports car that stopped in front of the house was a classic. A man, someone she didn't recognize, got out of the car, waiting while the convertible top closed. Another set of headlights directed her away from the sports car. Phil's reliable silver Mercedes crept down the drive. He stopped far enough away from the car so there could be no question of his car even coming close to this swanky ride.

Dressed in charcoal gray slacks, with a silvery blue shirt, Phil reeked of sexy, Toots thought as she watched him walk over to the veranda. His brown hair looked wet from his shower, and she thought about that time so long ago on their first date when they'd showered at Diamond Head. The night Abby had been abducted. She'd been in such a hurry to leave, she remembered baring it all in front of Phil as she'd hurriedly dressed. He hadn't seen her nude since. Maybe now was the time, she thought as she felt a familiar pull in the pit of her belly. Abby was right. She still had desires, and right now, Phil Becker was her total focus.

He kissed her cheek, and she inhaled the clean scent of Dial soap and his spicy aftershave. She closed her eyes for just a second, savoring the moment. "I have a guest, and I have no clue who he is," she said, nodding to the man who was now removing luggage from the passenger side.

"You really don't know who he is?" Phil asked, his voice a bit stiff.

Toots shook her head. "I guess I should find out, huh?"

With Phil at her side, she walked down the steps and down the drive to the flashy car, which she saw was a Porsche 911, an older model. A classic, she guessed. The man was bent over, searching inside one of the open pieces of luggage, when Toots spoke. "Excuse me?"

"Tootsie?" The man stared at her, apparently baffled.

Toots felt her heart skip a beat. "Daniel Alan?"

He immediately wrapped Toots in a bear hug. He squeezed her so tightly, it took her breath away. She kissed him on both cheeks, pulled his face away so she could get a good look at him, and then kissed him a second time.

"The one and only," he said.

"This is the surprise of the year. I can't believe you're actually here. You don't look like yourself. . . ." Toots paused, afraid she might've insulted him. "I mean, you look fantastic—just not the Daniel I'm used to seeing."

Taller than she remembered, and certainly thinner than he'd ever been, she raked her gaze up and down, then back to his face. Glossy black hair, now speckled with gray, twinkling cobalt eyes. *Daniel Alan is hot,* she thought as she smiled at him.

"It's been a long time," he said, as if it explained the physical changes.

Phil cleared his throat. "Toots?"

She whirled around. "Oh, Phil, I'm sorry. I am just so shocked to see this young man."

Phil shot a look Daniel's way. "And you're going to introduce me when?" he asked in a tone that let her know he was not happy with the turn of events.

Flabbergasted and a little embarrassed, Toots shook her head. "Phil, I'm sorry. I'm still floored. Daniel, meet Dr. Phil Becker."

The two men shook hands and gave one another the typical male proverbial nod of acknowledgment, each unsure of where he stood.

"Daniel, Dr. Becker . . . Phil," she said, letting him know this was not *her* doctor. "Phil saved your mother's life last year."

If there had ever been a stunned moment in Phil's relationship with Toots, it was then. Relief flooded over him like a ravaging waterfall. He'd thought this handsome, much younger man might've been more than a friend to Toots. And he'd been right, just not the kind of friend he thought. He felt as giddy as a kid going to the prom. He shook Daniel's hand so long that Toots had to pry him away.

"It's good to meet you finally," Daniel said. "Mom told me all about you in her letters, and, of course, she can't sing enough praises, since she believes you brought her back from the dead. I just want to thank you both." Daniel stepped back, tears shimmering in his dark blue eyes. "I haven't been the best son. I had to come home to see Mom." He raked a hand through his glossy hair. "Is she here?"

Toots was in a semi state of shock over the change in Daniel. She was finding it difficult to carry on a normal conversation.

"Your mother is next door with her new friend, Robert," Phil informed him.

Perplexed, but in a good way, Daniel asked, "Mom has a male friend?"

Toots was surprised that Bernice hadn't mentioned Robert in her letters, but she must have had her reasons. Should Phil have kept this quiet? It didn't matter. Daniel was here, and he would meet Robert soon enough.

"Your mother has so many friends—some you know, some you don't. It will take weeks for her to introduce you." That was stretching the truth a bit, but Toots still felt very protective of Bernice. They were as close as sisters, and that would never change. Daniel hadn't been a perfect son, she knew, but he was here now. That had to count for something. Now the question was: Would Bernice have a heart attack when she saw the new and improved version of her long-lost son?

"Then let's get started. I drove all the way from Seattle. I'm ready to call it a day," Daniel said. Toots sneaked a peek at the license plate. Sure enough. Washington State. Bernice never told her she knew where Daniel was, but

Toots figured she must have had her reasons. Bernice didn't have to reveal every secret to her.

"Oh, damn me and my lack of manners. I imagine you're tired and hungry. I can help with the tired part, but the hungry . . . Well, if you remember, I'm not much of a cook. Phil and I have dinner reservations. I suppose we can add one more person?" She directed her question to Phil. While thrilled that Daniel had come to visit his mother after all these years, Toots didn't see this as a reason to postpone her evening.

"No, no, you all go ahead. I just want to see Mom, catch up, and maybe have a shower. I drove with the top down most of the way. I'd forgotten how hot it is in the South," Daniel replied.

Toots wanted to remind him that summer was just around the corner, but she didn't. If he stuck around long enough, he would soon find out. "Phil, would you come in and fix Daniel an ice tea while I call Bernice?" Toots asked, turning to go inside, expecting the men to follow. She wasn't sure if Bernice and Robert were bouncing away on his new mattress. No way was she going to say this to Daniel, so a phone call was best under the circumstances.

"I'll just grab my bags," Daniel said. He took the smallest piece of luggage, and Phil carried the larger one inside. The two men set them next to the staircase.

"I'll get that tea," Phil called to Toots as she raced upstairs.

"Wonderful! I'll be right back," she replied when she reached the top of the stairs. Once inside her room, she used the house phone to call over to Robert's. She hoped Bernice wasn't taking her advice just now, because it wouldn't be the greatest time to get frisky with her pal.

Three rings. Four. Five.

They're probably going at it hot and heavy, she thought. Eight rings. She was about to hang up, when a breathless Robert answered the phone.

"Good, you're there." Toots voiced her thoughts before filtering them.

"Toots? That you? Why are you calling? Is everything swell over there? You need to speak up. I can't hear you." Robert chattered on like a Chatty Cathy doll.

Poor Robert, he needed a hearing aid and was too vain to admit it. Toots cupped her hand over the phone, speaking louder than normal. "I need to talk to Bernice. It's important."

"Come on over. We've just finished making the bed with those new sheets. They are so soft. Bernice wants a pink set. I'm going to give them to her for Christmas this year. Do you think that's a good idea?"

Toots hung up the phone. At this rate, she could slip out the side entrance and tell Bernice in person. Quickly, before Robert realized she'd hung up on him, she raced downstairs and out the side door that led to the potting shed, which Pete, her gardener, used to work in before he retired.

With her heels sinking into the grass and slowing her down, Toots removed them; then she ran the rest of the way. She banged on the front door. "Bernice! It's an emergency! Open this damn door, or I'm going to kick it in!" she shouted as she continued to pound on the door. Hell, they were both losing their hearing. "Bernice! Get your ass out here now!"

The door swung open. Flushed, Bernice looked like she'd been caught with her hand in the cookie jar. Toots was sure the cookie jar was Robert's new mattress, with the new sheets. "Thank God!" Toots said.

"What in the hell are you in such a tizzy for? Robert said you hung up on him. That's rude, Toots. Even for you. I thought you had manners, but, apparently, I was wrong. Now, what's so important that you have to come over here and interrupt us?"

Toots raised a brow. "So you *are* screwing Robert! I knew it!"

Bernice took a deep breath; then she rolled her eyes. "You nasty old woman. I am not screwing Robert. Now. We're trying a new recipe. He just bought that new conduction stove, and we're trying it out."

Toots didn't care if they were doing "it" on top of the new conduction oven. "Bernice, I want you to listen to what I'm about to tell you, and I do not want you to interrupt me. Do you understand? This is important."

Bernice crossed her arms. "Go on."

"Do you feel okay? You haven't had any chest pain lately or anything I should know about?"

"No, Toots, I haven't. If I had, I'm sure Dr. Becker would've told you already." Before having her surgery last year, Bernice had given Toots power of attorney, and Toots was privy to her medical history. It still pissed Bernice off to no end.

"He hasn't. Now listen up. I don't have a lot of time. Phil and I have dinner reservations at eight o'clock."

Tapping her foot, Bernice said, "I'm waiting."

Shit, Toots hated this, but once Bernice was over the initial shock, Toots knew she would be the happiest woman in the world. She just didn't want the news to send her friend's fragile heart into another attack. Taking a calming breath, Toots burst out, "Daniel is at the house." There, she'd said it!

Bernice continued to tap her foot. She pursed her lips, making her resemble one of those wrinkled-up potato-faced caricatures she'd seen at the Cracker Barrel.

"Did you hear what I just said?" Toots demanded loudly, no longer caring who overheard.

"Yes, I did."

"Well?" Toots leaned as close to Bernice as she could without touching her.

"You're a mean woman, Toots."

"Son of a bitch, Bernice! Your fucking son is sitting at my kitchen table, sipping a glass of sweet tea, as we speak, and you're calling me *mean*?"

Right before her very eyes, Bernice turned fifty shades of red, then settled on white. "What did you just say?" she muttered, her words barely audible.

"You heard what I said," Toots repeated.

"You're really serious, aren't you?"

"If I weren't serious, do you think for one minute I would trudge across the lawn wearing these?" She held her green heels up in the air.

Bernice dropped her hands to her side; then she brought them up to cover her mouth. "Oh, my God. For once, you're not pulling my leg! Woo-hoo!" Bernice shouted, and pounced off the porch like a gymnast bolting off a balance beam.

Toots cackled and took off across the lawn after her.

Chapter 17

Goebel and Sophie parked her newly purchased SUV next to a gray Volvo. "This place feels creepy," Sophie said.

Goebel hit the key fob unlocking the hatchback. They'd purchased new equipment as soon as they had received the final certificate of occupancy for their new office space for Psychic Investigations. They discussed their plans in private before revealing them to Toots and the gang. Once they were out in the open, it had only been a matter of weeks before they'd located an office and set up shop. Though business wasn't booming, Sophie didn't care. For the past five years, since Walter's death, she'd been having the time of her life. Thanks to the $5 million in life insurance she had received upon his death—the payoff on a policy that she'd worked her ass off to pay for—she didn't have to worry about finances. She'd invested some of her newly acquired funds; and despite the initial decline in the stock market, she had almost doubled the value of what she had been paid by the life insurance company.

Goebel, being the man of honor that he was, the man she was going to spend the rest of her life with—come hell or high water, marriage or not—had insisted on footing all the expenses when they decided to go into business together. Sophie purchased the SUV with her money because she didn't want to continue borrowing Toots's vehicles. She'd had magnetic signs made up last week with her and Goebel's pictures, and their business name spelled out in a freaky bloodred scrawl: PSYCHIC INVESTIGATIONS.

Goebel removed three large cables of electrical cords from the backseat. He really didn't think Sophie needed any of the equipment, but it looked good for the clients. A square black case that held most of Sophie's electronic gadgets was a must, she'd said. There were meters that measured electromagnetic fields, infrared video cameras, and the ghost box, which she still used, saying that it picked up voices from beyond. Another bag contained holy water, several branches of dried sage, and three cigarette lighters.

Between the two of them, they were able to carry all the equipment to the clients' front door.

"You ready for this?" Goebel asked before ringing the doorbell.

"Always," Sophie replied; then she stretched on her tiptoes and kissed him on the cheek.

"Hey, none of that, or we won't make it past the front door," Goebel said; then he kissed the top of her head. "Now let's get this show on the road."

After the young couple called, Goebel did a bit of investigating on the history of the old place. The mansion located on Legare Street had originally been built in the early eighteenth century. Once a boarding school for daughters of wealthy South Carolina cotton and rice planters, admittance to the elite school meant that one had attained the highest social standing. The school was run by a Frenchwoman, Madame Veronique Louise Barteau. She was known for her firm discipline and strict guidance. Most of all, the girls left Madame Barteau's School for Young Ladies prepared for their social roles as members of high society. All married within months of leaving the school.

One of the girls, however, Elise Montague, had failed to follow the rules laid down by Madame Barteau. She would often slip away at night to meet her lover, a man of low social standing, who, it was said, worked for a wealthy rice planter. While still in school, the girl became pregnant and gave birth to a son, who died a few days after his birth. It was rumored that her secret lover wanted nothing to do with her after she became pregnant and she suffocated her son, hoping that she would be reunited with her lover. It didn't happen, and the girl threw herself from the veranda, broke her neck, and was found by her lover the next morning. He was hanged, since it was believed that he was responsible for her death.

After this tragedy, the wealthy plantation owners refused to send their daughters to Madame Barteau's School for Young Ladies. The school was forced to close; and many years later, a newspaper tycoon purchased the home and restored it to its previous splendor, only to be driven away by the continuous cries of a baby who didn't exist. All those who'd lived in the mansion since then have told of hearing an infant crying at night. Some even reported seeing a young girl flying off the veranda on the fourth floor.

Wesley and Julianna Tarwick, who'd recently purchased the home, were experiencing things that were unexplainable to them. They'd called Sophie and Goebel, asking them to come to the house. They said they needed their help immediately.

Goebel rang the doorbell.

A tall, slender woman, with beady brown eyes and a sour expression on her face, answered the door. "Yes?" she asked, but she didn't invite them inside.

Sophie spoke up. "Are you Mrs. Tarwick?"

"No. Are you the ghost people?" the woman asked, her distaste for the subject apparent.

Goebel took over. "Mrs. Tarwick is expecting us. Can you tell her we're here?" Goebel used his most commanding voice. The woman stood aside and motioned for them to enter.

"I'll bet she wins 'Employee of the Month,' " Sophie mumbled.

"Shhh, not now."

"Wait here," the disagreeable woman ordered, then disappeared.

Sophie raised her brow. "What a hag. Reminds me of a character out of those old gothic Victoria Holt novels I used to read. She probably needs to get laid." She grinned. "It's a definite mood fixer."

"I can't disagree with that. Save those thoughts for later," Goebel said.

She teasingly elbowed his side. "I promise."

The older woman returned, followed by a much younger and prettier version of herself. Tall, rail thin, small brown eyes, which held a trace of sadness. She smiled, and her face lit up like candles on a birthday cake. *If only her mother would smile like that,* Sophie thought, *it might take that sour expression off her face.*

The young woman held out her hand. "Thank you for coming. I really appreciate this." She looked over her shoulder. "Mother, you can go now. I want to talk to these people. Alone."

"You're a stupid girl, Julianna," the mother said, sharing her opinion before leaving the main hall in which they were standing.

"I'm sorry. Mother is very skeptical. She thinks Wesley and I are crazy, that we're imagining all these . . . sounds we've been hearing."

"Most people are skeptical, which really translates to fear of the unknown. It's quite common," Sophie said as a way of easing Julianna's embarrassment.

She nodded. "Thank you for that. Mother can be difficult at times. Now if you want to get started, I have the room ready." Julianna eyed their equipment.

Looking at his watch, Goebel asked, "Just one room?"

"Yes."

"Then let's get started. I want to get the cameras in place before dark." He and Sophie grabbed their equipment, leaving two of the rolls of cable behind, since they would only need enough for one room.

Julianna led them up a staircase, which was unlike any Sophie had ever seen. They followed Julianna up three stories; the staircase widened the farther up they climbed. It was solid oak, with carvings from the early eighteenth century. Sophie thought of Toots, who would croak if she saw the interior of this place.

"Down here," Julianna said when they reached the end of a narrow hallway, and she opened the door. "This is where"—she paused, as if afraid to speak of the sounds she heard in the actual room—"we hear what sounds like a baby crying. It starts out as a whimper, then gets louder, and suddenly stops."

Sophie stepped inside the room. Immediately sensing a presence in the room, she set the equipment case down on the floor, raising her hand to indicate no one should speak. The room was small, maybe ten feet by twelve feet. A rocker and cradle were the only pieces of furniture in the room. A long, narrow window directly across from the bedroom door drew her in. As though she were led by unknown forces, Sophie crossed the room, stopping when she reached the window. She placed her hand on the glass and instantly jerked it away.

"What?" Julianna asked, her voice high-pitched from fright.

"Goebel, set up the infrared camera. Mrs. Tarwick, would

you mind leaving us?" Sophie asked from her position by the window.

"Is everything all right?" the young woman asked.

"Please, I need you to leave the room," Sophie said, her voice firm.

"Of course," the young woman said. "I'll be downstairs."

Sophie nodded. As soon as the door closed, a gust of cold air rushed through the room. Goebel stopped what he was doing. "Soph?"

"It's fine. Let me have a moment alone."

Since this was their very first psychic investigation working together as a team, neither knew what to expect. Goebel stepped out of the room, but not before turning on the infrared camera. It was almost completely dark outside. If it were to pick up any images, now would be the time.

Once Sophie was alone in the room, which she knew was the nursery where a little boy had briefly lived, she sat in the wooden rocker, its walnut wood dark and cracked with age. Next to the rocker was a small handcrafted hooded cradle made out of the same wood as the rocking chair. Sophie got up out of the chair and sat on the floor next to the cradle. She placed her hand on the smooth surface, amazed at the craftsmanship. All the joints were dovetailed, and the builder used square nails, quite common in the late eighteenth century. The two slats on top of the cradle were cracked, but otherwise, it was in excellent condition. Sophie gave the cradle a slight push. It rocked smoothly and without any creaks. As she was about to place her hand on the cradle to stop the rocking, she heard a very low whine, almost like a kitten's mewing.

Placing her hand in her lap, she closed her eyes and listened. The soft whimpering turned into what sounded like real-life cries. Sophie whispered, "Tell me, little guy, tell me what it is you want?" She knew from her research that the child was male.

Again, she placed her hand on top of the cradle, letting herself go as she did when she was in a trance. She could see the dark images of three girls. Sophie blinked several times. When the bedroom came into focus, she realized she was having another clairsentience vision. It was the same room, yet what she saw was the room as it had been in another time period. Closing her eyes, then opening them again to make sure this wasn't her imagination, she saw the three girls as they must have been in the late eighteenth century. A small cot placed by the window held a young girl writhing in pain. Two older girls were dressed in long, pale dresses, with the bodices forming a V that led to what must be an apron of sorts. Both wore white cotton bonnets with silk ribbons around them.

The girl on the cot screamed; then she wrinkled her face in a contortion that Sophie knew was agonizing pain during childbirth. She felt her own stomach clench, knotting in a pain so sharp, she lost her breath.

"Oh, my God!" she whispered, clutching her stomach.

Fighting her way through the pain in order to see her surroundings, she suddenly felt an overpowering urge to push. Though Sophie had never given birth herself, she knew she was experiencing full-fledged labor pains within her vision. Somehow, she was experiencing what the young girl on the cot was going through.

Sweat dotted her forehead, and she began to grind her hips against the hardwood floor. She grabbed her blouse and pulled on the material until it tore. Then the pain stopped as fast as it started. A warm feeling flooded over her—a happiness so momentous that she knew this was to be the highlight of her life. Limp with relief, she listened as the sounds from the newborn filled the room. The two women carried a bundle out of the room, and an older woman stepped inside.

The girl on the cot, Elise, began to cry when the woman spoke to her. Shaking her head from side to side, she wept uncontrollably. The two women came back into the room, still carrying the bundle, and placed it next to the girl. Love like nothing she'd ever experienced filled her being. She opened her eyes to gaze at her son. She would call him Liam, after his father.

Exhausted, Sophie's head dropped to her chest.

Chapter 18

Bernice stood in the kitchen doorway, her heart racing ninety miles a minute. For a split second, she thought it would explode in her chest. She took a deep breath, not believing what she saw.

In the flesh. At the kitchen table talking to Phil. Daniel Alan, the son she hadn't seen in twenty years. She watched him another minute before practically galloping across the oak floor.

"Mom," Daniel said; then he walked across the kitchen to meet her. He wrapped his arms around her and squeezed her tightly. He lifted her off the floor in a giant bear hug. "Damn, but you're a tiny thing." His cobalt blue eyes glistened with tears, and he didn't try to hide them. "I can't believe it's you."

Bernice wiggled out of his arms. "Daniel Alan, if I wasn't your mother, I would say you're about the best-looking man I've seen. Ever." Tears pooled in her eyes, and she didn't care. For the first time in twenty years, she was staring at her son. In the flesh.

"I don't know what to say," Daniel told her.

"You don't have to say a word. You're here now, and that's all that matters. I just can't believe how much weight you've lost. I want to ask how, but I don't really care. You are really here." Bernice started sobbing like a baby, not caring. This was another great moment in her life. Her son, here, alive, and looking damn good. Anything else was in the past. He was truly here, in the flesh.

Toots crashed through the back door, her heels dangling from her hand. Phil was sitting at the table, drinking a glass of tea.

"So, are you two going to just sit there making goo-goo eyes at each other? I think this calls for a celebration, don't you?" Toots directed her gaze to Phil. "Call the restaurant and add Bernice and Daniel to our reservations. I'm starving."

"No, Tootsie, really. I'm fine. I just want to sit here and catch up with Mom. It's been too long, and I have too many stories to tell her. You two, go on," Daniel said. "Unless Mom wants to go." He let the statement hang in the air.

Bernice finally came to her senses for a few seconds. "No, no, I want to stay here. I can fix Daniel's dinner. It's been so long! It will be a thrill to cook for my son again." Bernice smiled at him. "That is, if you're willing to eat my cooking. I don't do too much country-style cooking anymore, not since my heart attack, but I can tell by looking at you that's not going to be a problem."

She still couldn't believe her eyes. Daniel was not the same man he was when he took to the road all those years ago in hopes of finding himself.

He'd left for the hundredth time right before she and Toots moved to Charleston. In his early thirties, he'd been at least 150 pounds overweight, had an attitude the size of the moon, and, to top it all off, he'd suffered from an acute case of adult acne. He'd finished college, receiving a degree in elementary education. He taught fourth grade for a while, but his heart hadn't been in it. As soon as something went wrong in his life, he would pack up and travel to parts unknown in search of happiness, staying away for months at a time. Each time he returned, Bernice prayed he would have a new outlook on life, but it hadn't been so. If anything, he was more angry. They would fight, and he would leave again. This became their normal.

When Toots asked her to move to Charleston, twenty years ago, Bernice knew it was time for Daniel to do what he needed to do. She'd spent her entire adult life caring for him, and he'd been a good son until he became a nominal adult. Having grown up without a father had left a bit of a chip on his shoulder. Bernice felt as though he blamed her for his lack of a dad. She knew it wasn't her fault that he'd deserted them when Daniel was five years old and was killed in a gangland slaying two years later. However, Daniel seemed to blame her for some incomprehensible reason.

But now, here he was. Alive, handsome, and fit as a fiddle.

"I can see you're surprised," Daniel said. "I'm not that self-centered jerk I used to be. I decided I needed a change, and the only one who could make it happen was me. I went to work as a second-grade teacher and started working out at night. I learned to cook, and the rest just kind of happened. I did have those acne scars lasered off, though." He laughed.

Bernice giggled. "I didn't want to ask. It doesn't matter, Daniel Alan. Now, why don't you get cleaned up, while I fix you something to eat."

"Tootsie?" he asked. "You okay with my being here for a while?"

Toots had kept quiet, letting Bernice have her moment with Daniel; but now that he'd asked, she wanted to set some ground rules. "Daniel Alan, you are welcome to stay here as long as you want. My only condition is, respect your mother." Toots spoke kindly, but her words were firm.

"I'm fifty-three years old, Tootsie. Those days of my smart-ass mouth and running away when things didn't go my way are gone."

"Then it's settled. You can stay here until the cows come home. Now, Phil and I are going to celebrate his retirement—that is, if we haven't missed our dinner reservation."

"When you ran off after Bernice, I called the restaurant and bumped them up an hour. We're fine," Phil told her. "You still want to go?"

"Damn straight I do. I am hungry as hell. I want a steak, rare, with all the extra fattening stuff that people like you tell people like me to stop eating."

"Then let's get out of here," Phil said, and glanced at her feet. "After you wash your feet."

Toots looked at her grass-stained, dirt-covered feet and burst out laughing. "I'll be right back."

She hustled upstairs, cleaned her feet in the bathroom sink, found another pair of heels, and was back downstairs in less than five minutes.

"Let's blow this joint," she said, feeling as light as a feather. Happy, giddy. Shit, she was downright ecstatic.

Today had been a good day. She decided right then and there that tonight was Phil's night to celebrate his milestone. She was not going to ruin it by dumping him.

Chapter 19

"**O**f course, we can take them," Abby said into the phone. Chris was standing next to her, listening to her side of the conversation. "You can bring them whenever you're able. Doesn't matter what time of the day or night. I can't wait. Yes, we have one of the top vets in the country on our team. You bet." She hung up the phone and did a little happy dance.

"I take it that was good news?" Chris teased, knowing it was.

"Five dogs and three cats. They're left over from the fires in Colorado. They're flying them in first thing tomorrow. Two of the dogs are dachshunds with back troubles. I'm going to ask Phil if he can send for Dr. Carnes tomorrow. I know she isn't supposed to be here until our official grand opening, but the word is out now, and we're ready for the animals, so . . ."

"So, nothing," Chris said. He picked Abby up, swinging her around like a child. She was so petite; it was like lifting a small doll.

"Chris, put me down." She was laughing as he swung her around; then in the next minute, she started yelling. "Chris! Stop it! Seriously, I'm going to be sick."

He stopped spinning her around and set her down on the sofa in the formal living room.

"Move," she said. Shoving him aside, she raced to the bathroom off the kitchen, barely making it. On her knees, she threw up everything she'd had for dinner. Her eyes filled with tears because she was so sick of being sick. She knew something was very, very wrong with her. Right when life was perfect, she had to go and get sick. She heaved for another ten minutes.

Chris hovered by the door. "Abby, are you okay?" he asked, concern in his voice.

Weak and barely able to stand, she splashed cold water on her face and rinsed her mouth. She looked at her reflection in the mirror. "Total shit, Abby. You're screwed." Tears fell, and she wiped at them with her knuckles.

"Abby?"

She sniffed, grabbed a tissue, and blew her nose. "I'm good. Be out in a minute."

Tomorrow she'd make that dreaded appointment with Dr. Pauley, which she'd been putting off. If she was terminally ill, she wanted to spend whatever time she had left with her family and her husband. She was tough, like her mother. She'd get through this crisis, one way or another. She needed to talk to someone, but she didn't want to upset Chris. She'd call her mother first thing tomorrow morning. After she called Dr. Pauley. After the animals arrived and after she called Phil, asking him to call Dr. Carnes.

Chris tapped on the door. "Abby Clay, I am not going to ask you again. Are you all right?"

Taking a deep breath, she tossed the tissue in the wastebasket; then she opened the door. She knew she looked like hell, but there wasn't much she could do about it now. "I must have a bug again, or else that nasty dinner I made poisoned me."

Chris wrapped her in his arms, careful not to shake or jostle her around. "It must be a bug. I ate the same thing, and I'm fine. Make sure you call the doctor and schedule an appointment tomorrow. Come on, I want you to lie down."

Abby didn't put up a fight when Chris lifted her in his arms and carried her upstairs to the master bedroom. The room was the size of his old condo in California. He still found it weird living in such a huge house, even though he'd spent part of his childhood on the plantation. It'd been different then. He was young, running wild, and only there when he needed to sleep, shower, or eat.

Carefully he helped Abby remove her jeans. "Just because I'm letting you strip me, don't get any ideas, Mr. Clay." She'd no more said the words than Chester trotted in the room.

"Come here, boy." Abby patted the spot beside her. Like the obedient dog he was, he hopped up on the bed. He nudged her hand with his nose. "You're my main man, you know that?" She scratched him between his ears; then he curled up next to her.

Chris brought a cold washcloth from the bathroom. "Here, wipe your face while I go downstairs and make you a pot of chamomile tea. And I thought I was your main man," he added.

"Always," she whispered, unsure how long her "always" would be.

She closed her eyes, thinking of the zillion things she would have to do if she really was terminally ill: the animals, the house, her mother, the three g's, Chester. *Shit, shit, shit!*

She was not ready to die. She'd rarely been sick as a kid. Her mother was hearty, and Abby always thought she was, too. And she always had been. Except for the occasional menstrual cramps, and a few colds, she'd been as healthy as a horse.

She closed her eyes, visions of her mother's *events,* funerals. She imagined that her mother would be so grief-stricken. . . .

Wait! "Chris," she yelled, "bring my purse when you come back up!"

Abby instantly became alert, her thoughts taking her in a completely different direction. She wasn't sure, but still, it was always possible.

Chris came in the room, balancing a tray with a pot of tea, her purse slung over his shoulder.

"Smells good. The purse is so you, too," she joked.

"Smart-ass. Here, scoot over. I made you some raisin toast. I don't want you to dehydrate."

Suddenly Abby was ravenous. She munched on the toast and sipped the tea. Feeling almost like herself again, she reached for her purse.

"What are you looking for?" Chris asked.

"My date book."

"You of all people, I can't believe you still use one of those old-fashioned things. Why don't you keep your stuff stored on your cell phone?"

Abby found her date book at the bottom of her purse. She removed a melted piece of chocolate from the plastic and half a dog biscuit between March and April. "I need to clean this thing out. Now, let me look at this." She flipped through the months. Not seeing what she wanted, she flipped through them a second time, searching for that little red check mark. She looked at Chris, then back at the calendar.

"What?" Chris said, seeing the alarm on his wife's face. "Did we forget an appointment?"

Abby flipped through the past three months, desperately searching for that reassuring little red check mark. It was not there.

"No," she said, thinking, trying to remember the last time she'd had her period. When she couldn't remember, she plopped back on the pillows, so relieved, yet scared and excited, too.

"So, what's all this flipping pages back and forth for?"

"Chris, is there a CVS or a Walgreens close by? One that's open late?"

"Sure, there's a CVS a couple miles from here. Why? You need something?"

Yes, she did. But was she going to send Chris out at nine o'clock at night to get what she wanted?

No. She wasn't.

"Give me my jeans. We're going to the drugstore. Now." Abby took the jeans, which Chris picked off the floor, and put them on. Then she slid her feet into her hot pink flip-flops. "Come on, let's go."

"Abby, why don't you just tell me what you need. You're not feeling good. I can pick up whatever it is you need. Even if it's girlie stuff," he said, grinning.

If only, she thought, but laughed. *It is girlie stuff, all right.*

"For once, just don't argue with me. Just do what I ask without questioning it."

Chris held his hands out in front of him. "I thought that's what I always do."

Abby laughed. "Come on before the place closes. This is something we need to do together. Kind of a surprise." Again, she thought, *If only.* She could be wrong, but everything was making sense now. She'd been barfing, off and on, for weeks. More tired than usual; and now that she suspected what her problem was, she thought about the new and strange smells she'd sworn were there, when Chris swore she was losing it.

"I'm only doing this because I love you," Chris informed her.

"And when we get home, you'll love me even more," she teased. Chester rolled his head around. "You stay here, boy. This is man/woman time." She fluffed his fur; then she grabbed her purse from the bed.

Twenty minutes and a dozen questions later, Chris pulled into the parking lot at CVS. "Okay, we're here. Now you want to tell me what this is about?" he said, then cut the engine.

"Come inside, and you'll find out." She got out of the car before he questioned her again. She'd put off answering his questions the entire ride over. She wanted this moment to be special—something they would talk about in years to come, something they would tell their children and their grandchildren.

Chris followed her inside the brightly lit store. They had everything: Food, magazines, the latest "As Seen on TV" stuff. Soda, beer, dill-pickle-flavored potato chips.

"Abby, do you have the munchies?"

"God, Chris. You're acting like I've just smoked a joint or something. And, no, I don't have 'the munchies.' Follow me."

She was loving this bantering, the mystery of not knowing. Once she knew, once her suspicions were confirmed, their lives would change forever. She walked faster. When she located the aisle where they kept the pregnancy tests, she stopped and waited for Chris to catch up with her.

She eyed the pregnancy test kits on the shelf, then looked at Chris.

"You . . . are . . . is . . . are we? Abby!" Chris pointed to the many varied home pregnancy tests.

"That's what we're here to find out," she said, a euphoric smile curving her mouth.

He smiled back, and Abby thought it was as intimate as any kiss they'd shared.

"When?"

"Pick one," she said, indicating the variety of boxes on the shelf.

Chris grabbed an EPT kit. "Early should work, huh?" he asked, in somewhat of a daze, but in a good way.

"They're all good. Now pay for that and bring it to the ladies' room," Abby instructed.

"Here?" Chris asked. "Shouldn't we do this in the privacy of our home?"

"No! Why do you think I asked you to come along? Now get," Abby said. "And hurry!"

Chris took the pregnancy test kit to the front register. Abby searched the back of the store for the restrooms. Finding them, she waited for Chris to return with the paid-for test kit.

Three minutes later, Chris found her standing by the ladies' room.

"Come on," Abby said. "No, wait." She really didn't want to pee on a stick in front of Chris. Some things had to remain private. "Stay here," she said, taking the test from him.

Amused, he nodded. "Go on."

Once she was inside the ladies' room, she ripped the package apart, placing the supplies on the edge of the sink. Quickly, she skimmed through the directions, thinking a kid could do this.

Yeah, Abby. You are spot-on. A kid.

Hands shaking, she removed the plastic test stick, followed the directions, then placed the stick on the sink and washed her hands before opening the door.

Chris was pacing back and forth, just like one would expect an expectant father to do in the hospital.

Poking her head out, Abby said, "Come inside. It takes a whole minute for the results."

Chris entered the ladies' room hesitantly. "Looks just like a men's room, minus the urinal."

"That's it." Abby pointed to the white stick on the edge of the sink.

"Okay."

Chris stuffed his hands in his pockets. He looked everywhere, except at the stick next to the sink.

Suddenly, out of nowhere, Abby had a horrifying thought.

What if Chris isn't ready to become a father? And me a mother?

"You're too quiet. It's scaring me," Abby remarked, reaching for the test stick.

He gave her one of those special grins, one she knew he only shared with her. "Come on, let's not keep ourselves in suspense any longer. It's been way over a minute."

She nodded. "You're good either way, right?"

"You shouldn't have to ask. I believe we discussed this before we were married. You know how I feel. Now stop stalling. The store clerks are gonna think we're stealing, or something. Let's see those results."

"Okay." Abby crossed her fingers on her left hand; and with her right hand, she held the test stick close to the light above the sink. Her hands were shaking so hard, she almost dropped the stick and had to lean against the counter to steady herself.

Looking in the result window, Abby saw the words she'd hoped for.

"It's positive! We're going to have a baby!"

Chris grabbed her and tried to swing her around in the bathroom, but there wasn't enough space. He practically dragged her through CVS, shouting, "We're gonna have a baby! We're gonna have a baby!"

Their future was bright with promise.

Chapter 20

Toots and Phil arrived at McCrady's in downtown Charleston at two minutes after nine. "I hope you like the food here. It's supposed to be farm fresh. The chef has won numerous awards. One of my old partners recommended the place. Said the food was to die for."

Toots scanned the restaurant-brick walls and high ceilings, with one wall made entirely of glass. She was glad she'd accepted Phil's dinner invitation. "It's perfect." She'd never been here and liked the fact that he hadn't, either. New places, and all. Maybe it was a sign of things to come.

The hostess led them to a table for two in a private corner of the restaurant. Light green tablecloths, candles, and real silver. She was impressed, but she didn't want to say so to Phil. She didn't want to seem unsophisticated, like someone much younger would've been. Why she was having these thoughts was beyond her. A young man wearing khaki slacks, a starched white shirt, and a tie, with a long black apron to his knees, brought them ice water with slices of lemon in Baccarat water glasses. She knew this because she had Baccarat champagne flutes at home.

"I'm starving," she said, looking at the menu.

"I'm glad you're here with me, Toots. I want tonight to be special. It's only retirement, I know, but I feel like a boat without its oar. I was depressed for a few hours after I officially saw my last patient yesterday, but I kept telling myself this wasn't an ending but a new beginning. Now I'm probably the happiest man in Charleston."

Toots reached across the table for his hand. She squeezed, and he squeezed back. There was no way she could tell him about her past. At least . . . not tonight. "I felt that way for a while a few years ago." She didn't want to tell him how unsettled and useless she'd felt after Leland's funeral, because she didn't want to bring up her exes, dead or not.

"You don't strike me as the kind of woman who gets depressed," Phil said, smiling. "You're too damned ornery."

"You're right, but I had a spell a few years ago. I didn't know what direction my life was heading. That's when the three g's came to visit. I have to say, my life hasn't been the least bit boring since we all moved to California, then back here. I never thought in a million years we would all be starting new careers in our late sixties." She was rambling.

"I'm looking forward to moving to Myrtle Beach. I plan to spend my days relaxing, and in the evening, I'll write that novel that I've wanted to for as long as I can remember. I wish you would go—"

Toots's cell phone *pinged,* letting her know she had a text message. "Hang on a sec." She took her iPhone out of her purse and read the message. "Excellent," she said, more to herself than to him.

"What's so excellent?" Phil inquired.

Toots figured it was okay to tell him because he'd know soon enough. "You know that purple monstrosity a couple miles from the house?"

"It's hard to miss," Phil said.

"I bought it several years ago, with the intention of restoring it, but then we moved to Los Angeles. You didn't hear this from me, but you'll know soon enough, so just act surprised. Goebel and Sophie just purchased the place."

"And let me guess. They have no clue you're the former owner?"

Toots chuckled. "You're absolutely right. I told the Realtor to take whatever they offered. Goebel's had his eye on the place since he sold his apartment in the city. He has a condo in Los Angeles, but something tells me that's going to be on the market soon." Toots had the urge to smoke, but didn't. It could wait. She always liked a good puff when she heard good news.

The wine steward brought the wine list to the table, giving it to Phil. He quickly scanned the list. "Do you mind?"

She wanted to tell him she drank the cheap stuff, but she refrained. "By all means, please go ahead."

"We'll have a bottle of Syrah, Raven No. 10."

"Excellent choice, sir."

Toots recognized the name, as it was a California wine, but that was it. Boone's Farm was good with her and Sophie. She did like a good glass of scotch now and then.

Toots read the menu, and again she was impressed with the variety of entrees, except for the charred octopus. The wine steward returned with their wine. He went through the performance required for opening a bottle of good wine. Phil sniffed, sipped, accepted, then sent the steward away.

"Toots, I was serious when I asked you to come to Myrtle Beach."

Her heart raced, and she was sure she was blushing. It was the last thing she was expecting from him. Maybe later, but now? Taking a deep breath, she prayed for the right words. "I don't know what to say, Phil. I've never lived with—"

Her cell phone rang. Talk about being saved by the bell. "Sorry," she said, then answered the phone. "Abby, is that you?" All she could hear was bubbling laughter between words that were getting bleeped out by some electrical interference. "Abby, you're coming in and out. Call me later at the house. I'm having dinner with Phil now." She had clicked off and had put the phone inside her purse, when it started ringing again. "Yes?" she said, a bit aggravated at the intrusion, but she didn't want to turn her phone off in case Bernice needed her.

"Mom, can you hear me?" Abby shouted into the phone.

"Yes, dear, loud and clear. We had some kind of interference a minute ago. Is everything okay?" It wasn't like Abby to call her when she was out, unless it was an emergency.

"I have five dogs and three cats arriving tomorrow, two of the dogs are doxies with back injuries. They're coming from Colorado. They were lost during the fires. Do you think Phil could call Dr. Carnes and ask if she can come early? We'll send a Flexjet to Naples. I know she's coming for the grand opening, but these dogs need her now. I wouldn't trust them with just any doctor, especially after Frankie's miraculous recovery. But that's not really why I called. Can you stop over before you head home? Both of you. I wouldn't ask, but it's really important."

"Hold on." Toots placed the phone down. "Abby wants to know if you'll call Dr. Carnes. She's got two injured dachshunds coming in tomorrow."

Phil nodded. "Sure, let me do that now, while you're talking to Abby."

Toots picked up the phone. "Yes, he's calling her right as we speak. It might be late when we're finished. I don't suppose you've heard the news. Bernice has a visitor, so we got a late start." More static. "Abby?"

"Just stop over. I don't care how late," Abby said.

The call dropped. "Phil, something is up with Abby. She's asked me, us, to stop over on our way home. Something is wrong, I just know it. She would never call me, knowing I'm out for the evening, unless it was an emergency."

"Then let's go. We can eat later," Phil said. He motioned for the wine steward. "We have an emergency. We have to leave." He placed a wad of cash in the wine steward's hand, grabbed the bottle of wine, and pulled her chair out for her—all in record time. The guy was a gentleman of the first order.

Damn, Toots loved this man! If Ida knew her thoughts, she'd never let her live them down. Toots was prepared to eat a bit of crow if necessary. Maybe she needed to rethink her decision to stop seeing Phil. He was so easygoing with Abby. And Abby really liked him. Chris too. Yes, she was going to rethink her decision, the one that she really hadn't made yet. *That doesn't make one damn lick of sense,* she thought, but she sometimes didn't make sense.

Again, Phil was coming to her and Abby's rescue. Surely he would be understanding when she told him she'd had eight husbands. Yes, but then there was that dying issue. Maybe she should just forget a serious relationship and enjoy what they had while it lasted.

Yes, that's what she had to do. Phil was starting a new career. She couldn't jeopardize his life because she was a jinx.

Chapter 21

Goebel sensed that something wasn't right. He opened the door to the nursery. Sophie was lying on the floor, curled up in the fetal position; her blouse was torn on both sides. "Sophie?" he whispered as he lowered himself to the floor.

She rolled over on her back. "Help me sit up."

"What's wrong? You look like you've been through the fires of hell." Goebel didn't know what had happened in the room, but he didn't like what he was seeing. Sophie looked frightened, and that wasn't normal at all.

"This place needs cleansing, and there are souls here that need to move on," she said. "I've had another clairsentience experience, Goeb. This is unlike anything I've ever heard of. I don't even know if you'll believe me when I tell you what just happened in this room."

"Of course, I'll believe you. What happened? You're not yourself," Goebel told her.

"I need to send the spirits away first. We need to do this now. Right now, Goebel, as in me and you together. We have to do it in this room."

Alarmed, Goebel grabbed the case filled with the materials Sophie used.

"We don't need all that. Just sit across from me. Close your eyes."

He did as she instructed, knowing now wasn't the time to question her further. He trusted her, having seen her in action too many times to have doubts now.

Sophie reached for his hands and gently held them in hers. "I know you're afraid, and you are searching for your mother." A gust of cold air came between them. "You are here, little one. Your mother loves you so much. She is so sad that you didn't live. She wants you to see the light. She is there waiting for you."

The chill left the room. Eyes closed, Sophie gave up a little smile. "Yes, she is waiting for you. Your mother fell, and she's been waiting for you for a very, very long time. She needs you to be with her, to come to the light. She will care for you, Liam."

Sophie and Goebel sat in silence for several minutes. She felt a lightness enter the room, as though a heavy cloak of sadness had been lifted. She opened her eyes. "I need the sage."

Goebel removed several bunches of dried sage, a lighter, and a small metal tray. He gave them to Sophie.

"Pray."

She lit the sage, its pungent smoke swirling throughout the room. Sophie went to stand beside the small cradle. "You are with your mother now, and she is happy. We all pray for you and your mother. Please bless this room, this home, and those who inhabit this space. Leave and love, and allow this family to reside without fear." She waved the bundle of sage around the room, up and down, in the corners, across the floors, over the window. Every space was cleansed with the purifying smoke. When the bundle smoldered, Sophie placed it on a metal dish, where it could burn out completely.

She walked through the room again and closed her eyes when she stood next to the window. "I have experienced your pain. May you rest peacefully and forever."

Goebel stood by the door, waiting for Sophie's instructions. *Damn, but she's gifted,* he thought as he watched her. She was truly the real deal. Not many possessed her gift, and the handful who had any psychic abilities at all used them erroneously, took money. Not his Sophie.

Turning away from the window, she said, "We're finished here."

Goebel packed up the case and the infrared camera, hefting them in his left hand. With his free hand at the small of her back, he guided her out of the nursery and down the narrow hallway to the stairs.

"We have to talk about what happened tonight, but later. What I have to tell you will go down in the books. For now, let's get this family settled and leave. I want a smoke so bad, I can taste it."

Goebel chuckled. Now that was his Sophie. Spunky as hell.

Julianna Tarwick waited anxiously at the foot of the staircase.

"Do you need me to stay?" Goebel asked. "I can load the SUV while you speak to Mrs. Tarwick."

"Go ahead. I'll meet you in the car. This won't take long."

As soon as Goebel left, Sophie smiled at the frightened woman. "There was a baby born in the nursery many years ago. He needed a little help crossing over to the other side to find his mother. I can assure you, you won't be hearing any cries or seeing any strange shadows."

"How can you be sure?"

"I don't know. I just am. It's part of my gift, and I don't question it. I suppose there are reasons why. If I need to know, then I will. It's hard to explain. I'm a work in progress."

"I can't thank you enough. I guess . . . if I hear any more crying, you will come back?"

"Of course, but you're not going to hear anything. Like

I said, the little guy needed some help locating his mother. I helped him to find her, and he's at peace now."

Julianna smiled, her eyes sparkling like two shiny pennies. "I can't thank you enough."

Sophie simply nodded and allowed the young woman to guide her to the door.

As soon as it closed, she whipped a cigarette out of her purse and lit up. The inside light was on in the car, so she could see Goebel shaking his head. She took three drags, pinched the fire off the cigarette, and kept the butt in her hand. She might be tacky, but she wasn't going to toss a cigarette out on someone's lawn.

Relieved to be out of that house, she got inside the car and leaned her head back on the headrest.

"All is good?" Goebel asked as he shifted into reverse and backed out of the driveway.

"Yes, I think I can safely say the Tarwicks aren't going to hear any more crying, at least not from that nursery."

"Then I say we stop at Perkins, have a little bite to eat. I have something I want to show you after we finish. And they have a smoking section."

Sophie eyed Goebel in the semidarkness. "Is this something I need to be concerned about, something I won't like? You hate sitting in the smoking section."

He shook his head. "I'll manage. Now you're gonna have to wait and see. At the moment, I want something in my stomach. Aren't you hungry?"

"I'm always hungry," Sophie answered.

Goebel swerved into the nearest Perkins, which stayed open twenty-four hours a day. They had good coffee, and their omelets were some of the best.

Inside, the hostess led them to a booth in a quiet corner in the back of the restaurant, the smoking section. Sophie lit up as soon as they sat down.

Once they'd placed their orders, Goebel took Sophie's hand in his. His large hand was rough and calloused; it gave her a sense of protection. "You're gorgeous, you know that?"

Sophie's antennae instantly went on high alert. "I look like crap right now, and we both know it. Now you're really scaring me."

"You always look beautiful to me, Soph. Can't you sense when I'm being totally honest? I'm in love with you."

She smiled. "I try not to tune in to the vibes you give off. I'd be in trouble, otherwise. And the feeling is mutual, but, of course, you already know that."

The waitress brought their orders, and for the next fifteen minutes, the only communication between them was the clattering of silverware and slurps of hot coffee. When they were finished, and their plates had been removed, Sophie lit up. "I won't be able to smoke in public too much longer. South Carolina's sure to follow the rest of the country in banning indoor puffing."

"And they can't do it soon enough, as far as I'm concerned. I want you around for a long time. Tossing those smokes is a good idea."

Sophie crushed her cigarette out. "You're starting to sound just like Mavis and Ida."

Goebel looked at the check and removed his wallet from his back pocket. "You ought to listen to them, too." He tossed a twenty and a ten on the table.

"Oh, hush! I will quit eventually, just not today."

"Think about it," he said, reaching for her hand again.

She would, when the time was right. She'd tried to stop smoking more than once. She had to be mentally ready, and she wasn't. When the time was right, she would quit. *Toots too,* she thought, grinning.

Outside, they were greeted by a warm breeze, the night skies clear, almost blue-black. Stars shone so brightly, their brilliance illuminated the darkened parking lot. Sophie thought of all the years spent in New York City, stars blocked by the tall buildings and the thousands of lights. Oh, they were there, she knew that. It was just difficult to spot them.

Inside the SUV, Sophie couldn't help but wonder what Goebel had up his sleeve, especially so late at night. Maybe he'd rented some wild honeymoon suite at one of those fancy bed-and-breakfasts in Charleston. If that were the case, it wasn't a bad idea. They slipped in and out of Toots's place like two horny teenagers, which reminded her of Ida when she would sneak out to meet that fraud, Dr. Sameer.

Goebel had a small efficiency apartment in Charleston. The walls were thin, and the neighbors were nosy. And she was known to get a bit rowdy when *things* were going good. By *"things,"* of course, she meant hot and heavy sex.

"You're too quiet," Goebel remarked as they headed to wherever he was taking her.

"I'm wondering what you're up to, that's all. You sure whatever this is, it's safe? And legal?"

He laughed and reached for her hand. He did that often, and she liked it. Walter had been such an unaffectionate jerk.

"You can tell me in about five minutes. But just to ease your worries, it's safe and very legal."

"Safe" and "very legal," she thought, *not sure if I like the combination!*

"I trust you, Mr. Blevins." And she did. With her life.

Chapter 22

Bernice made a fresh pot of coffee, making sure to use Toots's Kopi Luwak special blend. "How do you take your coffee, son? Last time I saw you, you weren't a coffee drinker."

He took his empty ice tea glass and placed it in the dishwasher. "Remember, I live in Washington State, birthplace of Starbucks. You can't live there and not drink coffee."

"I didn't think of that. I don't like that old shit, uh, stuff. It's too strong," Bernice said.

The click-clacking of dog toenails announced Coco and her BFF, Frankie.

"And to whom may I ask do these adorable little fur balls belong?" Daniel asked.

"Frankie, the weenie, belongs to Dr. Becker, sort of. Toots takes care of him all the time. And her majesty"—Bernice nodded at Coco—"belongs to Mavis. Coco expects you to bow to her."

"Well, they're adorable. I've been thinking about adopting a pet myself." He scooped both dogs in his arms and carried them to the table, letting both of them sit on his lap. "And, Mom, it's okay to say shit in front of me." Daniel laughed, then pulled her close for a quick hug. "I've missed you. Missed being a part of a family. I like it that all you old gals are living together. From what you've told me, there's never a dull moment around here."

After Bernice made a light dinner of fresh salmon and a mixed green salad, she had talked nonstop, trying to fill Daniel in on the highlights since he'd been away. When she got to the part where Leland died—and how fast life had changed for all of them—she stopped, took a breath, then told Daniel about her near-death experience. She was just getting to the good part, when she heard someone come inside.

Coco growled, and Frankie raised his ears.

The front door banged extra loudly, startling Bernice. "Toots and Phil must be home," she said.

"I heard you, and, no, they are not home. It's me," Ida said, pulling a piece of Louis Vuitton luggage behind her. She peeked around the corner into the kitchen. "That coffee smells divine, Bernice. Pour me a cup while I change clothes."

"And who might that be?" Daniel asked when he heard Ida.

Hearing they had company, she entered the kitchen. When she saw the man sitting next to Bernice, she stared wordlessly. Her heart was pounding so rapidly that she thought she might pass out.

"Hello," she said, her voice rising.

"And hello to you," Daniel countered. Both dogs wiggled, and he set them on the floor. "Cute little buggers." They ran to their favorite corner in the dining room, where their daytime beds were located.

"Ida, this is Daniel Alan, my long-lost son," Bernice announced.

Clearly, she hadn't expected this. Bernice offered up a big grin. "Handsome, don't you think?"

Taken aback by her bluntness, Ida suddenly felt shy, not her normal confident I-can-have-any-man-I-please self.

"Nice to meet you, Daniel. Your mother doesn't speak of you often enough. I had no idea she had a son . . . your age." No, from what Ida had heard from Toots on the rare occasions they'd discussed Bernice's son, she had imagined an overweight, slovenly, lazy slob. This man now seated at the table was anything but. Tall, broad-shouldered, cobalt blue eyes, and hair with touches of gray, in just the right places, he certainly was not what she had envisioned. Looking at him through the eyes of a professional, she was positive that he would make an excellent model. With the dark blue eyes, strong jaw, and sharp cheekbones, she could definitely see him on the cover of a magazine. Quickly she did a mental calculation, according to what she knew. He must be in his fifties. He did not look his age at all. Ida wondered if he'd been using her creams, but she wouldn't dare voice her thoughts.

"Ida, don't get any ideas," Bernice warned.

Ida wanted to melt into the gleaming oak floors like the Wicked Witch of the West in *The Wizard of Oz*. Embarrassed, and surprised as she was, Ida smoothed the side of her hair. "I'm going upstairs to change. I'll come back down for that coffee."

"And you can pour it yourself, you demanding twit," Bernice called out after her.

"Mom, I've never heard you speak to someone like that."

"Listen up. If you stick around long enough, you'll understand. Ida is a spoiled, self-centered bitch."

"I heard that," Ida called from the other room.

Bernice flipped her the bird, another habit she'd picked up from Toots. When she realized what she'd done, her face turned beet red.

Daniel, on the other hand, began to laugh so hard he doubled over. "I can't believe I just saw you do that."

She shouldn't be acting this way in front of Daniel. Why, he probably thought she'd lost her mind, or was senile and in the early stages of Alzheimer's. She was starting to think and act more like Toots daily. She smiled because Toots was good people—foul mouth, flipping finger, and all. It wasn't so bad to think she was acting like her dearest friend. "Sorry, I don't know what I was thinking."

"Mom, stop apologizing for being yourself. Remember how you tried to teach that to me? Remember what an asshole I was for the first thirty-plus years of my life? I like that you know how to use that finger. I do it myself when the occasion calls for it. Now tell me more about Ida. Her face looks very familiar to me."

Oh, crap! If Ida heard that, her head would swell ten times bigger than it already was. But he was bound to find out sooner or later, so it might as well be sooner, and from her rather than Ida. "You *might* have seen her on The Home Shopping Club. She has a line of cosmetics, which are selling faster than ever. I think she's a great businesswoman, but she is a . . . spoiled old thing."

"Just exactly how old is she? She doesn't look very old," Daniel said, now more curious than ever. Bernice should have never mentioned her success. She wasn't so sure that Daniel wouldn't try and take advantage of a wealthy woman. And where in the world did that come from? This was her own flesh and blood. She had no clue if Daniel was a ladies' man. He'd turned into such a handsome man; why, she just assumed that he was like his father. That two-timing SOB had looked at everything in a skirt, and then some. She could only hope that this new-and-improved version of her son hadn't picked up that trait.

"Ida is just over seventy," Bernice said, knowing that they had celebrated that milestone birthday party only a few weeks ago. She was seventeen years older than Daniel. Not old enough to be his mother, but too darned old to be his girlfriend.

"She doesn't look a day over fifty-five," Daniel said.

Ida returned just in time to hear this. "Why, thank you."

She'd changed into what she called dinner pajamas. Black silk pants and matching top, which reached just above her knees. She'd added a touch of lipstick and run a brush through her hair. "Now I would love some coffee."

Bernice pointed to the coffeemaker. "Help yourself."

"Of course, I will," Ida remarked. "I don't expect you to wait on me hand and foot."

They both knew better, but neither commented. For a minute, Ida was slightly ashamed of how she had treated Bernice. The feeling left her as fast as it came. She filled her cup and brought it to the table. She sat in the chair across from Daniel. "So, what brings you to South Carolina?"

Bernice popped right in, answering, "Why, me, of course! Surely, you don't think he's here to visit you? He doesn't even know you."

"Actually, Mother is only one of the reasons I'm in South Carolina."

Instantly Bernice's face dropped to the floor and came back. What other reason could he possibly have? Curious, she asked, "What's your other reason for driving all the way across the country?"

Daniel took a sip of his coffee. "Business. During all those years I spent wandering around, trying to find myself, I went back to college. Teaching elementary school was all right for a while, but I needed to find something else that I really could delve into. I went to law school, so I've been practicing corporate law for the past eight years. I have a client in Charleston who's in a mess, and I decided to combine business with pleasure."

Bernice thought her teeth would fall out. "You're an attorney? Really?" She couldn't have been any more surprised. Yes, Daniel had done well in school, graduated near the top of his class in college, but she'd never pegged him for having an interest in the law. Of course, she hadn't been around him for over twenty years. He was virtually a stranger to her.

Ida perked up like an instant Powerball winner. "How exciting!" she exclaimed.

Bernice knew she was feigning interest in something she knew nothing about, all in the hopes of procuring the male approval. Sophie and Toots were right. Ida was a slut.

"The law is my life now. I couldn't ever go back to teaching," he added, more to Ida than to his mother.

"Ida doesn't have children. As a matter of fact, she hates all kids, except for Abby, Toots's daughter. Ida's one of her three godmothers. Ida isn't much of a people person, either. She likes herself too much." Bernice was not going to allow either of them to even act like they had any common ground. She would kick Ida so hard in her uppity ass . . . she'd have to yank her foot out with a crowbar! Miss Ida was not going to stick her claws into her son's anything.

"For crying out loud, Bernice, you're making me sound like an ogre. I do, too, like children, and people. I'm selective, that's all." Her gentle laugh rippled throughout the dining room. Daniel caught her eye; and in return, she gave him one of her sexiest smiles. She knew this to be true because she spent hours in front of the mirror practicing.

He laughed, too, the sound rich and vibrant. "Mother, I think you're embarrassing your friend."

"She isn't my friend," Bernice shot back, then backtracked. "I mean, I met her because she's one of Abby's godmothers. We became friends through Toots."

"Where is Robert tonight? I thought he would be here with another one of his dreadful recipes," Ida said, taking control of the conversation. "Robert is your mother's love, uh, I meant her male friend. They like to cook. Rather, Bernice does. Robert spends his days searching for recipes." Ida shot Bernice the fuck-you look.

Daniel laughed. "I see you two bring out the *best* in one another. Mom, I'd love to meet Robert. If he's with you, then he must be one of the good guys."

"He's a very nice man. We are just friends, nothing more."

Ida cleared her throat and raised her perfectly sculpted brows. "So you say."

"Ida, shut up, for Pete's sake! You have no clue what our relationship's about."

"Oh, hush! We sound like a couple of schoolgirls. You don't want to frighten Daniel away his first night, now, do you?" Ida said in her most pleasant, fake voice.

Bernice rolled her eyes. "Nope, I don't. Now, before you arrived, I was having a nice conversation with my son. If you will excuse us, I'd like to finish."

Daniel stood then, stretching. Bernice watched Ida ogle him as if he were the catch of the day.

And something told her this was just the beginning.

"Actually, I'm wiped out. If you don't mind, direct me to my bed, and we can start over in the morning."

Bernice pursed her lips, something she did when she was pissed. "You can stay in the room across from mine. The sheets are clean." She wanted to add it was the farthest from Ida's room, but she had a feeling that wouldn't matter. Maybe she should send him to her house. It wasn't like she lived there every day. She made sure to go over at least once a month to air out the place.

Ida stood, too. "I say we all call it a night. I've had such a long three days. Those lights are torturous on my skin."

Again, Ida rolled her eyes.

"I can't see the first wrinkle on your face. Your complexion is as smooth as a teenager's," Daniel said.

"Yeah, and teenagers have acne," Bernice quipped.

"You're mean-spirited, Bernice. You know that?" Ida said. "I'm going to bed. Good night, Daniel. I'll see you tomorrow." And with that, Ida headed upstairs, knowing Daniel's eyes were on her as she sashayed out of the room. Her hips were swinging like a young girl's walking on the boardwalk.

"Lead the way, Mom. I really am pooped."

Bernice nodded. "Come on, son. I'll tell you a good-night story."

It would go something like this: "Once upon a time, in a land far, far away, lived an old whore named Ida."

Chapter 23

The Clay Plantation was lit up like Dodger Stadium. "I can't imagine what's so important that it can't wait until morning. This is so unlike Abby," Toots said for the umpteenth time, in the last ten minutes.

Phil stopped at the gate and punched in the code. "She's fine, Toots. I'm guessing she's overly excited about the arrival of the animals in the morning. This is a big undertaking. I admire her."

"Yes, I'm sure you're right, but she said it was very important. Not that the animals aren't . . . I just know it's something serious. She's been sick a lot lately."

He steered the Mercedes down the long drive and parked next to Abby's yellow MINI Cooper. He opened Toots's door, and she practically leaped out of the car, running to the front door of the house. She knocked, then called out, "Abby, we're here!"

They stepped inside the entryway. "Abby? Chris?"

"Mom, we'll be right down!" Abby shouted from somewhere upstairs. Toots recalled when she and Garland lived here for the brief time they were married, before he died so unexpectedly. The furnishings were the same. Mostly, family antiques. Toots hadn't wanted to redecorate when they'd lived here because she knew the plantation would one day belong to Chris. Even though Garland had left a large part of his estate to her, she'd willed it back to Chris as soon as he'd graduated from law school. She'd wanted her stepson to make any and all decisions when it came to the family estate. Never in a million years had she thought that he and Abby would live here as a married couple.

Abby, followed by a smiling Chris, who looked how the cat who ate the canary was supposed to look, greeted them at the bottom of the staircase.

"Abby, I am so worried about you! What's wrong?" Toots asked.

"Do you mind if we go to the kitchen? I'm sure I have another pitcher of sweet tea." Abby made the best sweet tea ever.

"Of course not," Toots said, trailing her daughter. "Are you sick, Abby? Please don't keep me in suspense any longer."

Abby turned to face her mother. "Mom! I'm fine. I don't know why you would even think such a thing. I'm fine. Really. I couldn't be better. Right, Chris?" Abby winked at her husband.

"Yep, she's as fit as a fiddle."

"Phil, you want tea?" Abby asked.

"I wouldn't turn your ice tea down for all the tea in China," Phil cajoled.

Chris filled four glasses with ice, while Abby made quick work of slicing a lemon. She pulled a few sprigs of mint from the mini herb garden she'd planted in small, colorful pots positioned decoratively along the windowsill. Then Abby got the tea out of the refrigerator and poured the cold brew over the ice.

"Abby, hurry up. I know you're up to something. I've never in my life seen anyone take so long to pour a glass of tea."

Chris burst out laughing. "Your mom knows you well, doesn't she?"

"Shhh, this is important." Abby grinned and filled the

glasses, bringing them to the table, two at a time. When she was satisfied, she sat across from her mom and Phil. Chris took the seat next to her. He reached for her hand, covering it with his own.

"Abby!" Toots appealed. "Spit it out! If you weren't so damned adorable, I'd smack your little butt. We left dinner, Abs, so we're both starving."

They all laughed.

"I'm sorry, Mom, Phil. You want a piece of toast or something?"

"No, we do not. We want to know why we're here!" Everyone could hear the impatience in her voice.

"You want me to tell her?" Chris asked. "You've stretched this out too long, sweet woman."

"Tell me what!" Toots shouted, not caring.

"I'm pregnant," Abby confessed, with a giggle. Joy bubbled up in her laughter, and her eyes sparkled like the finest gold.

Overwhelmed and *shocked to the core* didn't come close to describing the emotions flowing through Toots. "Say that again" was all she could come up with.

Chris took this as his clue to speak up. "Tootsie, you're going to be a grandmother. A nanny. A mimi. A mamaw. You pick."

Suddenly Toots's eyes were filled with happy tears. She reached across the table, knocked her glass over, and took her daughter's hand. *No.* She practically jumped over the table. "Come here." Abby allowed her mother to hoist her out of the chair. Toots squeezed her so hard, but then stopped. "Oh, my God, I don't want to hurt the baby. Phil, did you hear this? I am going to be a grandmother. Oh, shit! I can't believe this. When did you find out?"

"Right before we called you," Chris answered.

Bewildered, Toots shook her head. "Details, please." She hugged Abby again; then she grabbed a wad of paper towels, tossing them on the lake of spilled tea.

"I've been so sick. Remember the other night when I had that coffee at your house? I thought I'd been poisoned. I've been telling myself I had a bug, the flu. Then, tonight, I made fish for dinner. I got so sick afterward—I just knew I was terminally ill." Abby glanced at Chris. "I know I didn't tell you, but it doesn't matter now, because we know that I'm not. Chris mentioned something about going to the drugstore to buy me 'girlie things.' I've always been a bit irregular, so I always put a red check mark in my date book so I can remember when I had my period. I flipped through my date book, and I haven't made a red check mark in almost four months. Then everything made sense. The throwing up, the tiredness, the weird things I've been smelling that Chris"—Abby turned to her husband, her blue eyes raised—"thought I was imagining. He said I was losing it. Chris and I went to CVS, bought a test kit, and it said *positive*!"

"I think this is worth celebrating. I'll be right back," Phil said.

"Mom?" Abby asked as soon as Phil was out of earshot. "Are you two . . . you okay?"

"Of course, we are. You don't need to worry about us. You have much more important issues to deal with. Oh, Abby, I think this is the most exciting news I've heard in my entire life!" Toots gushed.

Chris chimed in, "I second that."

Phil returned to the kitchen with the bottle of Syrah, Raven No. 10. Holding it up in the air, he said, "This was too good to leave behind." He gave the bottle to Chris.

"I'll get the glasses. Three of them." He nodded toward Abby. "You will have to celebrate with the tea."

She laughed. "It's fine with me. I rarely drink alcohol, as it is. Nothing I'll be missing here."

Phil poured the Syrah, Raven No. 10 into three glasses. Chris filled another wineglass with tea for Abby.

Phil raised his glass in the air. "I would like to propose a toast."

Toots, Chris, and Abby lifted their glasses high in the air.

"To love, happiness, and the beginning of new life!"

They all clinked their glasses—the sound music to their ears.

Chapter 24

"Why are we stopping *here*? This place has been abandoned for as long as I can remember," Sophie said when Goebel shut off the ignition.

"I know it has." He turned sideways in his seat so that he was facing Sophie. "While you were in the nursery sending that little guy to the other side, I received a text message from Alice Radcliffe. Before you ask who she is, she's Toots's real-estate agent. Toots put me in touch with her about a week ago, and I put in a bid on this place a few days ago. That text message I received told me the owner accepted my bid. So"—he let out a nervous chuckle—"we're stopping here because the key is under the first step on one of the little porches in the back. I thought you might want to see the inside of our new home."

Flabbergasted didn't even begin to cover what Sophie was feeling at that moment. "But . . . I . . . you and me? Here?" Rarely was she speechless, but she really didn't know what to say.

Goebel took her hand. "This"—he touched the two-carat diamond he'd given her when he suggested they team up as a permanent couple—"I was serious when I gave this to you."

"I know that."

"We both know I've never formally proposed to you."

With a bravado she didn't feel, she said, "Yeah, so what?"

"You're not gonna make this easy, are you?" Goebel teased.

Sophie wasn't sure what to make of anything just then. This was so out of the blue, so unexpected, she truly needed a few minutes to absorb the enormity of Goebel's words. Taking a deep breath, she said, "This is not what I was expecting. I thought maybe you'd booked a honeymoon suite at one of those fancy bed-and-breakfasts in Charleston."

Goebel appeared crestfallen.

"Wait, wait. . . . I meant . . . this is a good thing, Goebel. Don't get me wrong. I am just . . . surprised, that's all." That was putting it mildly. *Damn, I've taken the thunder out of his surprise.* "Okay, let's start over."

Goebel nodded, cranked the engine, and backed down the driveway. When he reached the main road, he turned back toward town. Sophie didn't utter a word. She wasn't sure if Goebel was pissed or hurt. He was probably a combination of both. Shit! For once, she needed to learn to keep her big-ass mouth shut. She owed him an apology, but didn't want to speak now. Highly unusual for her. She decided to remain quiet and allow Goebel to take back the control she'd whisked away with a few words.

He turned the car into the Perkins parking lot. Okay, maybe he was taking this a bit too far, but she refused to comment. Goebel parked the SUV in the exact place they'd parked less than an hour ago. He actually shut off the engine, waited a couple seconds; then he started it up again. She couldn't help but grin. The old coot, she knew what he was up to. No way in hell was she going to open her mouth this time around. She was along for the ride.

For the second time, Goebel pulled into the driveway at the purple house, shut off the ignition, then turned to face her. "Sophie Manchester, I am insanely in love with your smart little ass. You've turned this old man from a die-hard bachelor to a—a moonstruck piece of mush. I want to marry you, want to wake up every day knowing you're somewhere close by. I want us to spend the rest of our lives together, having as many adventures as we've shared already. I want to live in this house with you. I want you to work beside me while I make this house our home. I want to see the look of love that I see in your eyes right now for the rest of my life. Now, Sophie Manchester, will you do me the honor of becoming my wife?"

Tears streamed down her face—good tears—the kind that sent shivers along her arms, her legs, and the middle of her back. She let them fall, not caring about it one bit. Her nose stopped up, her vision blurred from the tears, but never in her seventy years had she ever felt so wanted, so desired by a man.

"Goebel Blevins, it would be *my* honor to be your wife." Enough said.

Before she knew what was happening, Goebel jumped out of the SUV, ran around to her side, opened her door, and lifted her out of the car. She wrapped her arms around his neck, placing her head against his chest. No words were needed, as they both knew where they stood.

He carried her around to the back of the house, which was huge, removed a penlight from his pocket and directed its beam across the back of the house, all the while still carrying her in his arms. When he spied the aforementioned porch, he stooped down to the ground, still holding her in his arms. Using one hand, he fumbled around for the key. When he located it, he said, "Eureka!" Repositioning Sophie, he marched to the front of the house and walked up the small stairs leading to the front door. He inserted the key with one hand, jiggled it a few times, then pushed the door open. He carried her inside, shone the light's beam around the main room, and then set her down.

"I've always wanted to carry you over the threshold.

Now I can take that off my bucket list," Goebel said, grinning, and just a bit out of breath.

"I've never been carried over a threshold, just so you know." She needed Goebel to know this was a first for her, too, even though she'd been married before. That schmuck Walter had been too drunk on their wedding day to do anything more than grab the last bottle of free champagne, then pass out as soon as they were alone in their cheap hotel room.

"Good, because I don't think I can do this again," he teased.

"Are you saying I'm too fat? Too old?"

"Not hardly. I'm just out of shape."

"Bullshit. You're in excellent shape. Remember when we first met? You were a bit on the heavy side then, but now . . . please. You're in better shape than some men half your age. I see what you eat, and I know you walk on that treadmill in your apartment."

"Thanks, Soph. I want to stay healthy as long as I'm able. Meaning I'll get to spend more time with you. Maybe you'll think about tossing those smokes?"

Yes, she should, but not now. "I will, someday. Right now, I just want to enjoy this time alone with you in our . . . new place." She wanted to say the word *dump,* but refrained. The place was old, yes; but from what little she could see, it looked as though much of the original lighting and woodwork were there, and in halfway-decent shape.

"Promise me you'll think about it. Now let's scope this place out. I stopped by, and let me tell you, the place needs some work, but, Sophie, it's a gem. I can't believe this hasn't sold before now. Most of the work needed is outside—the grounds are terribly in need of a good gardener's touch—and, of course, the outside color would have to be changed immediately."

Sophie got caught up in the excitement, too. Toots and

Abby were excellent decorators. She knew they would pitch in when the time came. "Let me look around."

Goebel directed the penlight through the downstairs rooms. "I can't believe what a deal, Soph. I'd tell you, but this is your gift, and you're not supposed to tell how much you paid. It's rude. Suffice it to say, when all is said and done, this place will be worth ten times more than the selling price."

"It does seem to be in decent condition. Exactly how old is this place?"

"Late 1800s according to Alice."

Sophie stopped when they entered what once might've been the drawing room. The built-in bookshelves looked to be in decent shape, as far as she could see. She'd come over tomorrow during the day, when she could really get a good glimpse at her—*their*—new home.

"Look at this," Goebel said, aiming the light across the middle of the walls. "This is the original wainscoting. All the fireplace mantels, there are five in all, are original. Hardwood floors are too. Doors as solid as a rock. They don't build homes like this anymore."

Again, Sophie heard the excitement in his voice. It wasn't hard to get caught up in it. *This is going to be fun,* she thought as she eyed the staircase.

"Let's go upstairs. I want to see the bedrooms," she said in her most seductive voice.

Goebel's cell phone erupted, the ring one of those high-pitched *do-da-do-da* sounds that grated on her nerves. "I need to take this. Sorry.

"Goebel Blevins.

"Toots? Yes, she's right here. Hang on.

"It's for you. It's Toots. Says it's very urgent." He gave her the phone, curious as to why she hadn't called on Sophie's cell phone. Then he remembered it was probably in her purse inside the SUV. He hoped the area was safe. Sophie would never let him hear the end of it if someone took her purse.

"You're kidding me, right? Do you know where I am right now? No, of course, you don't. Yes, if you think it's that urgent, of course. We'll be there in ten minutes."

Sophie clicked the END button. "Toots says it's urgent. She wants us both to come over now. You okay with that?"

"Hey, I've got the rest of my life to be alone with you. If Toots says it's urgent, let's go. I'll show you the rest of the place tomorrow."

"I hope Karen didn't take a turn for the worse. Poor girl," Sophie said, referring to the producer for her and Goebel's reality special, which most likely wasn't going to be a reality in their lifetime. She honestly didn't care.

"No, I'm sure it's something else. Toots would've blurted that out on the phone."

He was right. She would have.

Before Sophie could walk to the front door, Goebel pulled her close to him. "Let's set a date now so we can give Toots some good news, just in case hers is bad."

Sophie nodded. "Next week soon enough?"

Goebel lifted her off her feet and swung her around. "Damn straight!" He put her down, then pulled her close again. "Sophie Manchester, you've just made me the happiest man in the entire world. You know that, right?"

"Ditto, Mr. Blevins, with appropriate modifications, ditto, ditto, ditto."

Chapter 25

It was close to midnight when Wade and Mavis returned from their trip to Charlotte. They'd enjoyed the conference and the drive home, especially since they were rarely alone. When they drove through the gates, Mavis saw that the downstairs lights were on. "I wonder why everyone is still up? Toots must be having a party."

Wade parked beside Phil's silver Mercedes. "I say we go inside and find out."

"You don't want to check on Robert first?" Mavis asked before getting out of the car.

"He's probably inside with the rest of the gang. He doesn't like being away from Bernice. He's crazy about her. Almost as crazy about her as I am about you," Wade said, taking her hand and leading her up the steps.

Mavis was glad for the darkness, as she knew she was blushing like a girl about to receive her first kiss. "Wade," she whispered his name airily. Just saying his name sent shivers up and down her spine. She hadn't been this excited over a member of the male species since she and Herbert had met in college over fifty years earlier. She had a brief flash of George and that *thing* he owned, his VCD. Quickly she shifted focus to the here and now.

"Shhh," was his last word as he touched his lips to hers, devouring their softness. Mavis melted into his arms, giving in to the moment. She kissed him back, lingering, savoring every part of his mouth on hers. So lost in Wade's kiss was she, the space around her was nothing more than a blur. Seconds or minutes passed, she wasn't sure. When Wade pulled away, she felt a momentary loss. "The hall lights just came on," he whispered in her ear.

Again glad for the darkness, Mavis touched her lips as though she wanted to imprint the memory of his kiss on her fingertips.

"Who's out there?" Toots called. She'd heard footsteps, then nothing.

"It's just me," Mavis answered. "Wade is here, too."

Toots opened the front door. "Then why don't you both come inside?" She could tell that Mavis was a bit flustered. "Did I interrupt anything?" she asked coyly, knowing full well that she had. But at that moment, she simply did not care; she was jubilant, and they were throwing a party to celebrate.

"Uh, no," Mavis said; then she stepped inside as Toots held the door open.

"What's the celebration?" Wade asked.

"We're in the dining room. All of us. We've been waiting on you two," Toots said. "We have lots to celebrate. You won't believe your eyes when you meet our latest visitor."

When they reached the dining room, Mavis saw everyone who mattered to her gathered around the dining-room table, plus a handsome man whom she had never in her life seen before. They'd had to bring in chairs from the veranda so everyone would have a place to sit.

Toots gestured in Daniel's direction. "Daniel, this is Mavis and Wade. He lives next door with his brother, Robert. And this is Bernice's son, who's just arrived from Washington State. He's an attorney."

Bernice glowed like a kid at Christmas when she looked at her son. And Robert.

After the usual pleasantries, the chatter picked up.

"This is quite the surprise, isn't it, Wade?" Mavis asked. "What in the world could be so important? Daniel, I'm sorry if that sounds rude. I didn't mean it to be. Toots's and Sophie's ways must be rubbing off on me. Speaking of Sophie, where is she? And Goebel?"

"They're on their way. Have a seat because good news is only exciting the first time it's told," Toots offered up.

"Mother!" Abby said. "That is not always the case." She winked. Toots winked back.

"I'm teasing, but we can wait for Sophie. She'll be here any moment now."

Placed in the middle of the dining-room table were two carafes of coffee. Regular and decaf, along with a full sugar bowl and two cartons of half-and-half.

Toots had called Jamie, knowing she'd be awake, and invited her over as well. Lucky for everyone, Jamie had a batch of pralines, as well as some raisin cookies she'd brought home from the bakery. Toots absolutely loved the girl and felt like she was family. Add that her pralines were the best in the state, it was a win-win situation all around.

While they waited for Sophie and Goebel, they all started talking at once.

"Robert, you're feeling okay?" Wade asked as he poured a cup of decaf for Mavis and one for himself.

"Of course, I am. Why? Do you think just because you've just returned from the dead-people conference that I'm ready to kick the bucket?" Robert spoke extremely loud. Since they knew he was hard of hearing, they let it pass.

"You, my dear brother, are a cantankerous old man," Wade said, grinning. "We were at a convention for the owners of funeral parlors, not a 'dead-people conference.' I can assure you that there was not a single corpse there, much less any zombies. And while we're on the subject, and I know it's not everyone's favorite topic, but Mavis and I, well, we are going to open a funeral parlor together. Here. In Charleston."

All chattering stopped.

"I think that's an excellent idea. I'm sure I can provide your clients with their final exit shot," Ida said, without the first hint of conceit.

"Of course. We were going to ask you if you'd help out. I wasn't sure with all the success of Seasons, since you're always traveling back and forth to Wilmington. We've already got a place in mind. The owner wants to retire and move to Florida. We met him at the conference," Mavis said.

"Congrats, Mavis and Wade. You two will make great . . . uh, great funeral directors," Abby stated in her enthusiastic way, without a hint of sarcasm.

"Yes, and while we were there, I contracted with a company in Canada. They want to market Good Mourning. I am going to be so busy that I won't have time to"—flustered, Mavis finished—"to hang out with you all as much."

"Bullshit, you will make the time. We've all got projects going on. Abby is expecting five dogs and three cats tomorrow. You promised you would give her a hand," Toots said, spoken like a true ballbuster. Remembering Phil's phone call, she turned to him. "Dr. Carnes, what did she say?"

"She'd take the first available flight in the morning, so there's no need to line up the Flexjet."

"That's excellent news, and, Mom, Mavis's work is important, too. It should come first in her life."

"Oh, I know. I just wanted to yank her chain. You're a real go-getter, Mavis. Of course, we'll support you and Wade, just don't get offended if I say I really don't want to do business with either of you anytime soon."

They all laughed.

The front door banged, and they all knew who it was before she entered the dining room.

"This better be good is all I've got to say," Sophie said

to the group gathered at the table. Spying an unfamiliar face, she introduced herself. "I'm Sophie. This is Goebel. You must be one of Ida's hot young things from Wilmington."

The room went completely silent; then Bernice practically jumped out of her chair. "Sophie, you shit, that 'hot young thing' just happens to be my son. Daniel, meet Sophie, the biggest smart-ass in the bunch."

"Ah, frig, I'm sorry if I offended you. Daniel, it's good to meet you. We've heard a lot about you the past few years. I must say, I didn't expect you to be so damned hot. That's why I assumed you were with Ida. She likes men, and age doesn't matter."

Daniel had the good grace to laugh. "No offense taken. Actually, I consider it a compliment."

Ida shot a glance over at Bernice, as if to say, *Ha-ha, told you so*. Bernice stuck her middle finger up directly in Ida's line of vision. Ida just smiled.

"Okay, I, for one, want to know why we're all here. I was in the middle of something very personal when you called, so this had better be good," Sophie said to Toots.

"Abby, you and Chris want to do the honors?" Toots asked.

All eyes focused on Abby. She gave a sheepish grin; then her eyes lit up like fireworks on the Fourth of July. "In about five months, Chris and I are going to have a baby."

No one said a word; then they all started talking at once.

"When did you find out?" came from Ida.

"Is that why you've been puking your guts up?" came from Sophie.

"Oh, Abby, that's the most exciting news I've heard in forever! Congratulations to both of you," Mavis offered. "Just think, a little one in the house." At that moment, Coco, who'd been reclining on her bed in the corner with Frankie, started barking. "She's jealous already," Mavis added.

"So, was this worth coming out so late?" Toots asked, grinning.

Bernice finally spoke. "I can't wait. You know I practically raised Abby, and it looks like I'm going to be around long enough to show her the ropes of motherhood. Congratulations, Abby."

"Yeah, you raised her, all right. You cooked, and I did the rest. I distinctly remember you running for cover when she would puke or poop."

"Hey, I cleaned up my share of messes from your daughter. As I recollect, you were quite busy throughout her early years, searching for husband number . . . what? *Thirty?* I can't remember! There were so many."

The room went silent. Toots dared to look at Bernice. She didn't know that Phil was unaware of her many marriages. She wanted to strangle the life right out of her, but it wasn't Bernice's fault. It was her own. She'd hemmed and hawed, and now it was coming back to bite her in the ass, courtesy of Bernice. And she couldn't say a damned word in her own defense because there was no defense.

Toots sneaked a glance at Phil. He didn't appear to be affected by Bernice's statement. She crossed her fingers. If luck was on her side, maybe Phil thought this was just more old-woman bantering.

Sensing her mother's discomfort and knowing why, Abby raised her voice in mock anger. "God, Mother, do you have to be so graphic?"

"Well, I don't want Daniel to think I didn't raise you. Yes, Bernice, you helped. Abby would probably have had scurvy, had it not been for your cooking."

They all laughed, and again the dining room was full of laughter, shouts, and congratulations on the new life soon to come into the world.

"Toots, let's go outside and have a smoke," Sophie said. "I've been dying for a cigarette, and there's something you need to know."

"Me too," Toots said. "I have something to tell you, too."

On the back porch step, where they always sat and huffed, Sophie lit two cigarettes and handed one to Toots.

"You go first," Toots said. It was a way to stall what she hated to put into words.

"Tonight, when you called Goebel, we were at that purple house up the road. The old shit bought the place. Can you believe it?"

Toots smiled. Of course, she believed it. She was the former owner, but now wasn't the time to take the wind out of Sophie's and Goebel's sails.

"That's excellent news! Is he planning on living there?" Toots asked because she was nosy.

"Yep, and get this. He asked me to marry him. I mean a real proposal, and I said yes. We're getting married next week."

Toots appeared stunned.

"Congratulations again. Geez, there's a lot to celebrate in this house tonight," Toots said, suddenly overwhelmed with despair. Her news was such a downer. She was afraid if she told anyone else, she'd jinx them, too.

"How fast can you plan a wedding? If you can plan my wedding as fast as you planned those *events* of all your dearly departeds, then it shouldn't be a problem." Weddings, babies, husbands. A night Toots would remember for the rest of her life. Yes, she had screwed up by withholding her past from Phil, but she wasn't going to allow her screwups to put a damper on Abby's news or Sophie's upcoming nuptials.

"I can plan a wedding in a day if I have to." Toots forced herself to cheer up. This wasn't the time to wallow in self-pity.

"Then let's do it. I wanted to tell you first. If it weren't for you, I'd still be in my apartment in New York. Minus Walter, to be sure, but still." Showing a rare moment of affection, Sophie leaned against Toots, her dearest friend in the world.

Toots smiled. "Let's go inside and tell the others." She crushed her smoke out in the can.

"Let's do it," Sophie said, dropping her cigarette in the can, then smashing it in the sand.

Inside, Toots made a big production when she placed her fingers in her mouth, whistling so loud it hurt her ears. Silence.

"Sorry, but I need your attention. Not only do Abby and Chris have good news, but I think Sophie has something she wants to share with you all, too." Toots made a dramatic sweeping gesture with her hand. "It's all yours."

Rarely at a loss for words, Sophie felt tongue-tied as she stared at all the people she loved. She didn't love Daniel, but that was because she'd just met him. Who knew? By the end of the night, he very well could be her new best friend. She eyed Goebel. Damn, he was a good man. She briefly thought how their paths had crossed. She'd liked him the minute she laid eyes on him, and she was sure he had felt the same way about her. Now they were going to marry. A first for him. A real marriage for her.

"Sophie," Toots announced. "The floor is all yours."

"Okay . . . well, tonight Goebel and I set a date for our wedding. One week from today, and you're all invited."

Hoots and hollers, laughter, kisses and hugs, all flowed freely. Ida even gave Bernice a hug. A miracle in and of itself. The night was a time for love, friendship, new beginnings, and, most of all, a celebration of family.

Toots watched the scene as it took place. A warm sensation spread throughout her body. *This is life. This is love.*

Phil came up behind her and wrapped his arms around her waist. And it was finally time to tell the truth.

Chapter 26

"We need to talk. Privately," Toots said to Phil. "We can go upstairs to my room."

"Whoa, I guess all this love and happiness has made you change your mind, huh?" he joked, but Toots didn't answer. As much as she wished that were the case, it wasn't.

"Come on," she said, turning her back to him. He followed her upstairs to her room. She turned on the lamp next to the bed, then sat down. She patted the spot next to her. "Sit down."

Phil sat down beside her. "What's going on, Toots? You don't seem too happy right now. Is it something I said? If it is, let me apologize now."

She shook her head. "No, it's nothing you've done, or anyone. It's me." She took a deep breath, hating what she was about to do, but knowing it was time. Phil meant too much to her to continue the lie. With Bernice's outburst, she was surprised he hadn't questioned her already.

"Okay," he said, his voice soft and soothing. The one he used with his patients.

"Phil, I haven't been honest with you. There are things about me, about my past, that you should know." There, that was a start. She took another cleansing breath.

"I see."

"No, you can't say that yet, because I haven't told you

what and *why* I haven't been up front with you. Let me just get it all out, and then you can ask questions. It will be much easier for both of us. Trust me on this."

Phil nodded.

Shit, she thought. *He really isn't going to interrupt me. Okay, Toots, the floor is all yours. Now do it!*

"First let me say my dishonesty wasn't intentional. There really isn't any way to break this news other than to come right out and tell you." Another deep breath. "Phil, I have been married eight times, and all of my husbands died. I believe I'm a jinx, bad luck, whatever you want to call it. I'm afraid if you and I take our relationship to the next level, as you suggested, that you will die, and possibly you might think I'm a loose woman."

The truth was out. There were no more lies, nothing between them any longer.

Phil shook his head. "Can I just ask you one question?"

"Of course."

"Why do you believe you're a jinx, or bad luck?"

Toots wanted to shake him. "Phil, I have been married eight times. They've all died. There were no divorces, just death. I've buried and fried so many husbands, I've become quite the expert at planning funerals. I like to refer to them as *events*."

"I still don't see what this has to do with us."

Toots almost choked on her own saliva.

"You're a smart man, Phil. You're a heart surgeon. You make your living saving people's lives. I marry men, and it seems to take their lives. I don't want anything to happen to you because I . . . I care about you too much to take the risk."

"And don't I get a say in any of this?"

"Of course, you can say whatever you like, but the fact remains, there is something not right with me and my relationships with men. They all fail by death."

Phil touched her shoulder, gently guiding her to face

him. "Toots, first of all, I don't believe for one minute that you're a jinx, bad luck, whatever you want to call it. People die. It's part of life. Secondly, I don't care about your past. I care about you, about us, and about our future. When I said I wanted to take our relationship to the next level, I didn't mean I just wanted to jump in the sack with you, though I do, but that's beside the point. I didn't ask you to come to Myrtle Beach with me just to . . . shack up. I want you to be with me, Toots. Always. However long that may be. I'd much rather take a chance with you than spend the rest of my life alone. I've been alone too long, and that's my own fault. Yes, there were many opportunities for me to get married, but I chose work over a family. You didn't do that. You chose your family, and if that meant you had eight choices, then all I can say is, more power to you. But to think any of this matters to me is crazy. I know you've been married before. I'm good with that. Hell, I can't wait to become a grandfather to Chris and Abby's child, and we haven't even . . . you know what I mean. I want a family, Toots. I want you, pure and simple, bad luck and all."

Surely, Phil had drunk too much wine tonight. Add all the caffeine they'd consumed, and he was probably talking out of his head.

"Aren't you going to say anything?"

"I don't know what you want me to say," Toots whispered. She could not believe he was in his right mind, but she didn't want him to know what she was thinking.

"I want you to say what you always say, 'The past is prologue,' and let's take our relationship to the next level. What I don't want to hear you say is, it's your fault that your husbands died. They were damn lucky, if you ask me. You've been the light of my life this past year. I didn't really live until I met you. I hate to say it, but I'm glad Bernice was brought to the hospital, even more glad that I was able to save her life and give her a few more years of happiness. That's what I want for us, to live the rest of our lives—however long that may be—together. As man and wife."

Phil got off the bed and stooped before her, literally on bended knees. He took her hand in his. "Toots, I want to marry you. I love you more than any woman I've ever known. I love Abby and Chris. I adore Mavis and Sophie. I'm learning to like Ida." He grinned up at her. "Now, can you put all that craziness out of your head and answer me?"

She stared down at him in a sort of bemused wonderment. *Is this guy for real?* she thought. *Yes, he is.*

And life was short. Too damned short for her past husbands, but Phil was right. She hadn't caused their deaths. So much of her life during the past five years had been centered around death, and ghosts, and superstition. It's no wonder she'd started thinking of herself as a jinx. Phil was right. Life was too short *not* to live to the fullest.

She was going to start living in the present, and let the future bring what it may.

"Yes, Phil, I can do that."

"You really mean it?" Phil asked.

"Yes, I do, but I have one stipulation."

"Name it."

"I am going to be a grandmother, Phil. There is nothing that will take me away from my grandchild, so Myrtle Beach is out of the question for me."

"I've never been a grandfather, either. I wouldn't think of missing this opportunity. I've spent my entire adult life watching people die. I think it's high time I got to watch someone grow, from the ground up. Besides, I can write my novel anywhere. If you want to know the truth, I hate Myrtle Beach. I thought it would impress you if I told you that I was moving there to write my novel. I can write a novel in the bathroom, in the kitchen, or right here in the bedroom. It doesn't matter where I am, Toots. What matters is that you're beside me."

"You mean it? I don't want you to have any regrets. Remember, I have been around the block a time or two. Some men wouldn't want to get involved with a woman with my past, and one my age. You're not getting the pick of the litter, Phil. I just want to make sure you have absolutely nothing to regret later."

"As long as you're with me, beside me, I can assure you that I will have no regrets. Toots, I am a man of my word. I love you, and I want to be a grandfather to Abby's child. That is, if she'll allow me to. I knew the minute I saw you in the hospital that you would have a major role in my life. Don't ask me how I knew, I just did. Pure and simple. I saw you, and thought, 'That's her.' "

Toots's heart flip-flopped, then did a backward handspring, she was sure, because it felt like it was going to explode with happiness. It was even better than she'd imagined. Her heart was light; and she felt like she wanted to jump up and down like a kid. And she would later, when no one was around.

"Then I say, let's tell the folks downstairs good night. And you can stay over if you want."

Chapter 27

At promptly 8:15 AM, the crew from Colorado arrived courtesy of an airport limousine van Abby had made arrangements with when animals were to be transported from the airport.

Dr. Carnes was due to arrive around noon. Last night, Phil had promised to pick her up at the airport.

The three vet techs waited in the intake room, the building closest to the house. There were three cats—one terribly burned, another suffering from dehydration, and the third, a tabby kitten, wore an oxygen mask due to smoke inhalation.

The two dachshunds, a brown male and an adorable black-and-brown female, were the most critically injured of all the animals. Dr. Gary Wright and his wife, Susan, both from Wright Medical Center, a local animal hospital, checked the two dachshunds as soon as they were brought in. The other three dogs, an older golden retriever, a black Labrador, and a mixed breed, weren't in bad shape considering what they'd been through. Right now, they needed food, shelter, and, most of all, love.

For the first time in weeks, Abby didn't feel sick, and she was thrilled because this was her first official day in action as owner and operator of Dogs Displaced by Disaster, or

3Ds as she referred to her organization. Dr. Wright took charge as soon as the animals' immediate needs were met by the volunteers. Today her volunteers consisted of her mother, Sophie, Goebel, Mavis, and Wade. Ida and Daniel were spending the day with Bernice and Robert. Jamie and Lucy had promised to stop by with the homemade dog treats as soon as the bakery closed. For safety purposes, Chris was in charge of Chester, Coco, and Frankie at the house.

The two dachshunds were brought into the state-of-the-art surgical suite Abby had spared no expense to furnish. "Do you think these little doxies will ever walk again?" Abby asked while Dr. Wright examined them.

"I can't say for sure, since we don't know how long they've been injured. What I can say is, if there is anyone out there who can save them, it's Michelle Carnes. She's the best there is. You were lucky to get her."

"I know. She saved my mother's dog. Well, not really her dog . . . Dr. Carnes performed a miracle with Frankie. We didn't know how long he'd been injured, either. The owners of the house died and he was left alone. We figure he fell. But that's how I came to know about Dr. Carnes. I haven't met her yet, but she'll be here around noon."

"That should give me enough time for the MRIs. You really have equipped this place with the best," Dr. Wright told her.

"Thanks to you and Susan. I wouldn't have had a clue if you both hadn't advised me," Abby said. "Can I help here?"

"Sure. Grab a couple vet techs and tell them we're ready to get started with these little weenies. I'm not a neurosurgeon, but I do know that the first thing we need to do is make sure that deep pain doesn't set in, or these little guys will never walk again."

As soon as the MRIs were completed and the results in,

Dr. Wright started a decompression treatment that would slow any further damage to the spinal cord until Dr. Carnes arrived to perform surgery.

Dr. Wright spoke as he worked. "I can't wait to meet her. I read on her Web site that she recently performed brain surgery on a baby panther at her hospital in Naples. I have been on Alligator Alley and have actually seen all the wildlife on and near the road. It's no wonder so many of them meet up with cars and human intrusions."

"She should be arriving soon. Dr. Becker is on his way to the airport now," Abby said, glancing at her watch, surprised at how fast the time had passed.

"I just think it's wonderful what you and Chris are doing here. I pray for your success, as animals have no greater allies than those humans willing to give of themselves. I know it cost a small fortune to equip this facility."

"We have a lot of private donors. My mother, for starters. Then, of course, my three godmothers all chipped in. Funding isn't going to be an issue, at least not yet."

Abby thought of her days at *The Informer,* her little ranch house in Brentwood. All of that could be sold, the funds put into 3Ds. And, of course, she couldn't forget the little one. She and Chris would set aside money for the baby, his or her education. No, as bad as the economy was, funding wasn't a problem at this stage.

"Well, you know Susan and I will do all that we can, free, gratis."

"I do, and I can't thank you enough," Abby said. "I'm going to check on the other dogs. Sophie and Goebel might need a hand. Just buzz me if there is anything you need." Abby walked over to the two metal cages, where both doxies were sedated. She reached in and rubbed the brown guy's long ears. She could have sworn the dog smiled at her. The black-and-brown pooch was awake. She reached inside the cage and rubbed her little black head. "You're gonna be okay, little girl, I promise." Abby's heart broke for these poor animals. Thankful she was able to help in a small way, she closed the cage and went in search of Sophie and Goebel.

Abby found the lovebirds in unit two. "Hey, how's it going?" She spied the three dogs, who were each splayed out on the giant dog beds.

"They're not bad, considering. The vet techs just left. Said these furry friends just needed a little bit of tender loving care." Sophie's gentle side showed as she worked with the dogs.

"Soph, I know this is probably stupid to ask, but those little doxies that are having surgery, do you, you know, have any insight into what their status is? Recovery-wise."

"Where are they now?"

"They're being prepped for surgery. I just left them. They're sedated right now."

Sophie stared at the three dogs on the beds. "These guys are gonna be just fine. One of their owners will come for them, the golden. The others, they'll be adopted. Good homes, too. Can I see the dachshunds? I might be able to get a take on them if I see them."

"Goebel, you okay here on your own for a few minutes?" Abby asked.

"Heck yes. Best day ever. Second-best day ever. I'm loving this, go on. Let Sophie do her thing."

Abby and Sophie slipped inside the surgical unit. Careful so as not to disturb them too much, they tiptoed across the newly tiled floor to the wall where the surgical cages were. Sophie grinned. "Look at the ears on this one." She stuck her finger through the door, touching the paw where the IV had been placed. She closed her eyes and stayed that way for a minute.

In the next cage, she did the same thing. Sophie smiled again; then she whispered to Abby, "I want to talk to that surgeon as soon as she arrives. There could be some complications with this one if I don't tell her something about a disc. There's something loose."

They left the surgical unit and returned to find Goebel snuggling on the floor with the dogs. "I think he likes the dogs, Abs," Sophie said.

"It sure looks that way. Now, tell me the truth, what kind of vibes did you get on those two?"

"They're both going to recover. The little female will need some extra therapy, but they'll both walk, and your mother and Phil will adopt them."

Abby's jaw dropped. "Are you pulling my leg, or are you really telling me you know what the future holds for those two?"

Goebel laughed. "Abby, you should know better than to question Sophie."

Abby nodded. "True. So they're gonna be okay?"

"Yes, they are. I promise. Don't ask me how I know this stuff, I just do. It just comes to me like a thought."

Abby wanted to ask her about her pregnancy, if she knew the sex of her child, but something held her back. Sophie was very accurate. Abby wasn't so sure that she wanted to know her child's gender before he or she was born. That seemed like it took all the fun and mystery out of the pregnancy. Just this morning, she and Chris had discussed possible names: Jonathan Christopher for a boy and Amelia Sophia for a girl. (Abby informed Chris that Amelia would be known as Amy.)

"I believe you, Sophie. Now it's about time for Phil to return with the great Dr. Carnes. You two okay here for a while longer? Mavis and Wade are with the cats. I'm going to peep in on them real quick before the surgery. And, Sophie, do me a favor, okay?"

"Anything your little heart desires," Sophie said as she joined Goebel on the floor.

"First of all, stop being so damned nice. It's not like

you. And secondly, if you get any visions, or have any sudden thoughts about my baby, the pregnancy, please promise not to tell me. I want to be surprised."

"Oh, Abs, I won't do that. Truthfully, I haven't picked up on any vibes since you told us about the baby. Maybe this is something I shouldn't know. But if I get anything at all, I promise to keep it to myself."

"Thanks, I appreciate that. Now I need to get out of here. Hey"—when she got to the door, Abby turned around—"I'm super happy you two bought 'the purple palace.' It's going to be great having another married couple as neighbors."

Sophie laughed out loud, and Goebel raised his bushy eyebrows up and down, Groucho Marx style. "Thanks, kiddo, now get outta here," Goebel said.

Abby arrived at the surgical center the same time as Phil and Dr. Carnes. "This is Abby, the woman who made all this possible," Phil said, introducing them.

"I can't thank you enough for coming. I've heard so much about you, and all that you do for animals. Little Frankie is thriving, too."

Dr. Carnes was adorable, Abby thought. Probably close to Abby's age, she wore her deep red hair in a casual ponytail. A spattering of freckles dotted the bridge of her nose, and her smile was as bright as the moon. She wore blue jeans and a T-shirt that read ANIMALS ROCK.

"It's my pleasure, trust me. This is what I live for, these little pooches. I guess we should get started. The sooner I can get in there and fix them up, the better chance they have of a full recovery."

"Before you start, our resident psychic, Sophie Manchester, whom you may have heard about in connection with the rescue of two children who were kidnapped here in Charleston, and the breaking up of the largest child-pornography ring in the state, wanted to tell you something she picked up about one of the pooches. I'll send her into the surgery to speak to you.

"Then I'm going to leave you both to work your magic. Dr. Carnes, Dr. Wright, thank you both. You're really helping me make my dreams come true," Abby said, and realized she meant it. No longer worried about chasing the next celebrity story, she was totally at ease with her new career.

She'd been in such a hurry, once she saw that Dr. Carnes had arrived, that she hadn't stopped in to check on her felines. After telling Sophie to alert Dr. Carnes about the disc, she went into unit number four, where she found Mavis and Wade sitting watch over the cats as they rested in their cages. The doors were open, just in case the animals wanted to move. Abby didn't want them locked up unless it was absolutely necessary for their safety and the safety of the staff.

"Abby, you look wonderful this morning. I take it you're feeling good," Mavis said.

"Thanks, I am. Actually, I feel better today than I have in a while. I don't know if it's because I know I'm going to be a mother, or this." She gestured toward the cat cages. "But whatever it is, I'm totally loving it. Add that I didn't barf this morning, and I'm sure that accounts for some of my good cheer. I just wanted to check the kitties."

Abby went to their cages and fluffed their soft fur. The kitten mewed at her touch. She wasn't sure if it was a male or a female, but whatever its sex, she thought the kitten adorable. Gray fur and bright green eyes. This little one would be fine, she knew, because it had perked up as soon as it was fed and had a chance to bathe when the oxygen mask was removed. The cat with the burns was sedated. Dr. Wright said it was best because the first few days would be miserable. The pain meds would help, but the biggest adjustment for this cat would be the collar it would have to wear as soon as it was able to move around. This, Dr. Wright said, would prevent it from licking its wounds.

"They're all so quiet. My neighbor in Atlanta had a cat. It was a male, and, I swear, he had the loudest meow I'd ever heard. His name was Harvey," Wade said.

"Well, we can only hope these girls or guys make a full recovery so they can meow as loud as Harvey. Dr. Wright seems to think they'll make a full recovery."

"Yes, she was just here. What a lovely young woman. So pretty and kind. We're fortunate we have them," Mavis said in her sweetest voice. "Are you sure Chris doesn't mind watching Coco and Frankie?"

"Not at all. Chester is having the time of his life, I'm sure. No worries there. You two mind staying for another hour or so? I have another group of volunteers coming in this afternoon."

"We can stay as long as you need us to," Wade said. "This is fun. Put me down as a daily volunteer. It will be a pleasure. Plus, it'll give me a few much-needed hours away from Robert. He and Bernice need some alone time anyway."

They all laughed.

"Okay, then, I'm going to check on Mom now. She's in the office. I'll see you two later."

In unit three, Toots was busy answering the phone and taking messages. She had a pile of pink slips waiting for Abby as soon as she walked through the door. "You're going to have a zoo here if the phone calls are any indication. We've got more animals coming in tomorrow. Two cats and a rabbit."

"A rabbit, huh? Well, we are prepared to take in almost any animal. Dr. Carnes is in surgery now. Sophie says the doxies will make a full recovery." Abby dropped down in one of the plastic chairs. "She told me this earlier. I believe her, too."

"You should, as she's rarely wrong."

"Mom, did Phil spend the night last night?" Abby asked.

"Yes, he did, and that's all I'm telling you," Toots said with a grin. "Neither of us got much sleep."

"Hmm, that explains the glow on your face and the gleam in your eyes."

"Let's talk about the baby. I don't want to speak of sex in his or her presence."

"Just exactly how do you suppose this baby came about? The stork? A magic rock? Come on, Mom, give me a break. This kid was conceived in a lot of love. Don't go getting all old-fashioned and grandmotherly on me. I want you to be yourself. Though I don't want to be near you when you smoke. Sophie either. And I will not let you smoke around the baby. Or kiss him or her if you've smoked."

"Abby! I wouldn't dare do that, and Sophie either. I can't believe you would say that."

"Oh, shit, Mom, come on. I know you won't. I'm a mother now, too. We have to say this stuff, right?"

Toots chuckled. "I suppose you're right. I thought you would at least wait until the baby arrived. Have you made an appointment with the doctor yet?"

The phone rang. Toots took down all the required information, then ended the call. "A rooster and one hen. Tomorrow. Now answer me. Did you schedule an appointment with your OB-GYN yet?"

"Mom, I just found out I was pregnant last night. Today is a big day for 3Ds—so, no, I haven't called the doctor, but I will later this afternoon. I promise."

"Good. I just want you and my grandbaby to be healthy, that's all. Abby, there's something I need to tell you. I want you to hear it from me and keep it to yourself. You can tell Chris."

"Okay, sure, whatever you want. What is it? I know you didn't tell Phil about your 'wicked' "—Abby made air quotes with her hands—" 'past' because you slept with him. So, what's to tell?"

"Phil asked me to marry him."

Abby looked at her mother, then said, *"And?"*

"Well, that's all. I just wanted you to know. I haven't accepted, but it's something I am considering. Now, I know I said there would never be a number nine. But I've eaten my words so many times, it's a miracle that I haven't choked on them. Just whatever you do, don't say this to Ida. I plan to tell Sophie and Mavis, but not now."

"I can't say I'm surprised. Phil has it bad for you. I knew that when I met him in California. *L-O-V-E* was written all over his face then."

Toots shot her daughter the bird for the very first time.

Both cracked up laughing. "Mom, you can't do that, either. I don't want my son or daughter thinking the bird is a proper form of communication."

"Did I do that to you when you were little?" Toots asked.

"Not that I recall."

"Well, I do, and I didn't. I don't know how that got started." Toots paused, then continued. "As a matter of fact, I do remember how that got started. It was *Sophie*! In the seventh grade. We'd just met—it was our first day of school. Seventh grade at St. Mary's, what fun we had. Anyway, Sophie was in math class, and we were seated next to each other. Sister Theresa was our math teacher. Meaner than a snake, too. She'd called on one of the girls, and she wasn't one of the brightest kids in the class. I can't remember what she asked her, but the girl didn't know the answer. The sister kept at her until the girl started to cry. I'm sure she was embarrassed. As a mother, I would have asked that she be removed from that class, but I wasn't a mother then. Sophie, being Sophie, raised her hand, and, of course, she spoke before she was called on. She said she knew the answer to the mathematical question. To this day, I don't remember what the answer was, though I'm sure Sophie does. Long story short, Sophie stuck her middle finger high in the air and kept repeating, 'It's number one. It's number one.' Most of those in class knew that wasn't the answer. Later, I asked her if she wanted the correct answer. She looked at me as though I'd lost my mind. Told me she knew the correct answer, but I was as stupid as the teacher. It was then that Sophie explained the middle finger meant 'fuck you.' And that's how it all started."

"Amazing what a good piece of ass brings out in one's mother," Abby said, and then burst out laughing. "I swear you are an ornery old woman!"

"I am, aren't I?"

"Yes, you are, and I wouldn't have you any other way. You're a fantastic mom, and a sneak."

" 'A sneak'? Why would you say that? You obviously know I've slept with Phil. I am not hiding it. I just don't want Ida knowing."

"Not that. I'm talking about your buying *The Informer,* keeping it a secret for as long as you did. I think that was pretty darn sneaky, but in a good-way sneaky. Josh is doing a fantastic job. He e-mails me daily."

"Yes, that was pretty sneaky, but we're over that, right?"

"Mom, you know I was okay with your buying the paper. I thought it was the greatest thing—well, one of the greatest things you've done for me. I'm glad you did. Ever think of selling out?"

Toots doodled on a pad of paper that had cat and dog heads on the border. "Not seriously. Maybe later when I have time on my hands, but for now I plan to let you and Josh make all the decisions. Of course, if you want me to sell out, I will."

"It doesn't matter to me anymore. I'll always have the newspaper business in my blood, but now I want to focus on 3Ds and my pregnancy, and Chris. I guess what I'm trying to say is, it wouldn't bother me one way or the other. It's yours to do with as you please."

The phone rang again. Toots answered, took the required information, then resumed her conversation. "Like I said, when I have the time to really sit down and weigh the pros and cons, I will. Until then, I'm happy being here with you and Chris."

Dr. Wright, the female half, stopped in the office. "I just wanted to let you know the surgeries are finished. Both dogs came through with flying colors. The female had a little problem. There was more disc damage than what showed up on the MRI, and it was fortunate that Ms. Manchester warned us about potential disc problems. Dr. Carnes seems to think she got the excess disc fluid out," Susan Wright explained.

"Wonderful! This is great. Can we see them before we go home?" Toots asked.

"Sure, but they're out cold. But sure, come on, and we'll go together."

Ten minutes later, they all remarked over the perfectly straight incision Dr. Carnes had made on the dachshunds' long spines. Both dogs were expected to make a full recovery.

"It's time for the second round of volunteers. Why don't we all head to the house. I could use something to eat and a glass of ice tea."

All three doctors agreed.

"I'll see you at the house. You can come in through the back door," Abby said.

Twenty minutes later, an exhausted group of animal lovers and professionals met in Abby's formal dining room, where she served them ice tea, along with ham-and-cheese sandwiches.

Dr. Carnes's return flight had been canceled, but much to her surprise, she received an emergency call from

Naples. "I need to get back to Florida as soon as possible. I've got another dachshund with back troubles."

"Give me ten minutes and I'll have a Flexjet waiting to take you home," Abby said.

Forty-five minutes later, Dr. Carnes was on a private jet heading home to Naples.

Finally, at the end of a very long day, everyone gathered at Toots's house for dinner. Bernice and Mavis spent the evening cooking and baking. Robert directed them and read the recipes as needed.

All in all, it ranked high on Toots's growing list of the best days ever.

Chapter 28

"You're sure I don't look like a slut in this dress," Sophie asked Toots.

"No, you look like a cheap two-dollar hooker, you slut."

"Bitch," Sophie shot back.

"You two, stop it right now. It's Sophie's wedding day. You both should show some respect. I bet Goebel isn't cussing and carrying on with the guys. You look like a fairy princess in that dress," Mavis said.

"Well, I am a *godmother*, so why not add *fairy* to the title? And I'm sure Goebel isn't cussing, either. He's probably worried about his sore back. He's really worked his ass off on the lawn. Poor guy probably hated to stop just to run and get hitched. The painters are supposed to finish the outside today. I told Goebel that was our wedding gift to the neighbors. I don't think I could stand another day of that purple shit."

"Sophie, watch your mouth," Mavis reminded her.

"Kiss my old ass, Mavis. I plan to cuss like a sailor today and smoke like a locomotive. It's my wedding day— I can do whatever I damn well please."

Mavis smiled and shook her head. "Oh, I suppose you're right, but once that justice of the peace arrives, I wouldn't cuss too much. Don't they have the power to arrest people?"

"Oh, Gawd, Mavis. You're as naive as a newborn babe," Ida said. "Of course, they can't arrest you." Ida looked like the famous cosmetic queen that she was. Her skin was as smooth as a pearl; her hair sleek and straight. She'd applied her makeup, and looked as glamorous as a Hollywood starlet. She wore a pale peach skirt and matching silk top. Her shoes matched, too.

"Yeah, you better hope not! Because if that's the case, Ida, you're liable to be arrested for robbing the cradle." Sophie cackled as Toots zipped her dress.

"You're just jealous," Ida replied smartly.

"I don't think so. Daniel is a great guy—I'll give you that. I just don't see what he sees in your *old* ass. Bernice hates you, you know that, right?" Sophie barked. "She really thinks you're too old for Daniel. We all do."

"That's not true, Sophie, and you damn well know it," Toots interjected. "I've said a million times, if they're happy with one another, so be it. 'Love the one you're with.' My sister-in-law Mary used to tell me that."

"And you took it to heart. Eight times," Ida answered in a singsong voice.

"Oh, fuck off, Ida. I think you're still pissed because I married Jerry, and he left me all that cold, hard cash."

They all laughed, even Ida. The subject of Jerry had been a longtime war between them. Ida swore Toots stole him away. And Toots swore that Ida was just jealous.

"I'm over it, trust me."

"Then get your ass over here and fix my face. Toots, you watch her just to make sure she doesn't paint tits and dicks on my forehead."

Ida had her case of "magic," as she called it, with her. They were all upstairs in Toots's bedroom. As promised, Toots had planned every single detail for Sophie's wedding day, right down to the silk panties the bride wore. Toots was a pro at weddings, too. Mavis had sewn her dress, a low-cut cream-colored sheath that fit Sophie like a glove.

"I ought to paint your face like Bette Davis's in *What Ever Happened to Baby Jane?* All that lipstick outside the lip line. Eyeliner so thick it covered her entire creepy eyelid. I laugh every time I see that movie."

Sophie perked up. "Me too. I like the scene where she throws her sister down the staircase and feeds her the dead bird."

"Sophie, you're much more nasty than you've been in a while," Toots commented as Ida did her eyes.

"Yeah, I've been too nice. Now that I've found a man to marry me and take care of me, I've decided to revert back to my normal behavior."

"Be still, or I'll poke your eye out," Ida said as she expertly lined the not-so-blushing bride's eyes.

"You're just happy because you know you'll be getting laid for the rest of your life," Toots added.

"Like you're not," Sophie challenged.

"Tell it to the world, why don't you! Yes, Phil and I are screwing. Damn near daily. My twinkle is sore 'cause we've gone at it so much. Best piece of ass I've ever had. And Phil doesn't need Viagra or a pecker pump. Is that enough detail for you?"

"What the fuck is a 'twinkle'?" Sophie asked, laughing so hard that Ida had to stop lining her eyes.

"Yes, I'd like to know that, too," Mavis said. "I've never heard of that before."

They all turned to stare at Mavis.

"It's her thing, Mavis," Sophie said bluntly.

It took a minute for Mavis to understand what they were referring to. When she finally comprehended, her face turned bright pink. "You girls are so . . . nasty. Promise me you won't say these things in front of Wade. It would embarrass him to no end."

"We promise, okay? Now let's hurry up and get this

show on the road. I want a cigarette before I head down the aisle. Hell, maybe I'll let one dangle out the side of my mouth as I'm walking down the aisle. What do you think, Ida? Classy or trashy?"

"I think it's *so you,* Soph. That's what I think," Ida said as she made the finishing touches to Sophie's makeup. "Now look in the mirror and tell me what you think."

Sophie whirled around to see Ida's artistry. "Classy, Ida. Very classy."

And it was. Ida had enhanced Sophie's dark features without making her look made-up. Toots inspected Ida's handiwork. "You look like Sophia Loren, only better. On the other hand, the Italian bombshell does have bigger boobs."

Sophie flipped Toots the bird.

"Did I tell you I told Abby the middle-finger story? She'll be a mother soon. She needs to be prepared for things like that. Kids learn quickly these days."

"Spare me the details, I was there. Now come on"—Sophie looked at the new Rolex on her wrist, a gift from Ida—"it's time for me to get hitched."

"Wait!" Toots called out before they left her room. "We need to do something to mark this as an extra special day. For Sophie."

They all knew what Toots referred to. It had been their special way of acknowledging momentous times in the past. They'd started the tradition in the seventh grade and continued it as adults. No one said a word, as each knew what to do.

Toots held out her right hand. Mavis placed her hand on top of Toots's. Ida placed her hand on top of Mavis's; then Sophie added her hand to theirs.

"On the count of three," Toots instructed. "One, two, three!"

" 'When you're good, you're good!' " They tossed their hands high in the air. This was the secret handshake, meaning everything that happened among the four stayed among them.

"Now, let's not keep my future husband waiting. You girls ready?"

"Let's go," Toots said, and led the other three downstairs.

Toots had arranged for a pianist and violinist to play music on the back lawn, where Abby and Chris had married. Sophie had wanted a simple wedding, but Toots had to add something special, hence the musicians. All of Sophie's favorite flowers were placed in giant urns along the pathway that led to the splendid garden. Giant oak trees provided shade. The gardenias were in bloom, and traces of night-blooming jasmine still lingered in the afternoon breeze. At the end of the path, Toots had placed a simple archway made from bits and pieces of wood from Sophie and Goebel's new home. Goebel had given them to her, asking her to do something special with them, as he wanted something sentimental to add to the ceremony. She'd hired a team of Charleston's best carpenters. Their work was perfect. Mavis and Abby wove flowers from all the gardens through the spaces provided. Toots thought it resembled a wild tree of sorts, with wildflowers growing randomly from its branches.

Jamie and Lucy had insisted on making the wedding cake. Of course, Toots agreed. It was a surprise gift from the girls. She'd seen it this morning when Jamie delivered it. Sophie had been forbidden to enter the kitchen until the cake was out of sight. It was a fantastic cake. Naturally, Jamie insisted on making Goebel a groom's cake, and it, too, reflected his personality.

As they'd practiced, they waited at the bottom of the stairs. Toots was the maid of honor, and Ida and Mavis acted as bridesmaids. Sophie refused to make them wear traditional gowns, so they spent an afternoon shopping for dresses. They all agreed on something peachy, but it didn't have to match; nor did the designs have to be the same. Sophie was as unique as they came and deserved a one-of-a-kind wedding. Ida sprang for the peach shoes, but Toots and Mavis opted for taupe-colored sandals.

And now, with nothing left to do, Toots gave the signal to the pianist and violinist. "Close to You," performed by The Carpenters, was one of Sophie's favorite songs when they were young. Toots thought it appropriate that this should be the first song played.

Sophie raised her eyebrow at Toots, surprised by the music. "Shhh, it's my gift to you."

Sophie nodded and tried not to cry. This was too perfect a day, nothing like her last marriage. She quickly shoved those thoughts aside, as she didn't want any bad memories to touch the magic of her and Goebel's day.

Ida followed Toots down the path to the archway. Then came Mavis. Sophie blinked back tears, and as soon as Mavis took her place next to Ida, the traditional version of the bridal march echoed softly through the garden as Sophie made her way down the path to meet and commit herself to the man of her dreams.

When she reached the archway, the tears flowed, and she didn't try to stop them. Goebel, dressed in a light gray suit, with a peach silk shirt, looked handsome and debonair. His eyes were moist when he gazed into hers. "You look beautiful," he said.

Music continued in the background while the justice of the peace read the vows that Sophie and Goebel wanted. Simple, and sweet, filled with love. Sophie gave Goebel a simple gold band; he placed a matching band on her hand. Then the justice of the peace said, "I now pronounce you man and wife. You may kiss the bride."

Everyone clapped when Goebel dipped Sophie, then brought her up for a long, passionate kiss.

"May I present Mr. and Mrs. Goebel Blevins," announced the justice.

Again, they all clapped and threw birdseed as they retraced their footsteps up the path and inside the formal living room, where Toots had had all the furniture removed and small tables, with peach-colored tablecloths, placed strategically, allowing half of the room to act as a stage and dance floor. The pianist and violinist were for the ceremony only. Toots had hired one of the best local bands in Charleston to entertain them. They played 1960s rock and everything in between. Sophie would love them.

For the next three hours, they danced until their clothes clung to them. The men ripped off their ties; the women tossed their shoes. The champagne flowed freely. Goebel and Sophie were excellent dancers. They bopped to Marvin Gaye's "I Heard It Through the Grapevine," and Creedence Clearwater Revival's "Proud Mary," then slowed down to the sexy, soulful tunes of Al Green. The band, The Mimics, did just that. The music was excellent and enjoyed by all.

Bernice and Robert danced to Wilson Pickett's "In the Midnight Hour"; Mavis and Wade tore a rug to Martha and the Vandellas' "Dancing in the Street." Toots and Phil swayed to Sam Cooke's "Bring It on Home to Me." Abby and Chris took their turn dancing to Lady Gaga, The Beatles, and some songs that only they knew the names of. Jamie and Lucy alternated dancing with Daniel and Chris. Ida wrapped herself around Goebel more than once, but Sophie didn't say a word. He was her husband, and Ida could flirt all she wanted. Actually, Sophie told Toots she thought it a bit flattering that a woman as hot as Ida showed an interest in Goebel. She made Toots swear on her tits that she would never repeat those words to Ida. If so, Ida's head would swell to the size of the Goodyear Blimp.

When Jamie brought the cake out, Sophie cried. It was an exact replica of her and Goebel's house, minus the purple. Lucy had painstakingly decorated it right down to the last detail. No, it wasn't a traditional wedding cake, but Sophie was anything but traditional. She didn't want to cut the cake when it came time, but Jamie promised to make another just like it when they finished the renovations.

As the evening wore on, and everyone started to wind down, Sophie dragged Toots outside for a smoke. "Toots, I don't know how to thank you. This is simply the best night of my life. Well, almost. I'll have to wait and see how Goebel performs tonight."

Toots lit the smokes, handing one to Sophie. "I don't want to hear those details. I just want you to be happy, Soph. Goebel's a good man. You're very, very lucky."

Sophie took a long drag from her cigarette. "I am, and so are you. Phil's running neck and neck with Goebel. You know that, right?"

Toots smiled. "I do."

"When are you gonna say those words to Phil? Have you decided?"

"No, not yet. There's no rush. I don't want to make any drastic decisions until Abby has the baby. After that, well, I promise to think about it. Phil started his outline for his novel. You should have seen the way his face lit up when he was telling me the plot. I have a sneaking feeling he's going to be successful in his new career. How about it, Soph? Any insight into our future?"

Sophie sighed. "You really want to know?"

"Yes, but not if it's bad. I've had way too much bad in the man department."

She took Toots's hand and held it for a few minutes, then squeezed it before letting go. "Okay, what do you want to know?"

Did she really want to know what her future held? A little, maybe. "Just a little bit of the highlights, the good stuff."

Sophie lit her second cigarette off the first. "I can tell you this and be one hundred percent sure. Phil Becker is the next Robin Cook, only better."

"No shit?"

"No shit. Promise me you won't tell him, Toots?"

"Why not?"

"If he knows, he won't be hungry. A writer has to be hungry, and the only thing that can feed his hunger is publishing a book. If Phil knows he's going to be successful going in, the drive and hunger won't be there to push him to write the best book he can. So don't tell him, or it might not happen."

"You're really seeing his future? Or are you just telling me what I want to hear?" Toots asked, and lit another cigarette.

"When have you ever known me to do that? In a psychic way."

Toots thought for a moment. "Never."

"Then there is your answer."

"It'll be hard not to tell him, but I don't want to ruin his chance for success. Anything else you see that I should know about? Anything good?"

Sophie grinned. "Toots, you're about to have more good than one person deserves. Now, I have a husband who's probably tired and horny. I can't thank you enough for making this day so special. You're a good egg, but you know that already."

They both stood up; but before they went back inside to join the others in the winding-down celebration, Sophie and Toots hugged each other. Then they both cried tears of happiness. When they were finished, they blew their noses on the hem of Toots's peach skirt.

"I'll pay for the dry cleaner," Sophie said.

Toots rolled her eyes, and they wrapped their arms around each other's waist, like they used to when they were in high school.

After everyone offered up best wishes and congratulations, Goebel took his bride home. Chris and Abby had a doctor's appointment the next day. Wade and Mavis were supervising the sign for their new funeral parlor, and Bernice and Robert planned to spend the day at 3Ds.

Ida hadn't shared her plans, but everyone knew she and Daniel would probably spend the day screwing in Bernice's house, which Daniel had moved into.

And that, in summary, was Sophie's wedding day.

Chapter 29

Six weeks later

Today Abby was having her second ultrasound. Because Chris was so excited, he couldn't stop pacing.

"Look, Chris, if you don't stop, you're going to wear holes in this antique rug."

Abby finished blow-drying her hair. She was beyond excited. The last time they'd tried to do the ultrasound, there was a glitch with the machine. Abby had been so upset, she cried. She was almost six months pregnant, and she'd yet to have the pleasure of seeing her son or daughter inside her womb.

She and Chris both decided last night they would ask the doctor to tell them the sex of the child. Both were betting on a boy, since Abby had blown up like a house in the past few weeks. Given that the baby kicked so much and so hard, she and Chris were sure she was carrying a future star quarterback in the NFL.

"Wanna bet on the sex?" Chris asked Abby as she applied her makeup.

"You're kidding, right?"

"No, I'm serious."

"What's the payoff?" Abby asked.

"I don't know. Give me a minute to think of something . . . good," Chris teased.

Abby knew he was referring to something sexual. "As long as it doesn't involve taking off my clothes."

"Shit, you're no fun. I was going to say the winner gets to spend an entire day in bed with the loser. But since you say no taking off clothes, I guess I'll have to come up with something else."

Abby finished her makeup. "And how, exactly, does that make the winner come out on top of the loser? Whoops, strike that question. Well, I'm sure you can come up with something equally enticing, Mr. Clay. Now, if you want to see this football player, we'd better get going. I don't want to be late. Remember, today is the grand opening for The Canine and Feline Café. I can't wait to see the place. Mom hasn't been too forthcoming with the details."

"She wants to surprise you," Chris said as they headed downstairs.

"I'm sure she does," Abby agreed.

They drove Abby's MINI Cooper, since Chris's new Jeep was in the shop for a recall repair.

Abby had chosen a female OB-GYN because she felt more comfortable with a woman who'd actually given birth. Dr. Logan had four children, so Abby felt confident she would be a compassionate doctor. She'd liked her immediately, and so had Chris. She was in her late forties, a graduate of Harvard Medical School. Abby wanted her baby to have the best care possible, and Dr. Logan fit the bill.

Her office was in downtown Charleston. Early afternoon, they had no trouble being stuck in traffic. When she'd moved back to Charleston, Abby had soon learned that the traffic had its moments here as much as it did in Los Angeles. To the good, the traffic jams didn't last as long here.

Chris found a nearby parking spot, and Abby was thankful. July in the South was hot and muggy. That part she did not like, and the summer months were when she missed living in Los Angeles the most. The weather was perfect there, year-round. But as her mother always said, "It is what it is." She suddenly had a flashback of that hot, claustrophobic closet in South Central LA. No, she'd live with the humidity.

A gush of cool air greeted them when they entered the Logan Professional Building. Abby sighed with relief. The air conditioner in the MINI Cooper needed to be recharged or something because it wasn't cooling as well as it used to. And that was another thing. She wanted to get a larger vehicle before she had the baby. Chester sat in the front, and there wasn't room in the back for an infant seat, so a new car was in order. Chester would understand. She smiled at the thought.

"What's so funny?" Chris asked as they entered Dr. Logan's office.

"I was thinking about getting a new car. Somehow, I don't think Chester will mind, as long as he has his treats. I always kept treats in the trunk when I was working. I never knew how long I'd be on a star stakeout. Chester was such a good sport. Do you think he'll be okay once the baby arrives?"

"As long as you do what Dr. Wright suggested, I'm sure Chester will do just fine with the baby."

"I'm sure he knows what he's talking about."

Abby had asked Dr. Wright what to do to prevent Chester from being jealous when the baby arrived. He'd advised her and Chris to let Chester be a part of everything, as though he were a sibling. Only, instead of showing him the baby's things, Abby should let him smell things, let him get the scent of all the new "toys" they were bringing home. Once the baby arrived, Chester would only have to get used to his or her scent, having already been introduced to the other possessions.

Once they were inside the office, Abby signed the sheet. The waiting room was packed, and she had a feeling she

and Chris were going to be here longer than they'd antici-
pated. She prayed that the ultrasound machine didn't fail
this time. She and Chris were so excited. She could feel the
baby move all the time now. Her stomach would stretch as
though she had a box of Mexican jumping beans inside
her. She didn't mind; she really wanted to enjoy every
minute of her pregnancy: the good and the bad. The nau-
sea had passed. That part she would have willingly done
without, but now she felt like a new and improved version
of her LA self. She ate three meals a day. She tried to get as
much sleep as she could, and she and Chris had started
taking Chester to her mother's house in the evening. She
got her exercise; Chester and Chris got theirs. Plus, she
was kept in the loop on her mother's and godmothers'
comings and goings. And it was nice to have a married
couple living in what used to be the purple house. Life was
good, she thought as she flipped through a copy of *Parents*
magazine.

"Abby Clay," the nurse called.

She looked at Chris. "That's me. Come on, let's go see
our son, the quarterback."

The nurse wore scrubs with storks flying in the air, holding a blanket with a baby in it. Abby couldn't help but
laugh. "The storks get 'em every time," the nurse said.

"I'll bet it does," Chris commented.

"I'm surprised we didn't have to wait longer," Abby
said as they followed the nurse through a maze of hall-
ways.

"You're here for the ultrasound. We do that in another
part of the office. Dr. Logan's partner is in today, so you
lucked out."

Dr. Logan's partner was her husband. And that was all
well and good, but Abby would stick with the wife.

"I guess so," she remarked, for lack of anything better
to say. She looked at Chris and made a face.

"Okay, here we are."

They entered a small, dark room. There were no windows, no decorations; just a countertop with a bottle of gel and a stack of paper towels. A single cabinet hung above the counter. To her right was a long table with the ultrasound machine positioned off to the side.

"If you'll remove your top, we can get started."

Abby looked over at Chris, who stood by the door. "I promise not to stare," he said to break the moment of awkwardness.

"You can put this on until the doctor gets here. The room is cold because of the heat the machine puts out." Abby did think the temperature on the chilly side. She took the paper top and placed it on the table. Turning her back to Chris and the nurse, who seemed to stare excessively, Abby unbuttoned her cotton blouse and wrapped the paper top around her before climbing on the examining table. "Chris, come here and sit with me." Abby scooted over close to the wall to make room for him.

"You're not allowed to sit there," the nurse told them.

"I'm going to sit here with my wife until Dr. Logan arrives. When she tells me to get up, I will."

"Sorry, I didn't mean to come off as bossy." The nurse stepped out of the room, allowing them a few minutes of privacy.

"I don't like her," Abby said. "I'm going to tell Dr. Logan to make sure I don't have to see her on my next visit. She's nosy, and I caught her staring at my boobs."

"Hey, I was staring at your boobs, too. Nice rack," Chris teased, knowing how much Abby disliked the term *rack* when referencing her breasts.

Thankfully, Dr. Logan made her appearance. "Sorry to keep you folks waiting. I had a little emergency I had to take care of. Now let's get started." The doctor pulled Abby's medical chart from a holder on the door. "Ann, you can go now. Dr. Logan needs you in the lab."

"Uh, sure," they heard her say from her position out in the small hallway.

"She's new," Dr. Logan said to explain her odd behavior.

She flipped through Abby's file, made a notation, and then placed it on the countertop.

"Okay, Mr. Clay, you can sit in this chair here." She pulled a rolling stool out from beneath the counter. "You'll want to sit so you can see everything we're doing. Abby, go ahead and remove your paper outfit, and we'll get started.

"I'm going to rub this gel on your belly. It's warm now. Used to be icy cold, but someone thought to invent a way to heat the stuff without destroying its purpose. Most likely, it was a woman," Dr. Logan said, grinning. She rubbed the warm gel all over Abby's belly, top to bottom and side to side. "Okay, now I'm going to use this." She held up the transducer probe. "This part sends and receives the sound waves and receives the echoes. It's kind of like the eyes and ears of the machine. I won't go into all the mechanics, but it's pretty simple. I'm going to push a little so we can get a clear image. You tell me if I'm pushing too hard or if you need to stop." Dr. Logan used her left hand to type on the keyboard; with her right hand, she ran the transducer across Abby's belly.

Anxious, Abby asked, "What's that beeping sound?"

"It's just the machine doing its job. There's nothing to be alarmed about. Try to relax."

Abby nodded. She was anything but relaxed. She gave Chris a nervous smile.

"It's okay, sweetie. I'm right here."

She nodded, letting him know she heard him.

"Okay, now comes the fun part." Dr. Logan moved the transducer slowly, with a bit more pressure.

All of a sudden, the room was filled with a loud, pulsing

sound. "What's that?" Abby asked, more alarmed than before.

"That's your baby's heartbeat. And the swishing sound is your amniotic fluid."

Tears fell from Abby's eyes. "Oh, my gosh, this is amazing."

"Okay, now I'm going to position the screen so both of you can see your baby."

Abby was so excited; her heart rate noticeably increased. "Don't be afraid," Dr. Logan said in a soothing voice. "This is the best part of my workday."

"I'll try," Abby said, a slight tremor in her voice.

Dr. Logan fixed the screen so that all three of them would be able to view it. She rubbed the transducer back and forth. "Look, there's the head," she said.

"Oh, my God, it's real!" Abby exclaimed. "I mean, I can see it! Chris, look! That's the head!"

He chuckled. "Indeed it is."

"Oh, wow," Dr. Logan said.

"What?" Abby asked. "Is everything where it should be? It's hard to tell." She stared at the image on the screen, saw her baby's head, but it was hard to make out the rest of its little body.

"Look closely." Dr. Logan ran the transducer over her belly and pointed at the screen. "This image is a bit awkward. It's a little hard to know what you're actually seeing, but I can tell you this." She pushed down a little harder, causing Abby to wince. "Sorry, but I need to push a little in order for you all to see what I'm seeing."

"I'm good," Abby said.

"This is the baby's head, as you can see, though over here . . ." She pointed to another part of the baby, which didn't look like a baby should look.

"Oh, my God, is something wrong with my baby?"

"Calm down, Abby. Your baby is perfect. It's just that

there seems to be two of them in there." She pointed to the other head, and Abby almost fainted.

"Does that mean what I think? They're twins? Oh, my gosh! Oh, my gosh! Chris, there are two of them. *Oh. My. Gosh.*"

"Yep, you're having twins. Congratulations, Mom and Dad. Now, do you want to know the sex? I saw a 'no-tell' mark on your chart. You're still good with that?"

"No! I want to know! Right, Chris? We want to know." Abby was so overcome with . . . She wasn't even sure, but it was a good thing—whatever it was.

"Yes, we want to know," Chris parroted.

"Well, it appears you've hit the baby lottery. I see a little boy and a little girl."

Abby broke down and cried. Chris went to her and held her in his arms, not caring about the machine or proper protocol. "We did good, huh? One of each. Hot damn. Sorry," he said.

"Hey, 'hot damn' all you want, Mr. Clay. You're the proud papa of a pair. Now let me take a few pictures for you to take home and brag about, and then we're through." She punched a couple of keys on the machine, then hit a button. "Let's get this gel wiped off. Then you can put your top back on." The doctor wiped Abby's belly with a warm, wet wipe; then she gave her one of the paper towels to dry her stomach. When Abby reached for her blouse, her hands were shaking badly. She couldn't do the buttons.

"Here," Chris said, and buttoned her up, but Abby saw a tremor in his hands as well.

"Here you go. Bragging material." Dr. Logan handed Abby a copy of the ultrasound. "Abby, I'll want to see you twice a month, since we've got double duty in there. Don't worry—it's normal. The babies' hearts are strong. They have two arms and two legs. Continue to do what you feel comfortable doing. If you feel extra tired, that's normal.

Up your intake of good fruits and veggies, and you're good to go. Doctor's orders."

She patted Abby's shoulder and shook Chris's hand. "Now go tell the world you're having twins."

Abby was in a complete and total daze. She scheduled an appointment for two weeks; then the next thing she knew, she was back in the car.

Both were quiet, needing the silence to allow them to take in the fact that they were going to have two kids. A boy and a girl.

"We'll have to double everything. Two cribs. Two bassinets. Two dressing tables. Two . . . Chris, can you believe this? I am so totally in love with you right now! I could cry, but I won't, because I'm too happy. I am going to be the mother of twins! One of each! How blessed we are."

"I know, baby, I know. This is the icing on top of the icing. Man, I can't wait to tell Tootsie. She'll have a fit. I can't wait to tell her so I can see the excitement on her face!"

"Oh, my gosh! We're supposed to go to the grand opening of The Canine and Feline Café!" Abby looked at the digital clock. "We're late."

"Somehow, I don't think anyone will care if we're late. Especially after we tell them our news."

"You're right. . . . You're right. I'm so emotional right now. I can't seem to think clearly. Yes, let's go to the café. There's really no reason not to, right?"

"Right," Chris said; then he reached for her hand. "You and I and our son and daughter are gonna be all right."

Twenty minutes later, they were parking in front of The Canine and Feline Café.

Chapter 30

Toots was beyond pleased with the turnout. She'd been advertising the grand opening for the past two weeks. Pets and their owners lined up to have a turn inside the café.

The architect who'd worked on the project with her had a clear vision of what she wanted to achieve, and now here Toots was in her new, little doggy-and-cat café, which had a line at the door that went around the corner. They were handing out Jamie's homemade treats for both dogs and cats. They hadn't come up with a recipe for farm animals yet. Jamie, however, had assured Toots that when the time came, she would do her research and figure out something for them, too. Both Dr. Wrights had volunteered to spay or neuter the animals for free. Their appointment book was already full.

"You might regret this," Toots said, indicating the long line.

"Never. We love it. It's what we do," the Mrs. Dr. Wright said.

As usual, Toots had enlisted what she now called "the gang" to assist her with the opening. Mavis, being a true people person, greeted the pet parents and their pets at the door. From there, they were allowed to bring the pets inside. However, because it was so crowded today, the animals had to wear a leash if at all possible. Bowls of water were placed in the grooves specifically designed for this purpose. Toots and her architect pal, Rona Grandy, decided this would be perfect, so the dogs wouldn't knock over the bowls.

People next signed up to have their pets neutered or spaycd. From there they were given a brief tour of the café. Toots was planning on holding a pet event each week. She and Abby had a list to choose from, ranging from photographs for the holidays to specialized training for all breeds of dogs and cats, and all ages. The fees were minimal, just enough to keep the doors open. This was not going to be a profit-making investment for Toots. She didn't care. The satisfaction on the faces of the pet parents and their animals was enough.

Chester, Coco, and Frankie acted as mascots. Goebel kept them on a short leash while the animals took the tour. Abby had printed hundreds of flyers to pass out, letting the public know that Dogs Displaced by Disaster was up and running. They continued to have a full house. Abby and Chris hired a permanent crew to maintain the facilities, and to take care of the animals. Local vets were standing in line to offer their services.

Sophie walked around the open space, acting like the Dog Whisperer. She told Toots she could home in on the animals' vibes, too. And Toots believed her. She said that some of the owners she saw didn't deserve the animals. Not that they were mean, just neglectful. Dogs needed to have interaction with their owners; Sophie said she could point out the jerks if Toots wanted her to. Toots declined, suggesting another time when the place wasn't so crowded.

Glancing at the clock, Toots saw it was late, and there was no sign yet of Abby and Chris. She wasn't too concerned about it. Her first thought was that they had probably gone out for lunch after the doctor's appointment and forgotten all about her grand opening.

Then Toots thought, *No, that isn't like either of them. They always call if they are going to be late or unable to make whatever event they've scheduled.*

Growing worried, she found Sophie. "Let me use your cell phone. Mine's in the back, in my purse."

"Sure," Sophie said, taking the phone from her jeans pocket. She was rarely without the phone since she and Karen had become Facebook and Twitter buddies. They'd agreed to tape a special sometime next year, but Sophie or Goebel didn't care about the missed opportunity. They were so busy with their new home; and Psychic Investigations was getting more calls each week. Sophie said that before you knew it, she'd have to hire a part-time psychic just to keep the business up and running.

Toots dialed Abby's cell. Abby answered on the first ring. "Mom, we're looking for a parking spot. We'll be in as soon as we find one."

"Fantastic, I was getting a bit worried."

"Long wait at the doctor's office. See you in a few," Abby fibbed, and ended the call.

"They're here, but they can't seem to find a place to park." Toots gave Sophie's cell phone back to her. "And that's a good thing. Look at the turnout. You'll have animals from the entire state of South Carolina waiting in line. This place rocks, you know that?"

"I do."

"What happens when you guys have a cow or a pig waiting to be seated?" Sophie asked.

"I already told you, this place isn't equipped for livestock. 3Ds will be taking care of that. I'm just hoping to attract the locals. People love their pets, yet a lot of places won't allow you to bring them inside. Not here. This is just for the little furry friends."

"I'm sure it will be a success. Everything you touch turns to gold, but you already know that," Sophie teased.

"Not everything. Remember that flying car I invested in? And the charcoal underwear? I lost my ass on those, big-time." Toots laughed at her play on words.

"Well, as far as I can tell, it looks like it's returned, only it's new and improved, bigger and better." Sophie laughed so hard, even her mascara started to run.

Toots wanted to flip Sophie off, but it would have to wait until they were alone.

Ropes, chewies, balls, KONGs, catnip, cat grass, all the things dogs and cats loved most were there for them to have fun with; and if they really liked a toy, it was theirs. Frankie had become very attached to a rag doll. He carried it everywhere. When Coco came close to it, he would growl at her. So Toots decided if the animals wanted a plaything, they would be allowed to keep it. No fights at The Canine and Feline Café. When they were officially open to the public, the display case would be filled with Jamie's homemade treats. Just as with The Sweetest Things, Jamie planned to do all the baking for the café. If the time came, and they needed to broaden the palates of the animals who came in, Jamie said she'd been experimenting with a new recipe for all-natural dog food. Toots had tried it out on Coco, who was very particular, and she loved it. Frankie scarfed it up so fast—Toots knew he never actually chewed the food. Chester wasn't too fond of it, but he was used to fine cuts of beef, such as prime rib and the occasional porterhouse steak. Abby took very good care of her men. Toots just knew she would be the best little mother ever. And speaking of the angel, there she was.

The doors opened. Toots was thrilled to see her daughter and son-in-law/stepson. Both wore mile-wide smiles.

"I take it the ultrasound machine was working today," Toots said as she hugged them.

"Double time," Chris said; then he winked at Abby. They'd agreed to tell everyone about the babies, but not here. Abby planned to invite "the gang," as her mom now called her dearest friends and their mates, over for dinner tonight. Nothing fancy, Chris said. He would grill burgers and hot dogs. They didn't think the menu would matter, once they told them their news.

"What a great turnout, Mom. This is way more than we expected."

"Yes, and I'm totally thrilled. I'm sure things will slow down, once the novelty of the place wears off, but we'll have our regulars, just as a regular café does. It's a great feeling, seeing all these people with their animals. I know why you decided 3Ds was right for you. The satisfaction is so worth it. So, what's the baby news? Were they able to see the baby? Are we having a boy or a girl?" Toots spoke so fast—well, Abby could hardly understand her.

"Mom, not here! Listen, Chris and I are having a cook-out tonight. We want everyone to come over. Then we'll tell you what the doctor said—and not even one hint before then. So don't even ask, okay? Six o'clock. Tell everyone to be there, please, please, please. And, yes, I know I sound like a five-year-old. I'm going to go and say hello to the Doctors Wright. Then we've got to go grocery shopping for the cookout. You will be able to make it at six, won't you? Aren't you closing at four today?"

"Did the doctor give you a shot of speed today? I haven't heard you issue orders so fast since you were the editor in chief at *The Informer.*"

"Sorry, I just have a lot to do. Now, Mom"—Abby kissed her cheek—"make sure you're at the house at six. Where's Phil? I want him there, too. You know Chris and I are crazy about him."

"Yes, and I'm glad, because he won't stop proposing, and I might have to say 'yes,' just to get him to shut up.

Keep that between us. Now you go on. Let me take care of my canine and feline clients, and I'll see you at six."

Toots, Mavis, and Sophie spent the next two hours petting dogs, kissing cats, and cleaning hair off their clothes. They didn't mind—they were having the time of their lives.

Chapter 31

Abby practically cleaned out the grocery store. She'd needed to stock up on a few things anyway. They fed the animals free-range chicken, and they'd been on sale, so Abby bought every one available and stuck them in the freezer.

They were putting the groceries away, when Chris said, "We shouldn't have made Toots wait. She was hurt, I could tell. This is her first grandkid, scratch that. These are her first grandchildren. We should have taken her aside. I feel like shit for not telling her."

"Chris, why didn't you say something? You're right. I'm just so damned gung ho that I want to share it with everyone all at once. Do you think it would be cheesy if I called Mom and told her over the phone?"

Chris stacked cans of peas in the pantry. "Yeah, I do, since you had the chance to tell her at the café, but it's up to you. You asked, and I answered."

Abby unloaded the shopping bags, thinking. "You know that old saying, 'There is no time like the present'? Well, I am calling Mother now. I don't care what she thinks of me. She can call me a rotten daughter later."

Abby used the house phone to call her mother's cell phone. It rang six times; then it went over to her voice mail. She wasn't going to leave *this news* in a voice mail.

"I tried, and she didn't answer. I need to grow up and act like the mother of two children, instead of acting like a child."

"Oh, sweetie, I shouldn't have said that. These are *our* children. We decide what to do. And that doesn't make us bad people. We're kinda new at this, too, remember? We've only known for a few hours. Toots won't say anything, and don't mention this to her. It'll just hurt her feelings more, if we haven't already. Now, how would you feel about slicing the tomatoes and onions? You do such a nice job, especially with the onions. You slice them nice and thin, just the way I like them."

"Chris Clay, you are such a butt kisser, but I would be happy to assist you in your unending and dedicated pursuit of culinary excellence."

"And you call *me* a 'butt kisser'!"

"Hey, I'm calling it as I see it, and, yes, I felt your mouth on my right butt cheek this morning."

Chris held up his hands. "Guilty! But you need to keep that cute little rear end of yours out of my face. It's dangerous when I wake up with that as my first glimpse of the day."

"You can't hold me responsible for what position my ass takes during the night."

"Whatever you say, *Mom,*" Chris teased.

"You got that right, *Dad.* It's going to sound so odd, you and I referring to ourselves as 'Mom' and 'Dad.' "

Chris placed the packages of ground sirloin in the sink in a bowl of cool water to get the last bit of ice off the edges. "We'll get used to it. We don't have a choice in the matter now."

Abby dropped the paring knife. "Chris, you're not sorry, are you?"

He rinsed his hands, then came up behind Abby and looped his hands around her belly. "Now, how could you think this would make me sorry? Sorry it didn't happen sooner, *not sorry* it happened. Abby, other than the day you told me you loved me and accepted my marriage proposal, there is nothing that pleases me any more than you and I starting a family. We've lucked out, too, because we're getting a twofer. It's like a buy-one-get-one-free special at the supermarket. I'm looking on the bright side early, because when I look at double education, double cars, double weddings, well, then I'm not so sure of everything. Abby"—he turned her around so that she faced him—"don't ask me this again. I am the happiest I've ever been. I have you, these two babies, Toots, and the gang. Now tell me, what more could a sane man ask for?" He leaned in and gave her a soft, slow kiss.

"After that kiss, a lot. But you invited the whole gang over, so we need to make sure we have something to feed them before we tell them the good news."

"Abby, surely you're not telling me that you're going to wait until *after* dinner to tell everyone. That's just too cruel, and I won't let you do it."

Abby placed her hand on her right hip and jutted the other out to the left. "Well, of course, *husband,* I will do exactly as you ask. 'Your command is my wish.' Or is that 'your wish is my command'? I forget," she said, sticking her tongue out at him.

Unable to keep a serious face any longer, she burst out laughing. "Ha-ha, I had you for a minute. And, no, I am not going to wait until after dinner to share our news. See, that way, if I eat two hamburgers and two hot dogs, it will be understood that I'm eating for two . . . well, three, if I count myself in the equation, and I am, so no one can say I'm overeating. See, Mr. Clay, I've got this all figured out."

"Oh, yeah, Mrs. Clay." Chris grabbed a warm tomato from the bag sitting in the windowsill and acted like he was going to throw it at her.

"You put that down right now! Those are for dinner."

Chris tossed the tomato on the table. "You win, this

time. Next time, I might not care if I waste a tomato. Now let's get a move on before everyone arrives."

"Okay, but I am after your ass later. Promise."

"I'll look forward to it," Chris said. "I'm gonna run upstairs and take a quick shower before they get here."

"I'll be waiting." Abby loved the way they teased each other. This silly bantering could go on for days, and it had, more than once. She finished slicing the onions, washed her hands, then washed the tomatoes and peeled them, too. When she finished that, she shucked the fresh corn on the cob and wrapped each piece in foil so "Cuisine Chris" could throw them on the grill. She had bought potato salad already made and a container of coleslaw. She opened the cans of baked beans, scooped them into a large baking dish, and added her special ingredients. A little dry mustard, a little brown sugar, a little chopped onion, and they were ready to slide into the oven.

Chris came downstairs, looking handsome as ever. He wore a pair of khaki cargo shorts and a blue chambray shirt, with the sleeves rolled to his elbow. Abby smiled. "Hey, you look pretty darn sexy for a farm boy."

"And you look pretty good yourself for a semiretired hack and mother-to-be. You have the pregnancy glow."

"Thanks, I certainly feel the glow. Now, 'Cuisine Chris,' that's today's nickname, by the way. I have the corn ready, and the baked beans are in the oven. You get to make the burger patties, while I run upstairs to shower and change. It's almost five-thirty, so we gotta get a move on."

"Okay, I'll get the door if they get here before you're out of the shower."

Abby ran upstairs—well, she kind of waddled—her belly was big and, as of today, she knew why. Not only was she carrying a little football player, but she had a cheerleader, too. She liked the image. Abby made fast work of showering, shaving her legs, and washing her thick, curly blond hair. She slathered her favorite gardenia lotion on, sprayed

Jennifer Aniston's latest flowery spray on her neck and wrists. As an afterthought, she ran into the room they were using for a nursery and found one of the containers of baby lotion. She took it back in the bathroom with her and rubbed it on her belly. And the babies. She wondered if they could smell while inside the womb. She'd ask Dr. Logan on her next visit in two weeks. She added a bit of blush and mascara, scrunched her curls, and headed downstairs.

Chris had everything ready, plus the dishes were now set in neat stacks along the table. This was going to be a buffet-style cookout.

A loud knock, and Abby knew that her mother had arrived. And her godmothers. She could not wait to tell them her news.

Chapter 32

Chester waited by the front door. "You must smell Coco," Abby said as she opened the door. "Mom, Phil, Sophie, Goebel, Ida, Mavis, Wade, Robert, Bernice, and Daniel, please come in."

They all laughed at her. "I can't have you talking behind my back, telling your friends I'm not a proper hostess. Let's go to the kitchen and get our glasses. It's nice out, so I've got the patio set up. Is everyone okay with that? If not, we can eat in the formal dining room. I think the table seats, like, thirty people."

"Abby, we're fine. Now you go outside and look at your husband, while Sophie and Mavis and Ida help me with the drinks. Guys, go out and talk grill talk with Chris. Goebel, he may need some help. I'm not sure he's ever grilled anything."

Ten minutes later, everyone had a drink of tea or something alcoholic, which Toots and Sophie had poured. When Abby saw that all the people who mattered most to her were there, she stood up. "Okay, folks, I've kept you all waiting long enough. All of you know, I'm assuming Mother told you, that today Chris and I were going for a repeat of the ultrasound, which did not work last time. Well, what we have not told anyone until now is that we found out we are having a little boy." Abby couldn't help it; she had to pause for effect. "And a little girl."

"Twins!" Toots jumped out of her chair and did the best rendition of the happy dance that they'd ever seen. When she finished, everyone clapped. "Phil, I am going to be a double grandmother, and you girls are gonna be double godmothers. Does that sound right to you, Abby?"

Abby stood in a receiving line of sorts as every single one of her friends and family hugged her, shook Chris's hand, and asked if they could babysit. A night out on the town, once the babies were old enough to be left alone, was not going to be a problem. She would have an endless supply of sitters if she needed them.

"Thanks, everyone. I tell you, I almost fainted when the doctor said that I was gonna have twins. Then when she saw there was one of each, I truly felt like an over-achiever."

"Hey, I had a hand in that, too. Tootsie, were there twins in my family?"

"Your mother had twin brothers, but they passed away when they were very young."

Abby dropped her glass when she heard what her mother said and raced inside. Toots followed her. "Abby, I'm sorry for being so careless. I wasn't thinking. Your children are fine, and that was a very, very long time ago. Those kids would be close to a hundred years old, had they lived. Remember how much modern medicine has improved? Abby, look at me."

Abby blotted her eyes with the dish towel.

"You're going to be the best mother ever. I can tell because of the way you just reacted. That's the hardest part of becoming a mother. You will learn this, but not for a while. I used to say that 'when babies are little, they step on your toes. When they're older, they'll step on your heart.' Now dry your eyes and get out there and help Chris serve up those burgers. I haven't had a good burger since the last time I ate at the Polo Lounge in California."

Abby shook her head. "I'm sorry. That's not me, or the me I was before I was pregnant."

"It's all right. You will be emotional. You're pregnant, and we all love you and promise to tread lightly. Deal?" Toots asked the way she had when Abby was younger, and they'd had a disagreement.

"Deal."

"Now go on. Those babies need their dinner," Toots said, feeling very protective of her daughter and grand-children. Seeing that she was alone for a moment, Toots jumped up in the air, twirled around, then shook her hips left to right.

"Now, that's a damned happy dance," she said aloud to herself.

Seeing that Abby had platters of food in the fridge, Toots took it upon herself to help serve. There was some-thing in the oven. She carried the potato salad and the coleslaw out to the table. "Mavis, there's something in the oven. Can you come in and help me out?" As soon as Toots said the word *help,* not only did Mavis come run-ning, but Sophie and Ida came, too. Tears glistened in her eyes. These women were family to her and Abby. Toots had been the only one to have a child, and she'd wished the others could. But they hadn't, and she had Abby, so she simply decided she would have three godmothers. And here they were now, friends from more than fifty years ago who now made up her family. They'd bitched and griped, laughed and cried; but when Toots needed them, they were always there. She hoped they felt the same way about her.

"Mavis, can you take care of the stuff in the oven? So-phie, bring some more ice and another pitcher of tea out, if you don't mind. Ida, could you grab the condiments in that container Abby has in the fridge?" Toots looked around.

"Okay, girls, I think we've got it all. Now let's go talk about our grandchildren-to-be."

Abby raced back inside. "Mom, I forgot to make the coffee. Bernice and Robert are ready to croak."

"Go tell them to kiss your ass, and I'll get a pot going. Even I can make coffee, but don't tell Bernice I made it. Let's see if she can tell the difference."

Toots raced around the kitchen, which had once been her own. Abby had put everything in the same places that she had. She must remember living here as a child. Toots filled the coffeemaker with water, added four heaping spoonfuls of Folgers, and clicked the START button. Five minutes later, she had a tray with a carafe filled with coffee, surrounded by cream and sugar. She had even remembered to bring the cups and spoons. Not bad for an old broad who didn't know how to cook anything except toast and Froot Loops, and Froot Loops didn't really count.

She carried the tray outside. "Did you make that coffee?" Bernice asked.

"No, I'm just helping out." Toots set the tray on the table. "Help yourself, Bernice. I'm sure Robert needs some sugar in his system. Abby has lots of sugar."

Bernice slyly lifted her middle finger when Toots was looking. She returned the salute and didn't care who was watching.

The evening turned out to be another for the books. The food was good, the burgers fantastic, and they'd all spent the remainder of the evening discussing babies, The Canine and Feline Café, and Abby and Chris's future hopes for Dogs Displaced by Disaster.

Mavis and Wade had their new jointly owned funeral parlor up and running. No one had died, so they hadn't had a chance to see them in action, and Toots wasn't in any rush. The fact they touched dead people, and Ida made them look alive, totally creeped her out. But the success Ida and Mavis had had was phenomenal. Mavis's new line of clothes, Good Mourning for Canada, had added another large number to her annual earnings. Though Mavis wasn't about the money at all.

When you got right down to it, none of them were about the money itself. They were all about what they *could do* with their money to help others. They really were providing a service to the world, especially Ida. Her cosmetic line was so popular that Macy's had offered her tens of millions to sell it in their stores, but Ida had stayed true to her original vision. She wouldn't sell out yet. Let The Home Shopping Club make a nice hefty profit; then she would consider the Macy's offer. She wouldn't forget the people who had given her a chance. Ida was loyal like that.

She and Daniel were a couple now, and no one cared. Not even Bernice, because Daniel was happy—so happy, in fact, that he had set up another office, in Charleston, so he could be close to his mother and their new family.

Toots liked the feeling of family they all shared. She and Abby were the only two out of the bunch who were actually related by blood, but it really didn't matter where you came from. What mattered was how you got there and who stayed for the ride. Sophie, Mavis, and Ida mattered to Toots. They were her family and her life as much as Abby was.

"Mom, are you dreaming or something? You have the strangest look on your face."

"No, I was just woolgathering, something people my age do now and then. Now it's getting late. I believe it's time we left and called it a night. We need to get some rest. Especially you, young lady."

Abby and Chris thanked everyone for coming. They, in turn, thanked Abby and Chris for the wonderful babies, and decided that their next project was Abby's baby shower.

"Good night, Mom."

"Get some rest. I'll call you tomorrow."

"I'll look forward to it. Thanks for listening to me and giving me the advice. I'm guessing there's a lot I'm going to need to learn from you and my godmothers. I'm so glad you're all here." Abby kissed her mother, and then pushed her out the door. "Go."

Toots laughed and chalked up another perfect day on her ever-growing-best-days-ever calendar.

Chapter 33

Two months later

Jamie and Lucy baked every baby-themed sweet that had ever been thought up, and some that hadn't. Blue-and-pink cupcakes, in the shape of baby booties, with white icing that looked just like shoelaces. A pink bonnet cake, a blue bonnet cake, both chocolate. A red velvet cake for Abby, iced in her likeness. Lucy's idea, and Toots thought it cute. When she saw the cake, she changed her mind. *It was beautiful,* and looked exactly like Abby. It was the mommy cake. Abby didn't want to invite any of the girls from 3Ds, saying that she wanted to spend this special day only with her family.

They'd all discussed gifts out of Abby's earshot, and she would have everything on her babies' wish lists, and then some. Toots wanted to make sure the children were financially taken care of for the rest of her life. She willed her Charleston home to Abby, Chris, and the kids. The Malibu mansion would go to the grandkids, too, but that wasn't a gift. There were additions to her will. She was a very wealthy woman, and her family would be taken care of. All of them seemed to have great financial success. They were all blessed, and Toots never once took that for granted.

The girls placed their pretty packages on—where else?—the dining-room table. Nearing the end of September, it was still too hot to sit in the garden, so Toots suggested that they have the shower in her living room, where it was nice and cool. The guys had wanted to do something for Chris, so they all chipped in and chartered a boat for the day to go deep-sea fishing. Toots couldn't wait till they came back so she could hear their fish stories.

Abby was almost the size of a house. A small one, to be sure. She had gained more than sixty pounds, but she was healthy. Most important, the babies were healthy, and her doctor was fine with her weight. Abby was due in two weeks.

Sophie and Goebel had decorated a nursery at their house for the babies. Wade and Robert followed suit because they were sure Mavis or Bernice might want to babysit with them at their house. Just a good way for Robert and Wade to get their hands on the kids so they could spoil them.

Ida had purchased a mansion on The Battery, but it wouldn't be livable until next year. She, too, had come to love Charleston. It was a beautiful city, with history and culture. When she wasn't staying at Bernice's old house with Daniel, she would stay in her room at Toots's. Mavis still lived with Toots, and she really didn't have any plans to move out. She said she and Coco had spent too many years living alone, so she was content to stay with Toots, and it worked for both of them. She was close to Wade, and Bernice and Robert traipsed back and forth from her house to their place at least once a day. Abby and Chris and Chester walked over in the evenings to share a glass of tea and tell her about their day.

Jamie and Bernice had decorated the room in blue and pink. Balloons, streamers, and party favors certainly made the room take on the look of a baby shower.

Chris drove Abby over before he left with the guys. It was too hot for her to walk, and she was waddling like a duck these days. She made herself comfortable in the big plush recliner, which Toots had purchased for Phil for the nights they stayed in and watched television. It wasn't too often, but Toots couldn't see Phil reclining on the antique settees and love seats.

The women spent the next three hours playing games, laughing at dirty jokes, and oohing and aahing over the tiny little dresses and little pants. Knowing how much Abby loved her UGGs, Toots had ordered pairs for the babies. One in blue and one in pink.

"Thanks, Mom, they're just adorable."

Sophie gave her a double stroller that did everything but give lectures on how to raise twins. "This is so cool. It'll make it so much easier to take the babies out in this." Abby blew Sophie a kiss, because it was too hard for her to get up and down from the recliner.

Mavis, the purest and kindest, had crocheted each baby a blanket, though she hadn't used the traditional pink and blues. One was the palest peach, and the other a light green: Mavis's colors.

Abby rubbed the blankets against her cheek. "They're so soft, and perfect. Thank you so much, Mavis. I know it took a lot of time to make these. I'll treasure them. And so will the babies."

Next up was Ida's package. Toots thought Ida would go all out and bring a gift the size of a car, but she simply handed Abby a small square package wrapped in yellow paper. *Classy,* Toots thought. *Even at a baby shower, Ida has class.* However, Toots would die before she ever told Ida that. They all had class, each their own special grade.

"Go on, open it," Ida encouraged. Abby took the paper off and placed it in a box on the floor. Ida had promised her she would make her something from all the bows, because Abby swore she would not let them force her to make and wear a paper-plate bonnet.

Abby removed two leather books, both a creamy brown. Engraved in gold were the names that Abby and Chris would give their baby: JONATHAN CHRISTOPHER and AMELIA SOPHIA. Abby looked inside the books, and her eyes doubled in size. "My God, Ida, I don't know what to say."

" 'Thank you' always works," Ida said as she made her way through the boxes and papers to get to Abby. She gave her a big hug, and Toots saw that there were tears in her eyes. *Damn it, but Ida is good people, too. She's just a self-centered–bitch kind of good people.*

"Thank you, Ida. I'm stunned. This is beyond generous."

Bernice would try to get a dig in on Ida anytime she could. While she'd accepted that Daniel and Ida were in a serious adult relationship, despite their age difference, she still wasn't Ida's biggest fan. "Come on, Abby, tell us what it is. A lifetime gift card for The Home Shopping Club?"

"Shame on you, Bernice," Abby said. Knowing there was no love lost between the two women, Abby loved them both and refused to get involved in their silly love-hate games. "If you must know, these are bankbooks. I think they used to be known as *passbooks*. Each has a balance of one million dollars. When the children reach their twenty-first birthdays, it will be theirs to do with as they please." Abby grinned. "If I could get up to do the happy dance, I would, but my kids would kick my butt, so let me say 'thank you' again. My children will be set for a lifetime. Thank you for caring about them so much, Ida."

"Ida, that's very generous and kind, thank you." Toots meant it, too.

"They're family, Tootsie." When Ida called her "Tootsie," it was truly from the heart. Though Toots was beginning to think Ida's heart of stone was starting to crack, little by little.

"After that, I'm not even sure I want to give you my gift. Ida's always got to show off—let everyone know she's a millionaire. Well, Abby, I am not a millionaire, but Robert and I decided we would go halves on a gift that you might think a bit *crappy*—"

"Bernice, I would never think that," Abby declared.

"Hear me out. Robert and I have made a fund for you at CVS, where all of your diapers will be free forever, for as long as they're in diapers. It's at the CVS where you and Chris bought the pregnancy test."

Abby threw her head back and laughed. "Oh, Bernice, I think this is a fantastic gift, and sentimental, too. Now every time I have to go to CVS to pick up diapers, I'll remember that's where I was when I learned I was pregnant. Very nice. And thank Robert for me, too. No, never mind, I will do it myself."

Last, but not least, was Abby's gift from her mother. She hadn't the first clue what Toots would give her, but whatever it was, Abby knew it would be special, and from the heart.

"I have two boxes for you, Abby." They passed the largest of the two boxes to her first. It wasn't heavy, so she had no idea. "Go on and open it, but be careful."

Abby took her time opening the package, fearing she might break whatever was inside. When she took the paper off, along with a few pieces of tape, Abby removed two long, slender boxes. She stared at them for a moment; then tears fell like a waterfall. "Oh, Mom, you've bought christening clothes for Jonathan and Amy. It's perfect. I didn't even think to ask for this. Thank you so much."

"Abby, look at the boxes a little closer."

She did; then she gazed at her mother. "Those are your and Chris's christening gowns. I've kept both of them, praying that one day I could pass them on to my grandchildren."

"Mom, this is so fantastic! I didn't know you had these. And how is it you have Chris's?"

"He's my stepson first, my son-in-law second. I kept all of Chris's things when Garland passed away. He would like knowing that you and Chris have these."

"Well, I am going to cry again when I have to repeat this

story to Chris. I can't believe how good you all are to me. I am probably the luckiest woman alive right now."

They all laughed and agreed that she was.

"There is one more package from me. Here." Toots gave her a small gift, the size of a shirt box.

"Is it going to make me cry?" Abby asked, smiling while tears ran down her face.

"Well, I don't know. I guess it depends. But you won't know unless you open it, now will you?"

They all watched as Abby tore the yellow wrapping paper off the box. It was pretty paper, but not as pretty as Ida's. She took the lid off the box and removed a handful of papers. "What is this?" she asked as she skimmed through the stack of papers.

Toots didn't say a word. *Let Abby figure it out.* Abby flipped through the papers again and again. By looking at the expression on her daughter's face, Toots knew the moment Abby realized what she held in her hand.

"I'm speechless. Totally speechless. I had no idea. I am shocked." Abby kept shaking her head like she was in a daze.

"Well, what the hell is it?" Sophie asked.

"It's the deed to *The Informer.* It's mine now."

All eyes focused on Toots. "Just a little bit of her dream, you know, to hang on to. Just in case."

The baby shower was so much more than a baby shower. It was a life changer, and Abby knew she and her children had many material possessions, but, more important, they had love.

And Abby truly loved the ones she was with.

Epilogue

November 2013

Abby and Chris could hardly keep their hands off Amy and Jonathan. At four weeks, they were already two separate individuals. Abby knew their cries without looking. She knew who would wake up happy and who would wake up cranky because his or her diaper was full. She knew exactly how long it took them to fall asleep, exactly how many times they blinked their eyes before their soft eyelids would flutter and they finally gave up.

They looked exactly like Abby. Both were born with curly blond hair, and she was sure their eyes would remain the same light blue as her own. Unlike some babies, Amy's and Jonathan's eyes weren't dark at birth. They were as clear blue today as they had been the day they were born.

On Tuesday, October 15, 2013, Amelia Sophia "Amy" Clay was born at 2:19 PM. Jonathan Christopher Clay was born at 2:37 PM. Exactly eighteen minutes apart.

Chris and Abby knew Amy would never let Jonathan forget that she was the big sister by a whole eighteen minutes.

Abby had been downstairs in the kitchen, making herself a light breakfast, when she felt her water break. Chris was at the airport with Goebel and Phil to pick up two dogs that had been lost and injured in a flood. A good citizen found the dogs cold, scared, and hungry, and remembered Abby's flyer from The Canine and Feline Café. She made the call, and 3Ds arranged to have the animals flown to Charleston.

Knowing Chris wouldn't have time to come home, then drive her back to the hospital, she called her mom. Looking back, she thought it was a funny day, but it certainly wasn't at the time.

"Mom, you are not going to believe this, but Chris is at the airport with the guys picking up two dogs, and here I am stuck in the middle of my kitchen standing in a puddle of amniotic fluid, which I know means that my water has broken. I'm going to need a ride to the hospital. Then I need you to call Chris. Mother? Did you hear what I just said?"

Toots had taken a couple seconds to get her bearings. Phil—whom Toots had agreed to marry, though they had not yet set a date for the wedding—was at the house, and she told him what had happened. He made a phone call; within six minutes, a helicopter landed on the road in front of Abby's house. Phil and Toots drove to Abby's like a bat out of hell, and Toots ran inside and helped her to the helicopter.

Abby had the first hard labor pain as soon as they lifted off the ground. "The hospital is just minutes away, Abby. Hang on, sweet girl, just hang on." Toots had a death grip on her daughter. Any movement from the chopper scared her; then Abby would have another labor pain, and she would scream louder.

"MotherthisisntlikeIlearnedinmyLamazeclass!" *Mother, this isn't like I learned in my Lamaze class!!!!*

"Phil, something isn't right."

Toots grabbed Abby's hand. Abby squeezed hers so hard Toots was sure she'd have broken fingers when this was over.

"Thesebabiesarenotgoingtowaittheyarecomingnow!"
These babies are not going to wait; they are coming now!

By the time the chopper landed at the hospital, Amy was in her mother's arms, delivered by Phil. As they raced her to the delivery room on a gurney, Jonathan decided he wasn't going to wait any longer, either. Phil stopped the staff and delivered Jonathan in the hallway in front of the elevator that led to the psych ward. Abby was in hard labor for less than an hour.

And Chris arrived just in time to see his beautiful son and daughter after they were cleaned up and swathed in their pink and blue blankets. Abby cried because he missed the delivery, but Phil promised to give him a very descriptive play-by-play.

And today was their christening. Abby had wanted something simple, nothing quite as elaborate as a traditional Catholic baptism. She and Chris had spoke at great length to Father O'Neil, and they simply wanted the children blessed in the name of their loving Father, the Son, and the Holy Spirit.

Abby dressed Amy, and Chris dressed Jonathan, in the christening gowns that her mother had given to her at the baby shower. The babies looked like innocent angels in their creamy white, delicate lace clothes. The gang planned to meet Chris and Abby at the church, a small Catholic church that Abby had attended when she first lived in Charleston. Father O'Neil remembered her from her Sunday school days. Abby liked that, the beginning of a tradition for her children. Family was so very important to her and Chris, since both were only children. And now it was time to go, to meet the family, and come back here for one more celebration.

The church was only a ten-minute drive. Amy and Jonathan were sound asleep in their car seats in the back of Abby's new minivan. She had kept her MINI Cooper;

but for a while, she'd need the van to get the babies and all their equipment to and from wherever they needed to go.

The gang was waiting outside the church. As soon as Chris and Abby took the babies out of their car seats, the whole gang rushed over like a fast wind.

After everyone kissed and smooched the babies, leaving their plump little cheeks covered with lipstick, they took the children inside, where Father O'Neil was prepared to perform a brief baptism. She and Chris made a nice donation to the church and promised to raise their children in the Church.

The inside of the church was small, but beautiful, with stained glass and beautiful wooden pews. The scented candles provided an ethereal presence.

Abby held Amy, while Father O'Neil sprinkled water over her precious face, causing her to cry. After he blessed her, he followed the same procedure with Jonathan— though, brave soul that he was, he didn't cry.

They prayed and were all blessed. As everyone got ready to go over to Abby's, Sophie insisted that the god-mothers ride with Toots because she had something important to tell them. After they settled in, Ida asked, in her usual bitchy way, "What's so important that I have to ride with you old fogeys instead of with Daniel?"

Mavis, always the peacemaker, tried to keep the peace. "Come on, Ida, if Sophie says something's important, we need to hear it. Back off. I'm sure Daniel will understand."

With everyone settled in, Sophie told them about a dream she had the night before. The five of them were sitting around the dining-room table at Toots's. The guys were out doing some deep-sea fishing, a hobby they had taken up since the day of Abby's baby shower. They were all filling out what looked like applications of some sort. And from the snippets of conversation she could catch, they were applying for membership in that damned Vigilantes organization.

"What?" Ida said. "Are you saying that's something in our future? The Vigilantes?"

"Ida, I'm not telling you anything. I think the dream may have come from the interview I gave the *Washington Post*. There were these two reporters, Maggie Spitzer and Ted Robinson, and that good-looking photographer, Joe Espinosa, all of whom produced stories about the Vigilantes back in the day.

"And that same day I met the *Post*'s owner, Annie de Silva, who was one of them. But given my track record with dreams, I just thought you all needed to know about it."

"Okay, Sophie. You've done your duty and told us. Now can we go back to celebrating the christening of my grandchildren?" Toots asked.

"Sure, Toots, anything you say."

In less than half an hour, they were back at Abby's to celebrate. Both babies were sound asleep when they arrived. Toots helped Abby change them out of their delicate gowns and into their little nightgowns.

Downstairs, Abby and Toots placed the sleeping babies in the bassinets in the kitchen, where Mom and Dad could keep watchful eyes on them.

"So, why didn't we do the godmother and godfather announcements at the church? I thought that's how it worked," Bernice said.

"We wanted to do something a little different. Daniel took care of all the legal papers and it seems that Amy and Jonathan have four godmothers and four godfathers. Officially."

Before they'd made it legal, Chris and Abby asked Mavis and Wade, Bernice and Robert, Sophie and Goebel, and Phil and Ida if they would consider being the twins' godparents. Of course, they'd all said yes. But Abby wanted to make sure. She'd had three godmothers and had never thought it was strange at all. Now her children would have eight godparents: plenty of people to love her precious children.

Chester, who'd been feeling a bit left out, was allowed to look at the babies in the bassinets. Today, for the first time, he stared at Amy, and then licked her face. He went to Jonathan's bassinet and did the same thing.

"They've just received the Chester Simpson lick of approval."

Abby had hired a caterer for the day because she wanted to spend it with all the people she loved. After they'd served tray after tray of finger food, then little desserts plus drinks, Abby felt so full, all she wanted to do was lie down with her precious babies and husband. She whispered this to Sophie.

"Okay, we're finished here. Time to go. Abby's tired, the kids are tired, and I am tired." The caterers cleaned up quickly, and the gang hugged and kissed the babies. Before her mother and the godmothers left, Abby asked them to come upstairs for a minute. The guys guarded the babies while they went upstairs.

"Is something wrong, Abby?" Toots asked her daughter.

"No, nothing at all. I just wanted to know if we could . . . you know, do the secret handshake. Kinda like putting the icing on the cake. Today's been so special for all of us, I just thought it might be fun to end on a fun note."

"Girls, you game?"

They all agreed that they were. "Bernice, you want to be a true-blue member of the gang?"

"I thought I was," she said.

"Nope. Not until you've completed the official godmothers' secret handshake. You sure you want to do this? We do it a lot and in secret."

"Heck yes, I want to! Now tell me what to do."

"Just follow us."

Toots placed her hand out, and Sophie placed her hand

on top of Toots's. Mavis placed her hand on Sophie's; then Ida placed her hand on top of Mavis's.

"Abby, you're next," Toots instructed. Abby placed her hand on Ida's; then Bernice followed suit, placing her hand on Abby's.

"Okay, on the count of three. One, two, three . . . 'When you're good, you're good!' " They lifted their hands high in the air.

And they all knew that life was good.

THE SWEETEST THINGS BUBBLE GUM CUPCAKES

Ingredients

One boxed white cake mix (with oil, eggs, and water to make, according to package) [Jamie says it's perfectly okay to use your favorite mix.]
Pink food coloring (I use Wilton's icing for bright color, which doesn't change the consistency of things.)
One packet of Frosting Creations Bubble Gum Flavor
1 stick of salted butter
1 stick of unsalted butter
1½ c. powdered sugar
1 t. vanilla
18–24 gumballs

DIRECTIONS

Make cake mix according to package, add food coloring and fill 18–24 cupcake liners (in a cupcake tin) with batter. Most cake mixes say they make 24 cupcakes. I like big cupcakes so I usually aim for 18!

Bake according to package and cool completely.

Beat together (softened!) butters with vanilla and powdered sugar. Beat on high, until light and fluffy frosting develops.

Add bubble gum flavor packet to frosting and beat until well combined.

Cut a corner off a large zip-top bag and press a large star-shaped decorating tip into the hole.

Spoon frosting into bag and seal top.

Carefully pipe frosting evenly over cupcakes. (This recipe frosts 18 cupcakes perfectly. You will need to use a little less per cupcake to cover 24.)

Top each cupcake with a fun and colorful gumball.

I'd like to dedicate this book to some truly wonderful people who recently came into my life.

To Ben Harrison, the finest lawyer in Spartanburg, South Carolina. Many thanks for introducing me to Mark McManus, Kenny Church, Steve Duncan, Sam Maw, the owners of the Beacon Restaurant in Spartanburg, and to Tommy Lee, Barbara, Karen, Jerry, Cartwright, Calvin and Ruby for making me the best Philly Cheese Burger in the whole world. And there are no words to describe the Peach Cobbler that makes me wish I lived next door so I could eat it every day.

Thank you all,

Fern Michaels

Be sure not to miss the new book in Fern Michaels's
bestselling, action-packed Men of the Sisterhood series

TRUTH OR DARE

*The Sisterhood: a group of women bound by friendship
and a quest for justice. Now their male allies, the Men of
the Sisterhood, have formed a top-secret organization of
their own, with the same goal of helping the helpless and
righting the wrongs of the world . . .*

When the call comes, the Men of the Sisterhood drop
everything to help their friends. This time it's Cyrus, their
four-legged hound dog and unofficial mascot. While
member Joe Espinosa is driving along an isolated country
road with Cyrus in tow, he catches a glimpse of
movement in the woods bordering the road and notes
Cyrus pawing desperately at the car window. As soon as
he pulls over to investigate, Cyrus bolts out the door and
leads Joe to three children clustered together—
bedraggled, silent, and scared out of their wits. As soon
as he has brought the children to safety, Espinosa
arranges an urgent meeting.

Charles, Abner, Jack, Dennis, Harry and the rest of the
crew gather at BOLO headquarters to hear a shocking
story that confirms their worst suspicions. Many more
children are still in danger. But in order to protect and
avenge the victims, the team must use more cunning than
ever before. With so many vulnerable young lives at
stake, one mistake would be too many . . .

A Zebra mass-market paperback and e-book on sale now.

Keep reading for a special look!

Prologue

It was an enormous truck. White in color, with brilliant decals of fruit and vegetables stenciled over the wide side panels. In the center of the panel was large, vivid red lettering proclaiming that the truck was owned by B. M. Produce; then in smaller letters it read, "Fresh produce today and every day." At the very bottom, at the back end of the huge truck was ID for the company's business license.

There were four such trucks in the United States. One in Charleston, South Carolina; one in Falls Church, Virginia; one in Denver, Colorado; and one in San Diego, California. The company also owned twenty-four other trucks the size of a school minibus. Six each were allocated to the four geographical areas of the company that housed the bigger trucks.

The four large trucks were used for transporting produce. The twenty-four smaller trucks were used for promotional purposes to ensure that B. M. Produce became a household name. The only thing the smaller trucks did was roam the streets and towns so that people would see the trucks with the colorful decals and come to recognize the name of the company. The trucks patrolled the areas from six in the morning till eight o'clock at night.

The drivers were paid well for doing the cushy job.

B. M. Produce had been in business for seventeen years. To date, each and every employee had been hired seventeen years ago, when the company started. Not one employee had left the company, and no new ones had been hired.

The main headquarters for B. M. Produce was in San Diego, California, where the company was run by a man named Ortiz Ozay. He set up the driving schedules for the four big main trucks. He was the man responsible for the intricate locking mechanisms on the rear doors of each truck for special deliveries so that not even the drivers could open the doors.

The drivers called Ozay the traveling man because once a month, like clockwork, he would visit the other three locations to check on how things were going. At least that's what they were told.

In order to work, and keep working, for B. M. Produce each employee had to agree never to ask questions and to mind their own business and also agree not to talk to anyone about the company.

The employees agreed because who was interested in hearing about a load of overripe melons, stinky cabbage, and rotting lettuce?

None of the employees had ever seen the inside of the trucks they drove. If they had, they would have seen benches anchored to the floor and piles and piles of sleeping bags. They would have gagged at the sharp ammonia smell of urine and the fetid odor of human feces.

Because . . . B. M. Produce wasn't really in the business of transporting fruits and vegetables at all.

B. M. Produce was in the business of trafficking little blond-haired ten-year-old girls.

Chapter One

Demetri Pappas, doctor of veterinary medicine, dropped to his haunches to stare at his patient. There was a protocol to these visits that both doctor and patient adhered to every six months. The doctor spoke in Greek first, then back in English to see if his patient remembered his earlier teachings before having gone to live with Jack Emery.

Cyrus yipped, then yipped again.

"Fetch me the tennis ball. When you bring it to me, drop it into my hand." It was all said in Greek. Cyrus rose to his feet, all 160 magnificent pounds of pure dog. He raced to the end of the room, pawed through the toys, and found the tennis ball, not the red plastic ball, not the yellow rubber ball but the green tennis ball, and then carried it in his mouth back to where Dr. Pappas waited. He dropped the ball into his hands, offered up another yip, and smacked his paw into the doctor's open palm. He waited for the praise he knew was coming. No treat, however; Dr. Pappas was stingy with his treats, and Cyrus knew it.

"Well done, Cyrus. That was our last test. And you passed each one. Jack is going to be very proud of you. Go along, Cyrus, you have ten minutes to visit your old friends out in the yard. Ten minutes." This order was also given in rapid-fire Greek. Cyrus trotted off, allowing the doctor to home in on Joseph Espinosa, who was watching the scene play out in dumbfound amazement.

"Cyrus understands Greek?" He might as well have said, "Cyrus just returned from the moon," by the expression on his face.

"But of course. All my dogs understand my language. Every animal I breed is extraordinary, as you can see by Cyrus. His intelligence is superior to that of some humans. His stamina is equal to that of several men. He knows right from wrong. He is loyal to me and to his master, in this case, Jack Emery. He would and will kill for either one of us if he sensed our lives were in danger. He understands that children need to be protected at all times, at all costs. Cyrus graduated canine school at the top of his class of five."

"Uh-huh," was all Espinosa could think of to say.

"So, tell me, Mr. Espinosa, how is Jack and why did you bring Cyrus today?"

"Root canal. Jack had already canceled it twice, and the doctor told him no more, and the tooth was bothering him. Jack said he called to clear it with you."

"Yes, my assistant took the call. My checkups are mandatory, and I suffer no cancelations. Jack knows this, and that is why you're here. In other words, Mr. Espinosa, I run a tight ship."

"Uh-huh," Espinosa said again.

Espinosa watched as the doctor took a beef-flavored stick from a jar on the counter and slipped it into a plastic sleeve that he then placed in the cylinder that was Cyrus's report. A ritual. The doctor looked down at his watch just as Cyrus sauntered through the door. He looked around, then trotted over to the doctor, and waited for the doctor to tie the cylinder to his collar.

"Do not remove this cylinder, Mr. Espinosa. That is for Jack to do. It's part of our ritual. In addition to my warn-

ing, be advised that if you were to try to take off the cylinder Cyrus *would* take off your hand."

"Uh-huh," Espinosa said.

"This visit is now over. Cyrus, it was lovely seeing you
again. We'll meet again in six months. Take care of your
master and anyone else who needs your help. Let's have a
hug, and then you can be on your way."

Espinosa watched as Cyrus stood on his hind legs and
wrapped his front paws around the roly-poly doctor. Then
he nuzzled the man under the chin. He let loose with two
sharp yips, turned, and headed for the door. He didn't look
back. Espinosa scurried to keep up with the prancing dog.

Outside, the compound was quiet. Espinosa wondered
how many dogs were housed here. He asked Cyrus, not
expecting an answer. Cyrus barked seven times. So much
for being stupid. Seven dogs at fifty grand a pop was some
serious money. He could hardly wrap his mind around a
dog, any dog, being worth fifty grand. Except maybe
Cooper. *Cooper. Don't go there*, he warned himself.

Once inside the shiny black Silverado, Cyrus settled
himself, buckled his seat belt, and went to sleep.

Espinosa tooled along the winding country road that
would take him back to the District and the BOLO Building, admiring the trees on either side bursting with fall
color. Jack would be waiting to pick up Cyrus, he let his
mind wander. He was supposed to meet up with Ted and
Maggie after lunch to do a photo shoot with some gung
ho new congressman who loved getting his picture in the
papers. He hated puff assignments, as did Ted and Maggie. But those puff assignments paid the bills.

He sniffed and smiled. Alexis had used his truck a few
days ago to pick up some beauty supplies, and the scent
still lingered. He liked the powdery floral scent, whatever
it was. Lilacs, maybe. He missed Alexis, and she'd only
been gone for thirty-six hours. The girls were on a mission
that, according to Alexis, was so hush-hush she couldn't

even tell him where she was going, much less tell him what it was about.

Espinosa looked at the clock on the dashboard. He had made good time on the way out to Reston and was making good time on his return. His thoughts turned to how pleased Jack was going to be with Cyrus's stellar report.

It happened all at once. A flash out of the corner of his eye, a streak, movement of some kind. A deer? Cyrus's bloodcurdling bark, the dog's seat belt clicking open. Espinosa almost lost control of the Silverado. He took his foot off the gas pedal, slowed, and steered the big truck to the shoulder of the road. Cyrus pawed the window, then pressed the door handle. The door flew open, and he was out like he'd been shot from a cannon, sprinting, and then airborne down the embankment. He was lost to sight before Espinosa even got out of the truck.

Espinosa plowed through the brush, and before he knew what was happening, he lost his footing and rolled down the embankment, Cyrus's ear-pounding barks almost splitting his eardrums. He shook his head to clear it and then did a mental check to see if he'd broken or sprained anything. Other than a sore rear end, he thought he was okay. He opened his eyes wide, not sure he was seeing what he was seeing as Cyrus continued to bark relentlessly.

Three little kids, filthy dirty in equally filthy dirty clothing, clustered together, their frightened eyes on Cyrus. Espinosa swallowed hard. He came from a huge family of eleven siblings. He knew a thing or two about kids. First things first. "Cyrus, shut the hell up, or I'm going to call Dr. Pappas. I see them. I know what to do. Chill, okay?"

Either the threat of calling the doctor or Espinosa's calm tone or the big dog's just getting tired worked because he stopped barking. The fur on the nape of his neck stood straight up, his ears went flat against his head just as his tail dropped between his legs. Warrior pose.

Espinosa struggled to take a deep breath, the doctor's words ringing in his ears that dogs like Cyrus knew to protect children. Surely, the monster dog wouldn't turn on him. Or would he?

"Like I said, Cyrus, I know what to do. Just let me do it, okay?" He waited. Cyrus yipped and advanced a few steps, the children cowering against each other.

"Okay, kids, listen up. My name is Joseph. This is Cyrus. He means you no harm. I won't hurt you. How did you get here? Are you lost? Tell me where you live, and I'll take you home. Are you hungry?" When there was no response to his questions, Espinosa wondered why there were no tears. He estimated the age of the oldest girl going by how tall she was to be maybe seven, the other girl, almost as tall, six or so. Maybe they were twins. The little guy looked to be four, perhaps five years old. He was missing a shoe and a sock.

Espinosa tried wheedling. "Come on, tell me your names so I can take you home." The sudden thought that maybe they didn't want to go home hit him. Maybe they had run away from abusive parents. He corrected that thought. These kids, from what he could see by the layers of dirt and the condition of their clothes, looked to have been on the run for a while. All three were skinny and scrawny. They looked alike. Siblings.

Cyrus barked. *Do something already.*

Espinosa pondered the situation. How was he going to get all three kids to the top of the embankment without them cutting and running? Cyrus, of course. They were afraid of him. Cyrus could herd them to the top, and then he would secure them in the backseat of the Silverado and head for the BOLO Building. He'd send out a call for an emergency meeting. A *dire* emergency meeting.

"Okay, listen up, everyone. This is what we're going to do." Espinosa spoke directly at Cyrus, whom he knew would understand. "You herd them to the top of the embankment.

You watch, and I'll put them in the truck one by one. I'll call Jack and the others to meet up at the BOLO Building, and we'll work things out there. Right now, these kids are just too damn scared to do anything. Let's do it, big guy."

Cyrus barked. *At last, a plan.*

It took some doing, but they finally got the three kids into the back of the truck. All three were crying now as they clung to one another. Cyrus never took his eyes off them, even for a second.

Espinosa turned on the engine, then called the team. He ended each call with, *I'm forty minutes out. I repeat, this is a dire emergency.* After he ended the last call, to Abner Tookus, he put the truck in gear and headed down the road.

Connect with

Visit us online at
KensingtonBooks.com
to read more from your favorite authors, see books
by series, view reading group guides, and more.

for sneak peeks, chances to win books and prize packs,
and to share your thoughts with other readers.

facebook.com/kensingtonpublishing
twitter.com/kensingtonbooks

Tell us what you think!

To share your thoughts, submit a review,
or sign up for our eNewsletters, please visit:
KensingtonBooks.com/TellUs.